Bursting the

CHERRY

phyllis blunt

The
X
Press

Published in United Kingdom by:
The X Press,
6 Hoxton Square, London N1 6NU
Tel: 0171 729 1199
Fax: 0171 729 1771

Printed by Mackays, Chatham, Kent

Distributed in UK by Turnaround Distribution, Unit 3, Olympia Trading Estate, Coburg Road, London N22 6TZ
Tel: 0181 829 3000
Fax: 0181 881 5088

ISBN 1-874509-54-9

Thanks 2:
Dotun 4 igniting that spark!
Jacci - the best PA in the world, not 2 mention friend.
Diane, my U.S. connection - you're a star, girl!
Whahied 4 putting me in check!
My mother - 4 the ying in my yang!

Bursting the *CHERRY*

Prologue

IT WAS THE SWEET THOUGHT OF VENGEANCE — and only the sweet, sweet thought of vengeance — that drove Cherry along as she crunched over the pavement's thick frosty meringue-crust of hardened late-night December snow. An icy wetness began to slowly seep through the thin soles of her cheap canvas summer shoes, and the merciless evening chill hissed venomously through her flesh. She felt colder than a naked asshole sitting on the North Pole. But she really didn't give a shit. Her mind was so alive, and her heart was so full of the raging fire of revenge, that she felt like she was stepping across hot coals.

She'd been told her destination was 'five minutes' away from the bus stop. Five minutes had already turned out to be damn near twenty. She remembered the bus driver commenting, 'You'll catch your death of cold in those clothes, love'. No shit. Why did some people always have to point out the obvious? She was the one who had been freezing her ass off all day, so she *had* realised that her flimsy July clothes weren't suitable for December. But they were the only clothes that she possessed.

She finally caught her first glimpse of the tattered sign, glinting surreptitiously through the blackness. Its faded gold lettering, only faintly legible against the dimly lit street, read: *The Rosemead Hostel and Guest House.*

"You got yuh papers, love?"

Still shivering, Cherry handed over a bunch of forms to the kindly-faced, ebony-skinned Jamaican woman who was on night duty in the office of Rosemead. When the woman had flicked through the information and filled in the

1

relevant blanks, her soft, gentle features rearranged themselves into a hard and stony-faced expression.

Eyeing Cherry suspiciously, she said, "*Holloway* eh? Well, let me tell you that this hostel is quiet and *h*orderly, and our guests are civilised and well-behaved. De first sign of trouble and you'll be going right back to where you came from young lady. Y'understand?"

Cherry gritted her teeth. She longed to tell the woman where to go, but she needed somewhere to stay more than she needed her pride — for now. She replied tightly, "Yes."

She was led to a dormitory where several other woman were already sleeping in rows of low-slung, cast-iron beds under thin, dark-grey regulation blankets. An old woman was hunched in a corner, muttering to herself. She was wild-eyed, with long, wiry, unkempt grey hair and dressed in a crumpled, ill-fitting mismatched outfit.

Sensing Cherry's apprehension, the Jamaican night warden explained, "Don't pay Mad Mary no mind. Once you get used to her chatter, you won't even notice it." She paused to look Cherry up and down, disapprovingly. "Still, I bet there's worse where you've come from…"

Cherry matched her critical stare, and barely listened as the warden ran through her spiel. "You've missed dinner, which is served between six and eight. Breakfast starts at seven and finishes at nine. An' if yuh haffe go out in d'evenin', make sure you're back in good time, 'cause de main door gets lock off at midnight, and nobody is let in or out after dat, *h*unless yuh gran'mutha die." They had stopped at the end of the dormitory opposite Mad Mary, and the warder pointed to an empty cast-iron bed which stood uninvitingly in the far corner of the room. A single miserable grey blanket was tightly folded across its thin mattress, turned back to reveal well-worn white sheets and a flat white pillow. Although the sheets had obviously been boil-washed and bleached countless times, Cherry could still make out a variety of faded stains, left there by previous guests of the Rosemead Hostel.

"Right, this is your bed, and will be *h*until de end of your stay. She nodded at Cherry's brown leather rucksack, the only item she had brought with her. "An' yuh best not have much more than that, 'cause yuh don't get much storage space here. I'd advise you to keep anyt'ing of value with you at all times… Right, I'll say goodnight. If yuh need de bathroom, it's in de hallway."

Cherry wrinkled her nose, as she cast her eyes over her new home. The air was heavy with the heady odour of stale unwashed clothes, and stale unwashed people. Poverty seemed to cling to every orifice like a grimy tidemark. It was a truly gross, run down, end of the road, dirty, nasty, stinking shit-hole of misery. A half-way house in hell. But, as long as it would enable her to complete her transformation, Rosemead Hostel was going to be Buckingham Palace as far as she was concerned.

Cherry got into bed, and laid wide awake beneath the scratchy warmth of her regulation blanket. Mad Mary had started banging her head against the wall and her mutterings were even louder. The rest of the women's silence led her to believe that this was probably Mad Mary's regular routine.

Unable to sleep anyway on her first night of freedom anyway, she didn't give a damn. Cherry breathed a sigh of detached satisfaction. She was ready. Ready to kick some ass. And now, nothing and nobody was going to stop her.

A long overdue debt was about to get paid. In full. The first step in her plan had to be to get the fuck out of the miserable realms of the Rosemead Hostel and Guest House.

And fast.

Fate

"I DEALT WITH THIS WICKEDLY FIT GAL last night, y'know."

"What? Did she have a white stick?"

Yam kissed his teeth. "Cha. Me nah chat 'bout dem *nasty* 'foo-foo' t'ings you ah deal wid. This gal was *kriss*!"

DJ Yam, Mr. E, Fingers and D were sitting in the monitor room of Black Knight Productions for their late afternoon 'tea' break. The air was hazy with marijuana smoke, half-eaten patties lay on the coffee table and everyone's glass was filled with blackcurrant cordial — except Fingers, who had his usual brandy and coke. The walls were racked with all the latest and most expensive pieces of hi-tech recording equipment whose lights occasionally flashed green and red. The group was seated in front of a huge forty-eight track fully-automated Mackie mixing desk. Behind the desk was a floor-to-ceiling window which separated the control room from the vocal booth. As with most studios, Black Knight Productions was situated in a basement, so the spaces were lit with soft 'ambient' lighting, apart from the mixing desk which was spotlit from above.

Yam, resident producer at Black Knight Productions, was informing his associates of the previous night's events, with much interruption from D, the engineer.

"Jus' let me finish my piece, D, an' you might learn a few things, and even get your ugly ass some pussy!"

"Ya son of a—"

"D…" Mr. E cut in with a softly spoken authority. He was a sharply dressed Armani-clad black man who could have been anywhere between twenty-five and fifty-five years old, but he never mentioned his age, or any other personal details for that matter. The sole proprietor of Black Knight Productions and all its affiliated companies, when Mr. E spoke everyone listened. "Let de yout' finish up, nah."

Yam gave a grateful nod to Mr. E and, after a mock sigh

of exasperation at D, continued. "As I was saying before I was so *rudely* interrupted, I had this fine, *fine* honey last night. Though I'm still not sure if it was *she* who had *me*..."

"How ya mean?"

"Well, as I was deejaying my usual floor-stomping set down at Night Moves — where, as you know, there are 'nuff rude boys and 'nuff-nuff raggapussy — dis firing redskin sista walks up to me at the decks."

"Who was she with?"

"Just she one, star. Just she one. Anyways, this honey wasn't your regular raggapussy, no star, this gal was dread! Tall, long legs, one *big* booty and two phat titties wid de nipples dat just burst through one tight up top like yah soh."

Yam stopped to poke his two index fingers through his shirt at chest level to indicate two erect nipples.

D was getting excited, "Oh Lord..."

"Wait nuh — there's more! Her face was like one ah dem models 'pon cover ah *Vogue* magazine, wid the big soft red lips and the big doe eyes, all framed by some long silky black hair which did wave all the way down her back like yah soh..." Yam stopped again to imitate ocean waves running down his back.

"An' then what?"

"An' then she leant over the decks to reveal two huge, ripe melons that any red-blooded yout' would *kill* to rest his horny head upon, and asked me if I had any lover's rock."

D was unable to contain himself, and exclaimed in earnest, "You shoulda thrown her down right there!"

Yam was genuinely offended. "Yuh lickle raggamuffin! That's not how to treat a lady. Me's a genkleman, y'know!"

Satisfied he'd set D straight, Yam continued. "Anyways, I put on 'When I Hit Your G-Spot', and dis redskin gyal starts windin' and grindin' right there in front of the decks, and all the time looking straight at me wid her big doe eyes! It was my last record of the night, so I slid onto the dance floor and asked her her name. Guess wha' she tell me?"

Yam paused to drink in his rapt audience, making sure

he had their full attention. "She said her name was Cherry. So I asked her Cherry who? And she tell me 'Cherry Drop'... Then guess wha' she asked me?"

Yam stopped again, this time for full dramatic effect. "She asked me *if I want a suck*!! Well, I know an invitation when I hears one, so I took her back to the office..."

D, drooling in anticipation, said, "And then what?"

But Yam became cagey. "What we did then was the kinda t'ings man an' man don't talk about."

D was sorely disappointed. "Aw c'mon, Yam! Don't hold back on the small print!"

Yam refused to be drawn in. "Nah dread, as I said before me's a *genkleman*... I can only hope I get the opportunity to suck upon that sweet Cherry once again."

"Nah man! Ya—"

"D!"Mr. E broke in again."Hush yuh mouth — Yam's given me an idea." He looked intently at his associates, "That's what we need to make this thing work."

"What thing?"

Mr. E looked at them like they were crazy, and boomed, "Records, man! Yuh feget we're sittin' in my multi-million dollar studio to make hit *records* not chat 'bout foolishness!"

"Making hit records *is* chattin' about foolishness!"

D and Fingers slapped a high-five and fell about laughing, but Mr. E was oblivious to the joke. He continued, "What I'm saying is, *that's* what we need for this record — one slamming redskin gyal, with some crossover potential and 'nuff-nuff sex appeal! The kind of sista that all the girls want to be like, and all the brothas just wanna bend over!"

"Yeah, like Toni Braxton, or my gyal Whitney!"

Mr. E nodded as the others began to catch his drift. "Exactly! So, Yam, you reckon this girl can sing?"

The black cab pulled slowly into the Stockwell Park Estate in Brixton. It was four a.m. A clutter of high-rise tower blocks stood grim and forbidding against the black night sky. The Estate was a concrete jungle legacy of the misguided Labour government architects of the sixties.

"Will you watch me until I get in the door?"

"All right, love."

Cherry Drop looked sharply left and right before entering Byrant Court, which housed the one bedroom flat she called home. Not that she'd had any trouble here before, but you could never be too careful. That she was sure of.

The familiar feeling of relief melted over her when she entered her flat, with the door treble-locked safely behind her. All that could be heard in the still of the night was the faint thump of rhythm and bass from the flat two floors above. Most of her neighbours were pissed off that the kids in number nineteen were always holding late-night shebeens but Cherry didn't mind. She liked being reminded that she wasn't completely alone. Which she couldn't help thinking she was sometimes. Once or twice they had invited her to a party, but she'd declined. She'd no intention of getting close to her neighbours. Or anyone. Not even Babsy.

Cherry looked out of her huge ceiling-to-floor living room windows at the city streets that sprawled out beneath her. Every curve and corner twinkled with magical fairy light street lighting. Being on the seventeenth floor of Byrant Court, she had an almost panoramic view of London; it felt like she had the whole city at her feet.

And soon she would. She was certain of that.

She turned to walk through her sparsely furnished flat, which contained no TV or video. However, she had a mountain of CDs and tapes, which stood next to an expensive top-of-the-range hi-fi system. Although she'd lived there for three months, it still looked as if she'd moved in yesterday. Or was leaving tomorrow — which was probably nearer the truth. For the moment, it was like she was in limbo, waiting for her life to take its rightful shape.

Twenty-two years old, Cherry knew she had it going on. Young, beautiful, ambitious, talented and sharp. Very sharp. Her wisdom was not the kind that comes from books —

although she'd read her share. No, Cherry's real knowledge came from the infamous school of 'hard knocks', and it had been learnt the long, hard way.

But now she was ready. Ready to make it. And she was prepared to use W.I.T. — Whatever It Takes.

And as she sat down at her dressing table, all she could think about was what had happened earlier that night with DJ Yam. She felt a rush as she realised that her plan was already clicking into place.

Unable to resist sharing the details of her recent conquest, Cherry reached for the phone. "Babsy!"

"Who's this?" a sleepy voice croaked down the line.

"It's me — Cherry. Listen girl, I couldn't wait to tell you… guess who I've been with tonight?"

The voice was now slightly vexed. "Couldn't this wait until tomorrow?"

"What? You mean you don't wanna hear about me and DJ Yam?"

"No way!" The voice was excited and wide awake now. "Fill me in with the juicy bits! Is he gonna hook you up with a record deal?"

There was a pause, and then a reluctant, "Well, I'm working on it."

"What do you mean? You did tell him you're a singer didn't you?"

"Well… sort of."

"*Sort of*?" Babsy was confused. "Girl, exactly *what* happened?"

When Babsy had told her DJ Yam did a regular spot down at Night Moves, Cherry decided to go for it. If she was going to make it as a singer she'd have to start somewhere and DJ Yam seemed a good enough place. Both Babsy and Cherry knew that he was the producer for the infamous Black Knight Sound System, which had gained a name from the phat mixes they'd done for artists such as Mary J. Blige and

Jodeci. And weren't they the ones who'd bought Egg-Head — an old eighties English pop star — back from the dead with that wicked cover of 'Batty Rider'? Yep, Yam was the man — and Cherry had got him. Several times in fact! All she had to do was wait for the right moment and — *boom* — he'd be *gagging* to record with her.

A week later, that moment still hadn't arrived. Cherry had yet to make a move towards Yam with regards to her career. However, this was the last thing on her mind. A tremor of excitement rippled through her body as Yam traced the outline of her smooth stomach with his fingertips and reached up to squeeze her nipples. She was sitting astride his naked body and could feel the hardness of his shaft inside her soft grasping wetness. As she slowly gyrated on top of him, his penis began to swell and push against the walls of her vagina. God, it felt good. She looked down at her conquest, taking in his lean, dark torso, well-shaped pecs and chiselled jawline. Yep, Yam was definitely what you called handsome. Gorgeous in fact.

Yam suddenly flipped her over doggy style and quickened the pace until it was fast and furious. His left hand slid from her breast and rested on her clitoris. Cherry felt herself go weak as her body was overcome with pleasure. She knew she was going to come. They both were, and they both did. Together in fact.

As Yam lay in the aftermath of their love making, he felt quite pleased with himself. Life certainly was great — yes sir! He had *everything* — a budding recording career, great girl... *fantastic* girl. He looked over at Cherry who had her eyes closed. Beads of sweat clung to her full, sensuous mouth and when his eyes took in the large curve of her breasts, the smooth sheen of her skin, down to her silky curls of pubic hair and the long, long length of her legs, he felt like a king. She was quite a girl all right, a real handful — and it took a man like him to handle her. And he was probably the only one who had, by the look of complete satisfaction written all over her face.

Softly he called her name. "Cherry…"

She stretched out like a cat and slowly opened her eyes. "Mmm?"

"What made you come up to me the other night?"

"Huh?"

"In the club, what made you approach me?"

Cherry looked up at Yam and wondered if he suspected anything. "I don't know… I, er, just felt drawn to you somehow… Maybe it was fate."

Yam chewed over her words. *Fate*, could it be? He turned to face Cherry, "It's funny, I feel like I've known you my whole life. And I like everything I've seen so far. I like your…" he touched her lips "…smile. I like your…" he cupped her chin "…. eyes. I like your…" he reached out to run his fingers through her hair "… hair, and I like your…" he reached down and triumphantly exclaimed, "TITS!"

Cherry couldn't help laughing. His verbal was so extra. Yam was so naive, he was almost adolescent at times.

He puffed out his chest and stretched back, feeling a certain satisfaction in making Cherry laugh. But, as he basked in the glory of her joy, his eyes began to wander around Cherry's sparse bedroom, and he felt himself disapprove of the surroundings.

A black sheet had been used as a makeshift curtain and was nailed across the window frame, obliterating any chance of daylight. A couple of cheap rugs had been scattered over the standard council dark-green linoleum which covered the floor. The only piece of furniture in the room was a huge antique oak dressing table on which a clutter of large ivory scented candles had been arranged, their flickering light casting a low amber glow amongst the shadows. Mind you, he had to admit that the matching bedsheets and duvet set looked very luxurious, being deep burgundy and gold appliqué Ralph Lauren. However, they soon lost their grandeur, when all they had to adorn was the huge mattress on the floor, which acted as Cherry's bed. No, she was definitely too good for this. When they were together properly he'd rent a *pukka* pad — black leather sofas, four poster beds, the lot.

Suddenly curious, he turned to her asking, "Have you always lived here?"

"No, I got this place from the council when I left... when I left the home."

"The *home*?"

"Yeah, I grew up in a children's home, and when you're sixteen they just kinda kick you out into the world and give you a council flat."

Yam was incredulous, "What just like that? No money, no *nothing*?"

Cherry opened her eyes as wide as she could, looked straight up at Yam and hoped he was buying this. "Just like that. Hardly even a goodbye."

Yam looked back into Cherry's huge light-brown eyes, and at that moment she looked so vulnerable and alone that he felt a strange stirring in his heart, like nothing he'd ever felt before. He felt like he wanted to take care of her.

He pulled her close to his chest, "I'm here now, baby."

Cherry lay there and wondered if he was for real. The last time she'd believed someone who'd told her that, she'd been thrown into jail for five years...

She changed the subject. "Is Yam your real name?"

He laughed. "Nah, Yam's a nickname I went by as a yout', and it's stuck with me ever since."

"Why Yam?"

" 'Cause I love to 'nyam' food. Maybe because I was meant to nyam a certain Cherry I've become acquainted with." He rolled over on top of her until their noses touched. "In fact I'm starting to feel a little peckish right now."

Cherry rested her hand on his newly acquired hardness, and her smile widened. "Again?!"

"Uh-huh... again!"

The Proposition

AS HE LEFT CHERRY'S FLAT, Yam turned his collar up against the rain. Even though it was June, the sky was overcast, and London was blanketed in a thick hazy fog. He could feel the odd droplet of cool wetness slip underneath his collar and ooze down the nape of his neck and into the small of his back. But nothing could dampen his spirits today. No, today he was on top of the world, walking on cloud nine, higher than any drug could take him. He felt elated and scared shitless all at once, and the intensity at which he experienced these emotions almost took his breath away. Yam consciously checked himself. What was happening to him? How could he — the original Mr. Lover-Lover DJ playboy of London — be getting so excited over a babe? Was this that love at first sight stuff he'd read about in all those fool-fool women's magazines?

A roll of thunder rumbled across the sky. Damn! What was *with* this British summer? When he and Cherry got married they could move somewhere hot, like Jamaica or something.

Damn! Did he just think *marriage?*

Yam had arrived at the spot where he'd left his baby — a metallic-blue Ford Escort convertible with a souped-up engine, fastidiously clean alloy wheels, full body kit and a personalised license plate in italics. It was his pride and joy, the one thing he loved more than anything else on the planet — or so he'd thought until now. Now everything had changed. The whole world had gone and turned itself upside down, and all he had to hold onto was an overwhelming feeling of emotion for the woman he'd just left. And this was an emotion that he'd never even dreamed of before, never mind felt.

Cherry's words kept echoing around his head: 'Maybe it was fate.... it was fate'. It had to be bullshit. How could a young stallion like himself become a helpless victim of 'fate' and turn mushy over a woman? There was only one thing for it — he had to put it to the test. If he turned round and saw Cherry looking at him now, it was meant to be. If not, this whole love at first sight thing — and all this business about it all being fate — was just a stupid figment of his imagination.

Yam took a deep breath and turned round. What he saw almost knocked him for six. His sweet Cherry had wrapped herself up in her duvet and was on her balcony, waving goodbye to him in the rain! Stunned, and in slow motion as if in a dream he waved back. She started to blow him kisses…

It was all too much! Yam turned back to his car truly freaked out.

During the whole journey back, he thought of nothing but Cherry. In a daze he arrived home, parked his car and opened his front door.

"Is that you, Kenneth?"

"Yes, Mummy." Yam was in no mood for a conversation with his mother, or anyone else for that matter, so he went straight to his room and shut the door.

Even though he was in his room, the same room he'd grown up in, everything seemed different. His old Arsenal posters were still on the walls, together with the new ones; his model Ferraris and Porches still perched on top of the chest of imitation teak drawers; the same records were stacked neatly against the walls, and his mixing decks still stood expectantly in the corner. Yet today it was like they were all strangers, impartial onlookers, simply observing his dilemma.

Yam threw himself on to his bed, stretched his hands behind his head and looked up at the posters of Whitney Houston and Vanity that he'd strategically tacked to the ceiling. But even they seemed to have lost their usual lustre. It was like everything he'd ever known was just a dream, or an old, faded photograph. And the only thing that was real was the vivid thought of Cherry which coursed through his veins, pounded in his head and seemed to be the very air that he breathed.

"Kenneth! You want some chicken and rice?" The sound of his mother's voice cut through his thoughts like sanity in an asylum. As if on cue, hunger rumbled loudly through his stomach. He had to get back down to earth, and food was as good a way as any to get him there.

"Yes, Mummy."

The youngest of four children, Yam was the only one still at home, so of course his mother completely doted on him, which, as far as he was concerned, was how it should be. He was twenty-two, but he couldn't see the point of leaving yet, not with so many home comforts at hand.

He wondered if Cherry could cook... Probably not. It seemed like most girls nowadays weren't really interested in cooking and cleaning and looking after their man. Well, they'd just have to eat out.

"Turn it up, nuh."

Yam's mother handed him an exceptionally large plate piled high with chicken, rice and peas, and with big portions of yam and green banana teetering dangerously on the side. A thick, steaming gravy had been generously ladled all over the chicken.

"Turn up what?"

"The heat, man, this *h*english summer is freezing!"

Yam looked incredulously at his mother. Despite the cool temperature outside, inside the house was boiling hot. As it always was. Even in the middle of the coldest winter his family walked around the house in shorts and T-shirts.

The sound of the phone ringing interrupted their conversation. Yam took his plate with him to answer it.

"Yeah?"

"Yam." It was Mr. E.

"Yeah?"

"Have you spoken to dat redskin gal you were talkin' about de other day, yet?"

"Er, yeah."

"So when is she coming down the studio?"

Shit. In his excitement, Yam had forgotten all about asking Cherry if she could sing on the project they were doing. "Er… I'm not sure yet, I'm firming up the times and everyt'ing with her later."

"Well let me know when you can reach, man."

"Safe, safe."

"All right. Later."

"Yeah, later."

Yam replaced the handset. Where was that telephone number that Cherry had given him? He felt a hot flush of excitement as the thought of her ran through his mind. His heart began to pound as he dialled her digits, willing himself to stay calm.

"Hello?"

It was her.

"Er, Cherry, it's me, Yam."

"Hey you…" Her tone softened at the sound of his voice, and Yam felt his knees go weak.

"Er, I wondered if…" He paused. Oh God! He couldn't come out with it just like that. What would she think?

Cherry prompted him. "Yeah?"

"I… I wondered if you'd be able to, if you'd *like* to go to the cinema with me tonight."

"I'd love to."

"Cool, I'll pick you up around seven."

"See ya then."

Yam had decided to fill her in on the studio and everything later on. After all, it wasn't right to be making love to a girl one minute and then ask her to start working for you the next. She might think he was just using her or something. Anyway, it would be more professional to discuss it face to face. He replaced the handset and looked in the mirror above the phone. He did not like what he saw. His face looked mash-up after this morning's session and he had the living afro sprouting out of his head. There was nothing else for it, he would have to call Earl, his brother, to

15

come over with the clippers.

Monica answered the phone. She was his brother's baby mother.

"Oh hi, Monica, is Earl there?"

"Hold on, I'll call him for you."

Earl's gruff voice rumbled down the line. "What's up, pickney?"

"I need you to come over and cut my hair, bruv."

"No can do, Monica's goin' out and I've... got to look after... the kids." Earl was the kind of guy who left a long pause between every phrase. A two-minute sentence could turn into a ten-minute ordeal with him, but Yam was in a hurry and he had no time for it.

"Earl, ya gotta come round *now*! This is an emergency!"

"Well, why... don't you come over... here."

Yam began to panic as he quickly calculated how long it would take him to drive to and from Harlesden, where he lived and Hackney where his brother lived, then to get ready, and then go and pick Cherry up from Brixton. There was no way he could make it.

"Nah, Earl, I don't have time, man! Bring the kids over here — you know Mummy would love to see them."

"No way, I'm just gettin' ready to watch... football."

Yam began to feel desperate. "Oh please, bruv, I *beg* you. Listen, I'll sort you out..."

"What d'ya mean?"

Yam felt himself growing impatient. Trying to get his brother to do him a favour was like making peace talks with the IRA. "It means *I'll sort you out.*"

Earl mulled over the offer. "So is that sort me out a lickle or sort me out a... lot."

"A lot! *Whatever* you want man. Just get yuh *hugly black arse over here*!" Yam slammed down the receiver. His brother was the living wind-up. Anyway, he didn't have time for this, he had to make himself beautiful for tonight. He didn't want Cherry to think he was some lickle raggamuffin bwoy. Oh no, he was going to make sure that she knew she was dealing with one slick, big-time, superstar producer.

He made his way into the bathroom and lingered over the vast array of toiletries he'd amassed over the years. Aramis? Nah — too common. Kuros? Nah — too old man. Drakkar Noir? Nah, too eighties. Eternity? Yeah, Eternity! He was feeling *very* Calvin Klein tonight *and* he had the boxer shorts to match… He was yet to meet the lady that could resist him in his lucky *lurve* shorts! With all the difficult decisions over, Yam gave himself a satisfied smile in the bathroom mirror. Even if he said so himself, he was one slick dude. He *knew* Cherry was going to be impressed!

Just as Yam had finished scrubbing himself down and was lathering a generous amount of baby lotion all over his body, the doorbell sounded throughout the house. He heard his mother let Earl and the kids in and pictured her face lighting up at the sight of her grandchildren. He chuckled to himself as he heard her usher them into the kitchen for some food. His mother was always feeding everyone up like they'd just come out of Ethiopia.

Yam bounced downstairs to hear his mother say, "Oh Earl, this is a nice surprise!"

"Yeah, well, I just… thought it would be nice for you… to see the kids, Mummy." Earl got up and kissed his mother on the cheek. "And you know… we all miss you."

Yam's mother beamed as she gazed up at her favourite son. She made sure that she piled his plate extra high with food.

Yam eyed the scene with distaste. What a creep. And what a liar. He thought about telling his mother the real reason for Earl's visit, but he knew he wouldn't. He never did.

It had always been like this, ever since they were kids Earl always managed to twist any situation to his advantage. Not that Yam didn't love his brother. On the contrary, when they were younger he'd idolised him, entranced by Earl's highly developed manipulative skills.

Still, he felt that Earl was taking the piss on this occasion,

17

so he gritted his teeth and said, "So ya ready, Earl?"

Earl kept shovelling. "Wait up 'til I finish… this *righteous* food."

"Nah, dread, I need my hair fixing right now!"

Earl turned to his mother. "Sorry Mummy, it seems that… Yam does not want me to enjoy this delicious meal… so I'll have to leave you with the kids."

Earl caught up to Yam on the stairs. "You got my t'ings, bruv?"

Yam gave a defeated sigh."Yeah, I said I'll sort you out — just make sure you do my hair good."

Earl looked hurt. "Have I ever done it any other way? By the time I'm finished, you'll look like a… *Prince* and the gyal — whoever she is — will want to… throw herself down at your feet the minute she lays eyes on ya!"

Yam put a chair down in the centre of his bedroom. Earl arranged a towel around his shoulders and got to work with his clippers. Before long the whole of Yam's scalp was neatly trimmed, apart from the top of his head where he'd carefully nurtured a cluster of funki dreds.

Earl rubbed a fat glob of beeswax between his fingers and twisted it through Yam's dreds. "This is to shine up ya locks for the… lucky lady."

When it was finished, Yam jumped up, dusted himself off and took a critical look at the overall picture he created in the mirror. He was wearing a one-off flight jacket, courtesy of Tommy Boy record company, freshly pressed big and baggy black Karl Kani jeans, black Tommy Hilfiger T-shirt and black combat boots. With newly trimmed hair and his face shaved like a baby, the overall effect was SHARP.

Earl nonchalantly took in the show, confident in the knowledge that he'd done a great job.

Yam turned round and touched fists with him. "Respeck, bruv."

"Mmmm… well, 'nuff of the 'respeck'… What about de t'ings we agreed upon?" Earl stretched out his hand, ready and eager to receive a generous payment for his good work, into which Yam surreptitiously placed a crumpled five-pound note. Before Earl could register he'd been short-changed, Yam was down the stairs.

Earl was soon hot on his heels, ready to flick the sharp edge of the towel on his feisty lickle raas. "Come back ya lickle rude bwoy."

"Can't stop now, bruv! Catch ya later, Mummy."

And with that Yam jumped in his car and sped off towards Brixton.

Cherry had gone back into her flat, soaking wet after waving goodbye to Yam from her balcony in the rain, and began her daily wake-up ritual — voice practice. As she shaped the notes, her voice soaring, she felt the high that only singing could give her. This was what she lived for. It was the only time that everything seemed real. The only time that all the pain slipped away and she was somewhere else, up in the heavens shining with the moon and the stars. It was the only time she felt free from the memories that haunted her every waking moment and hounded her every waking thought.

After practice, Cherry sat deep in thought. How was she going to get Yam to hook her up with some studio time?

She'd thought guys like him used girls all the time for a quick roll in the hay, but there seemed to be no getting around what was happening in this case — he actually looked like he was falling in love. Which wasn't quite how she'd planned it. And they say that women are the weaker sex! If she hadn't known better, she would have thought that Yam was a virgin, and this was the first time he'd ever fucked by the way he was acting.

And none of that shit helped.

Not that he didn't seem like a nice enough guy. But then they all did. At first. Still, she didn't want to get into any of that lovey-dovey crap. She'd seen too many girls throw away their lives for 'love', and nine times out of ten it didn't

19

even last and they'd wind up all lonely and empty with no real career or anything to be getting on with, as they'd already sacrificed that, so they'd spend all their energy looking for the next man to fall in 'love' with.

Cherry had waited a long time to come out in the real world, and now she was here she was going to make sure that she focused on completing her plan — which meant there was no way that any rubbish like 'love' could be on her agenda. But now Yam was getting all emotional, it meant that she was going to have to worry about hurting his feelings if she asked him to help her. How would he react if he thought the only reason she was with him was to further her career? More importantly, would it blow her chances of getting into the studio?

Her train of thought was interrupted by the intercom.

"It's me!"

Babsy was downstairs for one of her regular 'surprise' visits.

"Come on up."

Byrant Court was like Fort Knox since Lambeth Council had decided to invest in security. Now each block on her estate had a concierge installed on the ground floor and any visitor had to pass through two camera operated intercoms before they even got to her front door.

"Hey, girl!" Babsy kissed Cherry's cheek and went into the kitchen to make herself a cup of tea. She was a mixture of Nigerian and Swedish, and was in her early twenties, with long red-brown corkscrew hair which exploded from her head every which way but loose. She worked as a model for the Queen of Sheba model agency and management company, and part-time as a waitress at Touchdown — a nightclub in the West End.

Despite the fact that it was only two-thirty in the afternoon, she was wearing full make-up and a skin-tight black lycra bodysuit, that showed off every inch of her perfect size eight model's figure. Babsy *always* dressed like she was about to have her photo taken for the cover of *Vogue*

— although some of her outfits would have been more suited to *Sports Illustrated*.

The girls had met each other at the Brixton Recreation Centre, where they both went to work out, and go for the occasional swim. Babsy, who'd been going there for years, was intrigued to see another black girl suddenly appear on the scene and quietly go about her daily workout. Cherry had seemed so mysterious, and yet her face had been somehow familiar to Babsy. So, after a few weeks of wondering who Cherry was, she initiated a conversation — some meaningless topic like the weather. Cherry hadn't been very forthcoming at first, but Babsy had persisted.

They'd been hanging out for a couple of months now, but Babsy had to admit that she still knew very little about Cherry, as she refused to talk about herself, or her family, or anything personal. All that Babsy really knew for sure was that she was having more fun than she'd ever had with any other girlfriend in her whole life. And that Cherry's sole aim in life was to make it as a singer.

Babsy sipped her tea, and turned to her friend."Hey girl, have you heard that Sharon Stone is dealing with a black man now?"

"No way! Who? Wesley Snipes?"

"No, this guy called Chuck Washington. Some big-time Hollywood film producer and restaurateur. They're calling him 'Mr. Grits'. He's cute too, check out this picture..." Babsy pulled out a copy of *The News*, a paper they religiously poured over every week, bitching and laughing about celebrities as if they were their best friends. She often joked that it was the only newspaper she could read from cover to cover.

"Been up for any jobs this week, Babsy?"

"Yeah, 'Sister Girl' magazine. But they turned me down 'cause I'm 'too light'."

"*Again?*"

Babsy sighed in a matter-of-fact manner. "Again."

She had a tough time as a model. All the black magazines

refused to use her, as they said she was too light-skinned for them, and all the white magazines usually dismissed her as too 'exotic'. An adjective they both hated.

Cherry consoled her friend, "I don't know, maybe we should start up a magazine for mixed-race people. We could call it: *It Doesn't Matter If You're Black AND White!*"

The girls cracked up. Then Babsy looked serious. "So you finally got your man. How did you pull it off in the end?"

Cherry looked at Babsy and wondered for the millionth time wether she had told her too much about her interest in Yam. As always, she argued with herself that it didn't really matter, because Babsy had no other kind of information on her. Still, it didn't hurt to be careful, especially if she wanted everything to go to plan.

She adopted a casual tone and replied, "Oh, it was no big deal actually. We just hit it off."

But Babsy wasn't going to be palmed off that easily. "Mmm, so I see. But what about your record deal? Have you got him to arrange some studio time for you yet?"

Cherry still kept her tone light and said, "No, not yet. It's kinda nice to be actually getting laid for once — y'know it's been a while, girl! The studio time has been relegated to second place on my agenda for a while, until I get a groove on!"

Babsy couldn't believe what she was hearing. "You what? All you've been talking about since I met you is how you're gonna hook up a record deal, and now you've finally got the chance to start making that happen, it's suddenly 'been relegated to second place, until I get a groove on'!"

Cherry sipped on her tea and leaned nonchalantly back in her chair, saying, "Oh, get real, Babsy! I've only mentioned it to you once or twice in the last couple of weeks. I just don't wanna rush into anything that's all."

Babsy looked confused, sometimes she just didn't understand Cherry at all. "Well I just hope that you don't give up on your dreams."

Cherry gave her most reassuring and enigmatic smile. "I won't, Babsy. I won't."

Yam and Cherry sat in the Haagen-Dazs ice cream parlour in Leicester Square. She was enjoying the delights of pralines and cream and he was mashing up a strawberry sundae with all the extras. He hoped that the snack would sweeten her up for what he was about to spring on her.

They'd just been to see the latest Sylvester Stallone film, which Yam thought was *fantastic*. Sly had slaughtered *everyone*. He hoped Cherry had enjoyed it too, as he'd pre-booked the tickets without consulting her first. It wasn't exactly protocol, but, he *knew* how women just loved off those lovey-dovey, weepy-weepy films that he *hated*, so he wasn't about to risk anything by letting her choose the movie. Anyway, if he had any doubts about this, they were quickly removed when she kept burying her head in his shoulder and gripping his arm any time there was bloodshed. Which was *wicked*. The rate Sly was going, she must have done it a *million* times! He just hoped that she'd noticed how firm his biceps were in the process. Lord knows he must have tensed them 'nuff times.

"Did you enjoy the movie, Cherry?"

"Yeah it was, er... fine."

After where she'd been for the last five years, the last thing she'd wanted to see was a violent action movie. But he'd bought the tickets without consulting her first. Anyway *he'd* certainly enjoyed it. She could tell that from the way he kept slapping her thigh and shouting words of encouragement every time Sly blew someone away.

Yam took a deep breath, he had to work his way around to asking her if she would sing on the studio project. "So, you never told me Cherry... what do you do for a living?"

Cherry was momentarily taken aback, she hadn't expected him to ask about her livelihood at that point. "A living? Oh, I'm... er... writing for the government at the moment."

"Writing for the government?"

"Yeah — signing on. But I'm... er... planning to start studying. Soon."

"Have you ever thought of doing anything else?"

"Like what?" Cherry felt worried. Did he suspect something?

"Well, I don't know how to put this, so I'll just come right out with it... Can you sing?"

Cherry nearly choked on her ice cream. She was certain he suspected something now.

Yam plunged ahead, "I know this might seem like it's a bit out of the blue but, er, I'm a producer and, well, we're doing this project in the studio and, well, I was telling the guys how fine you are and t'ing and, well, Mr. E — he who owns the studio — well, he thought you would be good for... that your image could be right for the project." Yam knew he was babbling on, but he couldn't help it. Cherry had looked horrified when he'd asked her if she could sing, he just knew she thought he was some music business hot-shot looking to exploit her.

He leaned forward and took her hands in his. "Look, I know we've just met and everything, but I... well, I really care about you. I mean this is *not* what our relationship's about as far as *I'm* concerned. I completely understand if you don't want to do it, so don't feel any pressure to say yes. It's just that the guys asked me to ask you..."

Cherry was sure he knew something, it all seemed to be falling just a little too easily into place, but she felt like she was on 'Mastermind' now — she'd started, so she'd have to finish.

Her voice came out as a whisper, "Well, I could give it a go..."

Yam breathed a sigh of relief. "Thanks Cherry. Don't worry, we won't get you to do anything embarrassing, I'll be with you the whole time. It'll just be a laugh, really."

The Black Knight

MR. E STEPPED OUT OF Black Knight Productions after setting the alarm, and performed his nightly ritual of double, treble and quadruple locking the solid steel security door that acted as a barrier between the studio and the outside world. Yep, security was tight. It had to be, because he wasn't insured. Insurance people always ask too many unnecessary questions.

Black Knight Productions was his dream. A fully fledged forty-eight track studio that you could record at, mix at, and then go straight to a mastering suite and cut a record! And it was all his. And everything that was recorded there was his. So Mr. E should have been a very happy man indeed.

However, Mr. E was not a happy man. He wasn't happy at all.

This was because he'd had the studio for over a year now and had, so far, made squat diddly, jack-shit, fuck-all. Not a raas t'ing, apart from the odd change from a remix or two. This was not because the songs they were doing weren't the shit. The product was firing. No, it was because the record companies weren't buying. They weren't handing out the dollars unless you practically gave the whole thing to them on a plate. Nowadays they wanted songs, artists, image, concept. Even a video! And all he had to work with was the songs, which left an awful lot of the package uncovered.

What he needed was an artist. Someone with megastar potential, like a Michael Jackson or a Whitney Houston. Something he could package up with the songs and sell to the record companies for 'nuff dollars.

'Cause he needed the money bad. Real bad.

Every penny he'd ever had was tied up in the studio, and the bills, which were coming fast and thick, all had to be paid. By him. And, even more worryingly, every single penny he *didn't* have was tied up in the studio. Which meant that he owed an awful lot of money to someone. And that *someone* was the kind of person that needed to be paid back. With interest. Or you'd find yourself losing a lot more than your livelihood if you couldn't clear the debt.

The truth of the matter was that Black Knight Productions was at least a hundred grand in the hole. It might seem a lot to some people but by the time he'd bought his Merc, the equipment for the studio, and spent the change on living expenses and rental space, it didn't actually leave that much. It had just been enough for starting costs really.

When he'd borrowed it, a hundred thousand pounds hadn't seemed like shit. He'd felt certain he could make at least double that within the first few months of running the studio. But things hadn't quite gone to plan. He'd had no idea what a waiting game the music business was. But he'd soon found out that you spent most of it struggling and penniless — until you had your first hit, and then you would be high-rolling it as the millions poured in. Unfortunately, as Mr. E was only too acutely aware, he was still at the penniless and struggling stage. And now, that hundred grand — the same hundred grand that had seemed so piddly when he'd first borrowed it, the same hundred grand that had seemed like a mere drop in the ocean compared to all the shedloads of cash he had been so sure he'd make, the same hundred grand that he had pissed away without a care in the world on a top-of-the-range car and all the latest high-tech studio equipment, weighed like a milestone around his neck. It was an ever-increasing burden that he bore on his back, day after day, week after endless week. An enormous, lavish, stupendous amount of pounds upon pounds upon pounds. A huge, copious, almost insurmountable pile of dosh. The kind of money that kings could live on. *The kind of money that men get killed for.*

Feeling short of breath, Mr. E clutched at his throat and loosened his collar and tie. There was no doubt about it, if he didn't sell some product soon or something, the whole of Black Knight Productions, and all its affiliated companies were going under, and the chances were that he was going to go right down with it.

With all this running relentlessly through his mind, Mr. E skulked over to his aforementioned brand new, top-of-the-range 500 series black Mercedes. Complete with tinted windows, soft black leather upholstery, a walnut veneer dashboard, and all the trimmings, it was the perfect chariot for the Black Knight. Or so it had seemed when he had a hundred readies burning a hole in his pocket.

Fingers and D were reclining inside its plush interior, waiting to be dropped home. "So I told my spar dat he better not test me, right, or he'd better be ready to deal wid some serious business—" Fingers stopped talking as Mr. E entered the car. "Everyt'ing cool, Mr. E?"

Mr. E glanced at their youthful inquiring faces. No, everything was most certainly *not* cool! He was a hundred grand in the hole, with a forty-eight track studio to run — not to mention a home, a car and wages to pay. And the only chance he had of saving his ass depended on these two clueless church-band muthafuckas comin' up with some hit songs and a megastar artist to match!

Mr. E turned the ignition, his eyes grimly fixed on the road as he replied in flat, lifeless tones, "Yeah, everyt'ing's cool."

After dropping off Fingers and D, Mr. E sped off into the night, thinking about the first time he'd met them. He had arrived in East London — from where, nobody knew. Having got together the studio, all that was left was to amass a team of talent to work in it. So of course he had gone to church. It was there that he'd first met Fingers and Yam. Fingers was on keyboards and Yam was on bass in the church band. Both of them had more talent in their little toes than all of the acts in the charts put together. Not that that cut any ice in the music business, as he was now — much to his chagrin — only too clearly finding out. It was only later that he discovered that Fingers was a multi-instrumentalist, playing keyboards, guitar, trumpet, whatever. There wasn't an instrument in the world that Fingers couldn't play. And he could play them all to the max. A genius really — but not even that was putting food on the table. Through them he had met Deckland, who was a recording studio engineer, and he had his team: Yam on drums and bass, Fingers on every other instrument, Deckland at the controls. And each of them wrote songs too.

And Mr. E owned them. And he owned anything they ever did in the studio. Not that they were really aware of that. The only thing they cared about was making music. Which was how it should be — you can't be creative *and* worry about business. That was his job.

Thinking of business, his mind turned back to the money he owed. Mr. E took out his mobile and dialled the number that was permanently tattooed to his brain.

An answering machine clicked on and said, "Hi, you have reached..."

Damn! When was this muthafucka going to be in? Three o'clock in the morning and still no reply. Maybe he was away or something. That was all he needed with his financial situation — an out-of-town muthafucka!

Having arrived at his destination, he parked his car, quietly unlocked the front door with his key, entered the house, climbed the stairs and went into the bedroom. He pulled off his trousers, slid in between the sheets and took a firm hold of Denise, his assistant at Black Knight Productions.

She awoke as she felt his familiar touch and croaked, "What time do you call this?"

"Shhhh."

Mr. E wasn't ready to take any attitude from a woman. In fact he was *never* ready to take attitude from anybody.

As usual, he went straight inside her, and after about two or three minutes of roughness it was all over. Denise still kept her position with her back to him, her buttocks pressed against his groin. Wide awake now, she asked herself for the millionth time, why she let him do this.

Mr. E got up and put his trousers back on. He had no time for all this huggin' and lovin', not when there was work to do. Silently, he stole back into the night.

Denise wondered if, when she woke up in the morning, she'd think it had all been a dream.

Monday morning dawned bright and early and it was with a light heart that Yam dialled Mr. E's mobile. He knew he'd be up — there wasn't a single time, day or night, that Mr. E wasn't wide awake and answering his phone. Maybe he never slept.

"Yo! It's me — Yam. Listen, Cherry's cool 'bout coming to the studio."

This was just what Mr. E wanted to hear, so he asked, "When can you reach?"

"Today if you want."

"Cool, hook it up for about six o'clock I've got a few runnings to take care of first."

"Safe. We'll see you later."

"Yeah, laters."

Mr. E called the studio. "Denise. Any calls?"

"The electricity board. They want to cut us off."

"What did you tell them?"

"That the cheque is in the post."

"Good girl. Did Warners call?"

"No."

"Polygram?"

"No."

"All right, tell Fingers and D to get de studio ready. We've got an artist coming down later on to blow 'pon some tunes."

Mr. E clicked off his phone. He knew the record companies wouldn't have returned his calls. He wasn't important enough. Yet. Maybe Yam's girl — Grape, or whatever her name was — would be the answer to all his prayers.

God knows he needed her to be.

When Yam entered Black Knight Productions with Cherry, his chest swelled with pride. She looked *fantastic*. She was wearing skin tight black PVC trousers that accentuated her every curve. A tiny black T-shirt that looked like it would be a snug-fit on a five year old, was stretched thinly across her breasts, with an ample amount of well-toned midriff on show. The guys would be trippin'!

He adopted a nonchalant air and sauntered into the studio, his right leg slightly dragging on every step. Triumphantly, he noted Fingers and D's jaws drop to the floor at the sight of Cherry.

Casually, as if it was quite normal for him to bring a beautiful girl into the studio he made the introductions. "Awright homies. Dis is Cherry. Cherry, meet Deckland and Fingers."

Cherry reached out to shake hands with each of them in turn and utter a very polite 'nice to meet you'. What a girl! She had the manners of royalty. His Nubian princess — and he was her king!

Fingers and D quickly jumped to their feet and ushered Cherry to the cleanest chair in the studio. Denise watched the whole scene with a bemused air. These guys — one pretty face and it was all over! You'd think they'd never seen a woman before. She thought she'd better rescue Cherry, otherwise the poor girl would never want to come back.

"Do you want some tea, love?"

Cherry smiled her thanks and D chirped in, "Yeah Denise, make dat a blackcurrant for me and Yam, and fix up a brandy and coke for Fingers, *s'il vous plait*."

"I think you know where the kitchen is *mon chere...*" Denise gave a conspiratorial wink at Cherry who laughed back.

"Yeah, but... but..." But it was too late as Denise was already out of the room.

Fingers turned back to the others shaking his head. "Yuh just cyant get de staff these days!" He looked at Cherry. He'd thought that Yam had been exaggerating, but it was no lie that this girl was supermodel material. She was dope. "Anyways, let's get down to business. Are you ready to hear the track?"

He played the song, and Cherry couldn't believe how great it was. It sounded like a number one record. Even though she felt excited, her first step in her master plan already in motion, she was a little apprehensive — unsure whether or not the whole thing might still be a set-up?

A low, gruff voice cut through the melodies of the track. "So… what do you think?"

Everyone turned round to see Mr. E standing in the doorway.

Yam stood up, and with a dramatic sweep of his hand, he revealed his prize. "This is Cherry… Cherry, this is Mr. E."

They nodded at one another. Cherry suddenly felt nervous. She had no idea that Yam's boss would be there when she came to the studio, so she kept her head slightly bowed and tried to remain calm as she answered his question.

"It's cool."

"So, you ready to blow 'pon it?"

"What?" Cherry felt uncertain, she thought she'd have time to practice the song before laying any vocals to tape.

Yam voiced her thoughts and protested, "We thought we'd give her a tape, so that she can go off and rehearse it first."

Mr. E kept his eyes on Cherry. He knew he was rushing things, but he couldn't hold himself back. Time was running out, and he felt like he had to know whether or not she could cut the tune there and then. She had the image all right — but could she sing? He pressed on. "Why? She's heard the song and you all heard her say she thinks it's cool. If she's *any* kind of singer at all, she'll be able to run through it right now… D, go and set up the mic."

D looked puzzled, like everyone else, he thought it was unfair to throw Cherry in at the deep end like this.

Mr. E's eyes bore into Cherry's skull as he asked, "So, do you think you're up to it, Grape?"

She bristled and rose to his challenge. There was no way she was going to let this asshole unnerve her *and* forget her name.

"My name is *Cherry*... Mr. *B*, and no, I don't see it being a problem."

The room fell silent as they watched D set up the mic. Nobody really understood the tension between Mr. E and Cherry and it made them feel uneasy. When everything was ready, D led Cherry into the vocal booth. Inside, she was shrouded in darkness, with just a tiny spotlight illuminating the lyric sheet which was balanced on top of a music stand. All she could see through the window of the vocal booth were the faces of Yam, Fingers and D, looking expectantly back at her.

"Okay Cherry, we need to get a level. If you could just sing a few words into the mic." Yam spoke softly, he felt worried for Cherry and extremely annoyed at Mr. E. He gritted his teeth and decided to just run with it for now — but he'd make sure to have a word with Mr. E later, let him know that he'd better treat Cherry with respect.

"One two, one two..." Cherry's voice was shaky. She felt nervous and intimidated with them all staring at her from the monitor room. She knew that she could sing the song, but now that she was in the vocal booth, she could feel her nerves starting to get the better of her. What if she made a fool of herself? What if they all laughed?

But she had no choice. This was her only chance, and if she blew it there'd be no way this asshole, Mr. E, was going to let her come back to Black Knight Productions for another try.

Before she could even finish her thoughts, the intro of the song began to play in her headphones. There was no time to back out now. Taking a deep breath, Cherry stepped up to the mic, her heart beat against her ribcage and butterflies raced around her stomach. It was now or never.

She opened her mouth and sang.

Yam hadn't expected much, but nothing could have prepared him for what he was hearing. No less than the voice of an... *angel*... rang out of the monitors and bounced off every wall in the studio. As it climbed its... *amazing*... highs and lows, he began to forget his manly self-image, and felt genuinely close to tears. This was was the kind of voice that could move you. His baby was *incredible!*

Yam thought that he had to be dreaming. To make certain that he wasn't, he looked around to check everyone else's reaction. Sure enough, Fingers and D were vigorously nodding their heads and muttering enthusiastic 'Yeah-yeahs' at every twist in Cherry's vocal gymnastics.

Meanwhile, Mr. E had leaned back against the wall, and melted even further into the shadows. He closed his eyes and let out a sigh of relief. The sound of cash tills rang in his ears and dollar signs danced before him. This girl was a goldmine! Finally — the answer to all his prayers. And then some.

Yam turned to him. Barely able to contain his excitement, he whispered, "So... what d'ya think?"

Mr. E stepped forward into the light. Deadly serious, he looked Yam straight in the eye and said, "Dat gal can walk on water... Finish the tune!" And with that he left the studio and went on his way. He had arrangements to make.

Cherry held her last note. As she opened her eyes she came out of the almost trance-like state that she always went into when she sang. Stepping out of the vocal booth, she noted the shouts of appreciation and respect from Fingers and D, and the smile that spread from ear to ear across Yam's face spoke volumes. In her moment of victory, she searched for Mr. E.

But he had already gone.

The Product

THE NEXT FEW WEEKS WERE FILLED with recording, recording and then more recording. The songs were polished and re-polished and polished again until they were perfect. It was exhausting and exhilarating at the same time. Everyone had a new burst of energy now that Cherry had come along to sing the songs, and it didn't hurt that she wasn't an eyesore either. Fingers and D dropped their usual routine of loafing around the studio with nappy hair and wearing any old wrinkled piece of clothing they could lay their hands on when they woke up. Instead, they arrived bright and early, all newly washed and pressed, curls all clean and shiny. Even Yam, who was always immaculate anyway, seemed to make an extra special effort.

Much to Cherry's relief, Mr. E was scarce to be seen the whole time, saying he had 'much runnings to be getting on with', and that they could 'do the business' without him having to be there to hold their hands.

Now, however, all the songs were finished and everyone was congregated in the office area of Black Knight Productions, ready for a meeting that Mr. E had scheduled at one p.m. sharp. That was, everyone apart from Fingers, who usually ran a bit late.

Bang on time Mr. E walked into the office, and greeted them. "Good afternoon, children!" He ushered Denise out the way, and sat down at the reception desk, from where he was to chair the meeting.

"I want to congratulate you all for working so hard over the past few weeks and comin' up with some dope tunes. Now we've finished the music, we have to package up our artist," he paused to indicate Cherry with a nod. "The next step is to arrange a photo shoot to get some glossy ten-by-eights of young Cherry here." He stopped to pull out a thick and important looking folder from his record bag. "Now, I've thought about this very carefully over the last few weeks, whilst you guys were working on the songs, and I've finally decided on the best image for our artist. Bear in mind that what we need is something that's gonna turn heads, something that the general public won't be able to get out of their minds. Something that millions of young girls will aspire to be like and even more young boys will fantasise over. Something dat's hard-hitting and contemporary, yet classic and timeless. An image that will appeal to all ages and make dem forget dat Whitney Houston and Toni Braxton ever even existed!"

Everyone was on the edge of their seats; after that build-up they couldn't wait to see what Mr. E had come up with. They sat mesmerised, as he slowly pulled out a magazine from his folder. He flicked it open to a page he'd already marked and, with a triumphant smile, turned it round to reveal a full-length picture of a stunning model, wearing one of the skimpiest bikinis they'd ever seen.

"*Wicked*!" D enthusiastically nodded his head, exclaiming, "Dis is *perfect* for you Cherry, the guys will be... will be..." He stopped dead in his tracks as he caught the look of horror on Yam's face. He turned to Cherry and saw that her expression mirrored Yam's.

Cherry was angry. Mr. E was taking the piss. Her voice was low and quiet, "What is this fucking bullshit?!"

"Baby!" Yam turned and looked saucer-eyed at Cherry. He could understand her being upset, but he didn't like to hear his angel swearing like this.

She turned to him, her face contorted with anger and spat out, "Shut the fuck up."

Yam recoiled like she'd shot a bullet through his heart.

Cherry turned back to Mr. E. "I'm serious, who the *fuck* do you think you are muthafucka — my pimp?"

"Well, I er..." Mr. E was at a loss for words, he'd never in his wildest dreams expected a reaction like this.

Cherry looked him dead in the eye. "Don't you *ever* think about dressing *me* up like a ho!" With that, she got up and strode out of the studio.

35

Mr. E looked incredulously at Yam. "Yam! Wha' kinda lickle roughneck rude gyal yuh bring me?"

Yam felt like the walls were crumbling around him, and his whole world was caving in. This was a side of Cherry that he'd never seen before, and it made him feel scared. How could Mr. E go and upset her like that? And turn her into the madwoman that had just sworn at him.

He turned to the reason for the change in his beloved Cherry and replied, "Just shut up, man," then brushed past Mr. E, D and Denise, and ran out of the studio.

Cherry was totally pissed off. Mr. E was an asshole that thought that he could treat her like she was just some slut off the street that he could do what he wanted with. *She hadn't spent five long years in jail to come out and deal with his shit.* And Yam, acting all hurt when she'd started cussing. It was about time that he woke up and smelt the coffee.

"Cherry! Wait up."

It was Yam. She turned round and looked at him defiantly. "What?"

"Are you okay?"

Cherry kissed her teeth, "Do I look okay?"

"Look, I understand how you feel. Mr. E behaved like an idiot in there. But his attitude is not worth throwing away everything we've been working for. You're not gonna achieve anything by blowing your top."

Cherry couldn't believe what she was hearing — who was *he* to reproach her? "Don't you care at *all* about what that asshole did to me in there? He made all the hard work I've done to make my voice what it is, and to lay all those tunes — that are gonna put money in his pocket — seem like nothing! He made me feel that my talent and who I am as a person doesn't mean anything whatsoever. All I am to him is some silly tart that he can dress up in a bikini or whatever else he feels like. If he thinks for one moment that he can play games with my life, he can think again! Guys like Mr.

E always get what's coming to them in the end — you can be sure of that. He's a fucking misogynist!"

Yam winced — she was swearing again. "A what?"

"A *misogynist* — someone who hates women."

Yam mulled over Cherry's words. Now that she'd mentioned it, he realised he'd never seen Mr. E treat any woman with respect. Not that he wasn't all right with the guys; he just didn't seem to have any time for women. "Y'know, I never thought of it before, but I think you could be right, Cherry. Look, I'm not gonna let Mr. E's stupidness blow the deal! You stay here, and I'll go and talk to him."

Cherry reluctantly agreed. Much as she longed to tell Mr. E where he could go, she was even more loathe to ruin all her plans by blowing this chance of getting a record deal. She gritted her teeth as she resigned herself to some sort of reconciliation with Mr. E.

Back in the studio Denise was having 'words' with Mr. E. "What did you go and do that for?"

"Wha'?" Mr. E was confused, what was *with* the women today? Even Denise was turning on him now!

"What possessed you to suggest a skimpy bikini as Cherry's image?"

"What's wrong with a *skimpy bikini*? I t'ink it looks great." He pointed to D, who seemed to have developed a deep fascination for his bootlaces. "D *loves* it — right, D?"

"Well I er…" D shifted uncomfortably in his seat his eyes even more firmly locked onto his feet.

Denise continued, "Exactly! Because it's just pure pathetic male fantasy. Have you ever stopped to think that Cherry might be a *serious* artist? You don't see Whitney Houston or Anita Baker running on stage in a bikini. Maybe — just *maybe* — Cherry might like to be perceived in the same way as them, rather than some… some Playboy bunny girl!"

Mr. E hated it when Denise gave him a 'talking to',

especially in front of the guys. Worst of all, he had a sneaky feeling that she was right. So he sat stony-faced and said nothing.

At that moment Yam re-entered the office. "Mr. E! I'm getting tired of you treating my woman like this. What are you, some kind of misogynist?"

Misogynist! What the fuck was that when it was at home? Mr. E had just about had enough of this saga, especially now Yam was flinging stupid words at him for no reason. He tried to make peace. "Look, look, there's no need to fall out over foolishness." He reached in his pocket and pulled out a wad of crisp notes. "Just take dis money and make sure Cherry buys something nice dat *you* all approve of. I'm just the one who has to pay all the wages here, never mind all the bills, so what does my opinion matter anyway! I'll check you lot later, I've got some business to take care of." And with that, he stuffed the handful of money into Yam's hand and was out the door.

Yam felt frustrated, he still felt that he had a few things to say to Mr. E. Denise sensed this and went up to him and put her hand on his shoulder.

"Don't worry, Yam, this won't feel nearly as important in a few days, when we've all calmed down. Mr. E knows he was wrong; leaving like that is just his way of dealing with the embarrassment."

Yam looked gratefully at Denise, she could always make things seem okay. He wondered, as he always did, why she never seemed to have a man. Before he'd met Cherry he'd tried to take her out once, but she'd turned him down. It didn't make any sense for a fine-looking woman like Denise to be on her own.

At that point Fingers sauntered in, not a care in the world, despite the fact that he was over an hour late. "Wha'ppen people. Did I miss anyt'ing?"

A laugh escaped involuntarily from Yam's lips as he turned back to Denise and said, "Thanks. Listen, Cherry's waiting outside, I'd better go and tell her the good news.

Check ya later, Fingers!"

Cherry's anger had only slightly subsided when Yam arrived back at her flat.

"Well?"

Yam puffed up his chest. "Well, I told him where he could get off. I'm not having anyone treat *my* woman with disrespect, studio or no studio! I said if he gave us any more attitude, I would have no choice but to lick him down! So he backed off and apologised for his misconduct and gave me some money, so you can buy whatever you want for the photo shoot!"

Cherry eyed Yam in disbelief, did he *really* expect her to swallow that? She decided to get to the point, asking, "How much money did he give you?"

Yam opened his fist. To both their surprise, he saw that he held a cool five hundred in crisp fifty-pound notes.

On their way back to Cherry's — Yam was more or less living with her now — Cherry sat deep in thought.

"Why is Mr. E called Mr. E? What's his real name?"

"That's why we call him Mr. E, because he's a mystery. None of us know anything about him. It was like he came from nowhere. I've lived in London all my life, and I've never met anyone who knew him before he set up the studio. We don't know where he lives or where he goes. No one — but *no one* — knows his real name or where he comes from. He's even got the studio bills in the name of Mr. Smith! To be honest we don't push ourselves up into his business anyway, 'cause the only thing we care about is that we can make music at the studio."

"Is that so?"

Cherry sunk deep down into the passenger seat. Her mind working overtime.

The Contract

CHERRY CAST A CRITICAL EYE over the glossies Yam had handed to her, trying hard to believe that she was looking at herself in the photographs. They were *amazing*. She had no idea that a photograph could be so flattering. The bright fluorescent orange velvet bell-bottom outfit that she'd got at Hyper Hyper looked fantastic, and the way Babsy had highlighted her eyes and mouth with a shimmery gold was nothing short of *genius*. Yam was just as bowled over. He'd always known it anyway, but here was the two-dimensional proof that his woman was like one of those supermodels that he'd previously only dreamt about.

He leaned back and nonchalantly said to Cherry, "Yeah, you're not bad to look at are ya."

Cherry shot back, "Oh Yam, I find it so hard to resist you, when you go charming me with all that sweet talk!"

The photos were what everyone had hoped for, even Mr. E was pleased. The 'product' was almost complete. Now there was only one more thing to take care of...

"Cherry, can I have a word with you in private."

What did he want? Cherry didn't feel like being alone with Mr. E, but reluctantly she agreed.

Everyone was in the 'office', so they stepped into the grey-carpeted monitor room.

Once they were inside with the door closed, Mr E turned to Cherry with a bright, sunny smile and said, "Now, Cherry, I know that we've both had our differences, but I want you to know that I'm very pleased with the way things have been running. We've almost got the package together and, when it's completed, I'll be hooking you up with a multi-million dollar record deal."

It was all very straightforward and pleasant enough so far, which made Cherry feel even more worried. She had a nasty feeling that Mr. E was like a cat ready to pounce. And she was definitely the mouse. She watched apprehensively, as he pulled out one of his folders and a pen and writing pad from his record bag.

"There's just a couple of t'ings we need to get out of the way first. To begin with, we need to write a bio about you."

"A bio?"

"Yeah, a *biography* — a brief history of who you are." Mr. E stood with his pen poised, "Now, what's your real name?"

Cherry's heart was in her mouth, she had no idea that Mr. E was going to pry into her background. "You know my real name," she said flatly.

"No I don't, I only know you as Cherry Drop."

"That's right. It's my real name." Cherry felt her cheeks starting to go red, Mr. E had really caught her off guard.

He gave her a knowing look. "Well, if you say so…" he jotted the information down on his pad. "Now, where do you come from?"

"Er… Ireland."

Mr. E was unconvinced. "*Ireland*? I can't hear an accent."

Cherry shrugged her shoulders, she didn't care if he couldn't hear English, all she wanted was for him to leave her alone. For this interrogation to be over.

"Well, okay… whereabouts 'in Ireland' exactly?"

"Er… Dublin."

"Yeah? Well you've completely lost your accent!"

"So what?" Cherry was getting pissed off, she hated the way he was looking at her, it was like Mr. E could see right through her, as if he could read her innermost thoughts — and through it all she could feel him silently mocking her.

Mr. E fought to retain his patience. "Okay, maybe you'll warm to this one a little more… What have you been doing over the past few years?"

"Growing up."

Mr. E finally lost it. "*Very* funny, young lady! What have you been doing with regards to *music*, prior to recording at *my* studio? Have you released any records? Done any backing-vocal sessions? WHAT?"

Cherry gave him a rebellious stare. "If I'd released a

record, I wouldn't be sitting here would I?"

Mr. E resigned himself to the fact that he was getting nowhere. "I tell you what, why don't I make some shit up, and you can approve of it later?"

"Great!" Cherry breathed a sigh of relief, maybe everything was going to be fine after all. She turned to go.

"Oh, just one more t'ing…" Mr. E casually waved a wad of papers at her, "If you could sign these…"

Cherry exhaled. "Sign what?"

"Jus' some papers for the business side of t'ings."

Quickly flicking through the papers she got to the last paragraph and asked, "Where's the pen?"

He handed her the pen and she signed the papers with a hurried flourish, then hot-stepped it out of the studio.

"What did he want?" It was Yam.

"Er, to sign some business papers and stuff."

Yam chuckled knowingly, "That's typical of Mr. E — he's always 'taking care of the business'. We've all had to sign certain 'papers'. Probably signing our lives away!"

They all laughed, although they didn't know how close to the truth Yam was. In a way they didn't care; all they desired at this point was that they could be in the studio making music. If that meant signing some of Mr. E's 'papers', then so be it.

In the monitor room Mr. E sat back in his chair and smiled to himself. It had been so simple to get that hot-headed bitch to lose her rag. Good job he'd tested her temper out first with that bikini photo. She'd gone for it like a lamb to the slaughter; it was almost too easy.

He'd known all along that she was frontin' it — like her real name was Cherry Drop! Not that he gave a shit. She could be the next Rose West for all he cared. Her ass was well and truly his now. No matter who the hell she was, or where the hell she came from.

The Record Company

NIKKI STIXX CRAWLED ALONG BAYSWATER ROAD in her brand-new burgundy Saab. Most people would be more than happy with a luxury company car, but Nikki hated it. What she really wanted was a just-as-new midnight-blue Audi convertible, with beige leather interior and automatic gear-shift. Just like Princess Diana had had. Of course, it was just a pretentious sloane wannabe car, but she didn't care. It was what she wanted. And so far, everything that Nikki Stixx had ever wanted, Nikki Stixx had got.

She breathed a sigh of frustration, and shifted the hated Saab gear-stick into neutral. The traffic was almost at a standstill now. Taking out her lipstick — Mac's rouge-noir — Nikki pouted into her rearview mirror and cast a disinterested glance over the perfection of the rest of her face. An Angela Bassett lookalike, some people she did business with found it difficult to get past her looks. Certain people refused to accept that an attractive woman could be intelligent and successful at the same time. It was like they didn't want you to have it all, no matter how hard you had worked for it. And Nikki Stixx had worked hard. Real hard. Without so much as a stitch of help from anyone. Not that she cared; always having to get past being typecast as a 'bimbo' had only ever served to add fuel to her fire.

However, none of this was on Nikki's mind this morning, as she sat sandwiched between a Range Rover and a Beetle, en route from her home in Notting Hill Gate to her office at the main B.U.L. Records building in Soho. She cursed the tube strike under her breath, seething helpless and impotent in the sea of immobile traffic. At this rate she was going to be late for her meeting — and, as always, but even more so today — she wanted to get there early.

Nikki was very excited about this one. Who'd have thought that a guy like Mr. E would have come up with product of this quality? He'd always been just another 'independent production company', that would come up with the odd groove now and then, and to whom she could toss the occasional remix. No-one could have been more surprised than her to hear his latest offering. If this package was for real, it was going to take her just where she wanted to go. Which was *all* the way. And then some.

That was, if she ever got to this meeting. Nikki felt herself starting to fret, she *had* to get there on time, before he took himself over to Warners, or some other bullshit. In her frustration, she beeped her horn at the stationary cars in front of her. When was the traffic going to get moving?!! In the midst of her anger, she mentally checked herself. She had to remain calm; it wouldn't do her any good to arrive at the meeting all sweaty and worked up.

So, Nikki Stixx leant back into her seat, took some long, deep breaths, closed her eyes and did some positive visualisation techniques on that Audi.

Meanwhile, Mr. E cruised his Mercedes along Brixton Road. He wasn't worried about being late at all. Nikki Stixx had called him personally when she got the tape with the bio and the photos — first thing in the morning, the very day after he'd sent it. She could have only listened to it once. Still, when the shit is that dope, one listen is all you need… The way she'd been all casual but sweet on the phone had almost given him a hard-on. He knew she was gagging for it… asking whether he'd sent it to anyone else! Of course, he'd told her the truth which was a 'No, *not yet*'. But he didn't want to mess around on this. This was one deal he wanted to happen fast. And it wasn't just the money, which he needed like yesterday; last week even. With the package he had sitting in his pocket, he suddenly felt confident that the dollars were going to start flowing now. The simple fact was that he was genuinely excited about the project. He couldn't wait to see the product in the charts. So there was absolutely no point in fucking around, no need to bullshit.

Because the shit he'd come up with was the real deal. And he knew exactly what he was looking for. B.U.L. Records was the company that could give it to him. And Nikki Stixx was the only A & R person that he wanted it from.

So, no, he wasn't worried about being late, the only thing he had to be worried about was that this lickle roughneck, raggamuffin rude gyal sitting right beside him, would say something stupid and mess up his business tactics.

He glanced over at Cherry, who had been sitting quietly ever since he'd picked her up in Brixton. He had to admit she looked hot today, squeezed into some bright shiny piece of something, which barely covered her ample curves. Looking all funky with her knee-length lace-up boots, and her hair gelled into big spikes. Pity she didn't have a brain to match, *unlike the sumptuous Ms. Stixx*.

"Are you nervous, Cherry?" he asked.

"No." Cherry wasn't nervous at all, she only felt the kind of serene calm that you feel when you're sure everything is going your way.

Mr. E disregarded her answer and continued in reassuring tones, "Well, you've got nothing to worry about. Your part is very simple — the only thing you have to remember to do is nod and smile."

"You what?" Cherry broke out of her reverie for a second. What was he going on about now?

"What I mean is, you just keep your mouth shut and let me do all the talking. You're only required to be there so that they can see that you're not a dog in the flesh, and that you look just as good in real life as you do in the photographs.

"I've got dis meeting very carefully planned and I don't need you butting in and confusing my tactics. So don't say anyt'ing at all. Just remember to *nod and smile* at everyt'ing I say, and if Ms. Stixx asks you any questions, let me answer them for yuh."

Cherry looked incredulously at Mr. E. Was he serious? It was so ridiculous, it wasn't even worth discussing.

She slumped back into her seat, cocked her feet up on the

dashboard and said, "Whatever."

Mr. E was beside himself, *did she have a death wish or something*? She couldn't *really* be putting her big, nasty boots on his freshly polished walnut veneer dashboard!

He hardly knew which cussword to say first, as he spluttered, "Tek yuh boot off me dashboard before I throw you outta my chariot. Record deal be damned!"

The B.U.L. building, in the heart of Soho, was all colour washed apricot walls with terracotta skirting boards. Bleached silver ash-wood furniture, and oversized burgundy soft cotton sofas littered the floor space. The black leather, chrome furniture and grey walls and carpets that symbolised the materialism and capitalism of the eighties, had all been ripped out and replaced with a softer, more laid back, new age type of sensibility. The new, gentler, colour scheme seemed to convey the message that music was no longer about chart positions, album sales and making money; instead it was about nurturing talent and sending out 'positive vibes *m-a-a-a-an*'. Of course it was all just a front. Record executives of the nineties were even more obsessed with sales and money than they were in the eighties. Because now money was more scarce. But instead of buying a Porsche convertible and a villa in the south of France with their pay cheques, they would go on equally expensive yoga retreats in pursuit of their 'inner selves'.

All this was lost on Cherry because, when she arrived at the waiting room for Nikki Stixx's offices, she just couldn't believe her eyes. She literally pinched herself to make sure she wasn't dreaming. Babsy would trip if she could see this... *any girl with a pulse would trip if she could see this*.

He was every schoolgirl's wet dream, and the most successful man in the music business to date. And here he was in the flesh, looking every bit as sexy and *fine* — if not better — than he did when he was gyrating his way through The Box and MTV.

Dressed in a bright red nylon Mecca tracksuit and matching red and white Sergio Tacchini headband, he was firing instructions at the receptionist. "Yeah, so when they represent with the orios, make sure ya send 'em up to me an' ma boyz."

It was Freddie Famous. Number one, bestselling male megastar in the world. The horniest, richest most famous man on the planet.

The wheels inside her mind already clicking into action, Cherry adopted a casual air and breezed past the scene at the reception desk, acting like she didn't even register his presence, never mind recognise him.

Mr. E, also determined to keep his cool whilst basking in the truly awesome presence of Freddie, strutted over to the receptionist and informed her in a loud and confident voice that he'd arrived for his eleven o'clock meeting with Nikki.

Within seconds they were being ushered into her office. Nikki Stixx was sitting on a huge, over-sized burgundy leather swivel chair, in front of a smooth, freshly waxed, bleached silver ash-wood desk, which matched the rest of the furniture in the room. Behind her, a floor-to-ceiling-window looked out onto the web of streets that made up Soho, the media and entertainment centre of London. Here a hotbed of the capital's hippest advertising executives, up-and-coming film directors and TV production companies rubbed shoulders with record company moguls, journalists and graphic designers. Throw in the odd tourist and the occasional prostitute from the 'red light' area, and you'd have a basic picture of Soho. It was a very impressive and exclusive location.

Nikki Stixx was all smiles, as she rose to greet them. "Mr. E, my main man! And this must be our new superstar!" After giving Mr. E two air kisses, she brushed her lips across Cherry's cheeks and gushed, "I have to tell you guys, I loved the tape, it's *incredible*. You don't know how excited I am, your stuff has definite superstar potential!"

She kept her eyes on Cherry, "It's great to see that you

look every bit as beautiful in the flesh as you do in the photos. It's not very often we hear a voice as amazing as yours from someone who looks as fabulous as you."

Cherry stayed silent and smiled an enigmatic smile, feeling that it was all going to be so easy; Nikki Stixx was practically pissing her pants.

Nikki continued, "So, your bio says that you spent the first ten years of your life in Mississippi, and that your father was a minister in the Pentecostal Church..."

Cherry felt herself begin to fume. What had Mr. E written in her bio? No wonder he didn't want her to read it.

As if on cue, he chimed in, "Dat's right Nikki, Cherry's roots are deep in gospel, which she has heard ever since she can remember, as it echoed around the four walls of her father's church..."

Mr. E barely noticed the words of his own spiel, as his eyes drank in the exquisite form of Nikki Stixx. Now this was a *woman*.

And he could feel that she wanted him — almost as much as he wanted her. What a team they'd make, they'd be invincible — the king and queen of the music industry!

Outside, Freddie Famous was quizzing the receptionist for details of Cherry. He'd been completely bowled over by the *vision* that had presented itself to him . What a babe! We're talking legs — *bam...!* booty — *bam...!* titties — *BOOMIN'*!

Of course, he had fronted like her shit didn't bother him, because he was Freddie Famous now, and Freddie Famous didn't need to be trippin' over no pussy — 'cause the pussy was trippin' over him, now he was hangin' on a superstar tip. Or at least, that's how it should have been. But the truth was, no matter how famous he was, or how many girls he was attracting, he still got that adrenaline rush, every time he clocked a fly honey. Admittedly, a girl had to be *very* fly nowadays to catch his attention, now there was such a selection available to him... But this honey had him feeling like he was just plain ole Felix Fitzroy again, back at the crib with his boyz, ready to hit a cutie for her digits right there on the street!

"So you ain't got a phone number, an address or *nothin'*?"

"No Freddie, just the details of the production company she's with."

The receptionist leaned forward to display her décolletage to its full advantage, annoyed that all Freddie could talk about was this new girl. "I've no idea who she is — this is the first time she's been here. We always get girls like that. They come here once, thinking they're gonna get a deal because of the way they look, and then — *poof!*" the receptionist clicked her fingers. "You never see them again. Now, *I* on the other hand —"

"Wait up!" Freddie silenced the receptionist mid-flow as some music began to pump from Jacqueline's office. An amazing voice filled the air. He felt sure that it belonged to the honey who'd just walked past him.

Unable to contain himself, he commanded, "Damn girl, gimme a piece of paper and a pen!"

The thwarted receptionist reluctantly handed him what he had asked for, and Freddie Famous hastily scribbled something onto the paper.

Just as he'd finished, the door to the office opened as Nikki ushered out her guests.

"You've really got an incredible story Cherry — the way your mother came to England on her own with nothing but a packet of Cherry Drops in her pocket... I've never heard of anything quite like it!"

"Oh, you haven't heard the half of it."

Cherry gritted her teeth. Mr. E could get a full-time job in pantomime with the fairy stories he'd been coming up with over the last hour.

"Well, if the rest of your life is anything like what I've just heard, I can't wait to hear about it. Anyway don't forget Friday, I want *everybody* in the company to welcome our new star! Mr. E, it was wonderful to see you again. Cherry, it's been a great pleasure meeting you. Until Friday!"

And with that she gave them both a dazzling smile and went back into her office.

Once she was on her own, Nikki started to pace her room. There was no way she could sit down after this.

Nikki Stixx was head of A & R in the R & B division of B.U.L. Records, but what she really wanted was her own label, with at least a million up front, and no stupid corporate suit to have to answer to every minute of the day. And now she was beside herself with excitement, because this Cherry girl looked like a one-way ticket to everything she'd ever dreamed of.

And she couldn't wait. Once this project was out there, everybody in the company would be kissing her ass like it was the Blarney stone!

As they made their way back through reception, Freddie Famous sauntered over to Cherry and Mr. E.

"Hey — your name's Cherry right?"

Cherry stood still and looked Freddie dead in the eye. So he'd taken the time to find out her name. Recognising this as a good sign, and realising the ball was in her court, she coolly replied, "Yeah."

"Was that you I heard singing?"

"Yeah."

Freddie Famous gave her one of his infamous slow, sexy smiles and slipped the note he'd just been scribbling, gently but firmly into the front of her jeans pocket and said, "You're cool baby."

And with that he went on his way.

The receptionist, green with envy, peered over her counter and said in her strong cockney accent, "He's been doin' that to girls all day. Do you want me to throw that in

50

the bin for ya darlin'?"

Trying to resist smiling, Cherry unfolded the note on which was written a telephone number and the word 'LATER'.

Mr. E was craning his neck to peek at the note. "What did he write 'pon de paper, Cherry?"

"He wrote that he likes my voice." What a cheek! as if she was going to tell him her business.

Mr. E was having none of it, and strained to make out the words of the note in Cherry's hand, saying, "Yeah, right! Like he was so *shy*, he had to write dat on a piece of paper! What about Yam? Ya soon dash him when a better proposition presents itself!"

Cherry swiftly folded the note and pushed it back into her cut-offs. "Don't be ridiculous, Yam will be just as happy as I am that Freddie likes my voice, so don't be running to tell him any of your fairy stories about me!" They were walking out of the building now, leaving behind a trail of blood-red burgundy leather and bleached silver ash-wood. "And while we're on the subject of fairy stories... what was all that crap you were telling Nikki Stixx?"

"Hush nuh, woman! Don't you know you gotta dress it up a lickle for these record company types?"

"Yeah, but do you really expect her to believe such dribble?"

Mr. E sighed and adopted the kind of tone you might use when explaining a very complicated task to a very simple child. "You're missing the point. It's not whether or not she *believes* me that matters; dis business is all bullshit anyways. It's whether or not she was *entertained*. And even you, with your talent for fault-finding, could not deny that Ms. Nikki Stixx has been well and truly entertained."

Cherry remained unconvinced. "I thought it was the *music* that's supposed to entertain in this business."

"Yes, but she loves de music already. So I was just throwing in a few more lickle points of interest for her."

phyllis blunt

Biting the Cherry

IT WAS ELEVEN O'CLOCK in the evening and Cherry and Yam were sitting in Cherry's living room. They were celebrating the good news of the record company 'biting the cherry' so to speak, with a bottle of ice-cold Moêt and a bag of weed. Cherry leant back and surrendered herself to the waves of pleasure that were washing over her as she sucked on her spliff.

Yam had long since moved his 'pre-production suite', which consisted of a four track, a drum machine and a keyboard, into Cherry's flat and he was playing her his latest composition — a slow and sexy groove that fitted perfectly into the mood of the evening.

"So d'you think you can come up with some lyrics and a sweet melody for dis yah groove, baby?"

"Sure." Cherry took hold of the mic with her free hand and began to sing a few lines in between puffs of her spliff.

Yam leant back in his chair and surveyed the scene. Listening to his music and hearing Cherry massage the notes over the throbbing groove with her incredible voice, he felt that this had to be the happiest time of his entire life. Ever since that fateful night when he had met Cherry, he felt like he'd been on a rollercoaster ride to heaven and it only seemed to be getting better. Now that B.U.L. Records wanted to be in on their project, the sky was the limit. Everything that he'd ever dreamed of could come true. He and Cherry could get one phat yard out in the country somewhere, with a heated swimming pool, tennis courts, snooker room and *everything*. Of course, they'd have to get a pad somewhere sunny as well, maybe Jamaica — someplace where they could just get back to their roots. They could even put a recording studio in there and do all the music right on the beach! Yam smiled to himself as he pictured himself lying on the Caribbean sand, rubbing copious amounts of sweet-smelling coconut oil all over Cherry's voluptuous curves.

He tore himself away from his daydreams to look at his baby. She was so fine. Even just casual in her yard, she was saying it. Cherry had swept her hair up in chiney bumps which showed off the long, elegant lines of her neck. All she was wearing on this warm summer evening was a skimpy white cotton vest, and a matching pair of panties. He could see the outline of her nipples, which were perky beneath her vest, her breasts dangling free, unrestrained by any bra. Her skin shone a rich chocolate brown in the soft candlelight as he became heady with the scent of their combined body heat filtering through the summer air. He longed to reach out and caress the silky smoothness of her skin.

He broke into Cherry's singing and indicated that she should sit on his lap. "Why don't you come over here, baby? You can get the vibes for the song much easier if I warm you up with a little lovin'."

Cherry looked at Yam and thought that it was a great idea, there was nothin' like getting horny to spice up the song.

Like a cat, she slowly uncurled from her position on the floor and moved over to him, taking her spliff and her microphone with her. Nestling her buttocks against Yam's crotch, she opened her legs and hugged the outside of his knees with her inner thighs. She arched her back, leaned her head against his shoulder and resumed singing, letting the notes shape low and husky melodies.

Yam felt the warmth of her body as it melted against his and he breathed in the sweet smell of her skin. He let his right hand slide underneath Cherry's vest and began to caress a nipple. As he felt it harden beneath his touch, a ripple of pleasure ran through his groin. Slowly, he took his left hand and slipped it into Cherry's white cotton panties. He made his way down through her silky curls, and plunged his fingers into the soft, warm wetness he had been hoping for.

As Yam's hand lightly teased her, Cherry felt herself go

weak with longing. The notes she was singing were taking their own shape now, dictated to by Yam's loving touch, and jumping to the constant throb of the sensuous groove. She felt her hips slowly begin to gyrate against his lap and the eager hardness of his wood press urgently against her buttocks. The firm ripples of the muscles on his chest and stomach tensed against the arch of her spine.

As the mic slipped from her hand, Yam turned her round and took her large, heavy breasts into his mouth. They were both beginning to melt into the rhythm of the moment. Almost roughly, he pushed her back on to the desk and pulled her legs wide apart. He leaned back and took a good look at his baby as she lay across the desk. The amber glow made her look like she had been dipped in chocolate and he definitely wanted a taste.

Taking off her panties, Yam began to live up to his name. As Cherry surrendered to the waves of pleasure that resonated throughout her body, and made her head spin, she felt certain that *this* was what music was all about. She stretched right back across the desk and, closing her eyes, she thought once again of Freddie Famous.

Mr. E sat in Josephine's — a disgustingly expensive French restaurant in Knightsbridge. He was wearing one of his favourite Armani suits in racing green, teamed with a pale pink Ralph Lauren v-necked polo shirt. He sat with his arms bent over the dinner table, so the sleeves of his jacket pushed back, and his solid gold Rolex watch — with full diamond bezel, dial and bracelet — could be displayed to its full advantage.

He felt his heart miss a beat, as he looked deep into Nikki Stixx's coal-black, almond-shaped eyes. She looked like a million dollars, in an ankle-length, navy-blue Calvin Klein bias-cut dress with flat matching brogues. Her only jewellery — apart from her stainless steel and gold Cartier Panther watch — was a small silver cross from Tiffany's, which dangled precociously between her breasts on a delicate silver chain around her elegant neck.

They were seated in the 'day room' of Josephine's, which allowed bright shafts of sunshine to filter through its huge skylights. Together with the array of over-large potted plants and baby trees scattered around the floor space, the impression was of a colonial dining room on a cool, but sunny day. Mingling with the low, hushed chatter of table conversation was soothing classical music, and the sound of water continuously flowing through the indoor miniature fountains.

It was perfect. The appropriate establishment for the king and queen of the music industry to tickle their royal palates and discuss the finer details of their imminent recording deal.

Mr. E was stabbing one of the three dainty buttered asparagus tips that made up the vegetable section of his scanty cordon bleu meal when Nikki asked, "So, Mr. E, where *did* you find an artist as incredible as Cherry?"

He smiled benevolently at her, "Well, she found us... As you know, the whole of London's buzzing about the phat sounds we've been creatin' at de studio, so we chose her out of all the hundreds of artists that keep hammering at our door every day, *begging* for us to hook them up with some of our kicking sounds. Of course she was a bit rough around the edges when we discovered her, but I know a genuine diamond when I see one, so I took it upon myself to develop her personally and polish her into the megastar that you've seen before you today."

"I see."

"Yeah, and when everyt'ing was done and dusted, I told the guys, 'Look, we have some multi-million dollar product at our fingertips now — what we need is a *major* record company. A serious player in the industry, with the *integrity* to share our vision, with the might and the power to this push dis product all the way — on a worldwide and universal tip'. I said I didn't wanna be playin' around wid any of dem fool-fool men in suits either, 'cause, as you know, they wouldn't know a hit record, or musical talent if it turned round and sucked their dick! No, what I need is a genuinely creative person, someone who can feel the grooves and know not to fuck-up de music when it's droppin' right. A 'key person', someone with a potent mix of creative talent and financial might. Because, as I'm sure you're well aware, whoever we decide to work with on this project is gonna be earnin' millions upon millions of dollars."

He leaned further forward onto the table, moving even closer to Nikki, making sure that his gold Rolex caught the sun from the skylight. And, looking directly into her eyes, he lowered his voice to a dramatic whisper, "And that person… is you, Nikki."

She gave him what she considered to be her most winning smile. She had to hand it to him, it was a great pitch — made even more brilliant by the fact that in this case it wasn't bullshit. He actually had the goods to back up his spiel. "So… exactly what type of deal are you looking for, E?"

Mr. E smiled inwardly, as he noted that she was dropping the 'Mr.' and getting all intimate. He now knew that he had Nikki Stixx exactly where he wanted her: right in the palm of his hand. Everyone had their price and he'd just made her an offer she couldn't refuse. He wondered how soon he'd be able to get her into bed.

Leaning back into his high-backed wicker chair, he said, "Don't worry about that, Nikki. I've got all the paperwork back at the office. I'll get my assistant, Denise, to fax it over to you this afternoon. At this point, I'm much more interested in enjoying a delicious lunch and getting to know my future business associate… a little better. So… what made a beautiful young woman like yourself want to get into the music business?"

Nikki knew exactly what kind of game Mr. E was playing. Lord knows, she'd been there so many times before. She might have guessed that the idiot was going to try and manoeuvre her into bed before they cut the deal. If only he knew how much he was wasting his time.

Still she needed this deal to happen like Santa Claus needs Christmas, so she decided to play along. For now.

Cherry sat and stared at the crumpled piece of paper in her hand, and considered her options.

She'd met everyone at B.U.L. Records earlier that day, and they'd all treated her like a queen. She'd never been treated so well in her entire life. It was certainly a far cry from the reception she had received at the Rosemead Hostel. *And a world away from her stay at Holloway*. Everyone had been falling over themselves to tell her how huge she was going to be, and how many trillions of records she was going to sell.

After the whole circus of it, Mr. E had gone off with Nikki to have a 'business lunch'. God only knows what fairy stories he'd been making up about her this afternoon. Still, as long as he hooked up the deal...

Yam had left to go up to his mum's — probably for a decent meal knowing him — and now she was staring at this note, trying to decide whether or not she should call Freddie Famous. Of course, she hadn't told Yam about the encounter, and if Mr. E went telling tales, she would just style it out like she had forgotten to mention it.

Meeting Freddie and him coming on to her had been an unexpected development, but the more she thought about it, the more she began to realise how useful this chance encounter could be. She bit her lip as she deliberated over just how much Freddie could accelerate her plans. The possibilities seemed endless. Pushing aside the fact that he was *totally fly*, he just happened to be the biggest star on the planet. If anyone could help her career, it was him. There was no denying it, this was an opportunity that didn't come along every day. The kind of opportunity that was good to miss.

Her mind made up, she dialled the digits.

An over-cheerful receptionist sing-songed, "Hello, this is the Lexon Hotel. How can I help you?"

"Yeah, can you put me through to room 201?"

Cherry heard the line click as the receptionist buzzed her through and a low, husky, male american voice cracked, "What's up?"

"Hi — it's me, Cherry, I met you at B.U.L. Records the other day."

"Yeah, yeah — the fine money in the tight shorts."

"Er... yeah, that's me."

"I've been tryin' to locate you. How come you didn't call me sooner?"

Cherry couldn't believe this, Freddie Famous was acting like an eager schoolboy, she played it cool. "Yeah, well, I've been busy recording and stuff."

"That's cool, money, and you should keep doin' it too, 'cause the voice that I heard is gonna take you places — an' I mean *all the way* sweet *thang*. However, tonight you should definitely take a break and come out with me and ma boyz. We're goin' to a club called Subterania. Do you know it?"

"Yeah." Cherry knew it only too well, it was a funky club in London's trendy Portobello Road area and tonight they played hip hop and soul.

"Okay, well give me your address, and I'll get my driver to pick you up around eleven."

Cherry gave him her address and then asked, "Er, is it okay if I bring my girlfriend?"

"Baby, you can bring your mommy, your daddy *and* your second cousin twice removed, as long as ya bring ya sweet self. I'll look forward to seeing you later. Peace." The line went dead.

Cherry replaced the handset and picked it up again to dial Babsy's number, "Girl, you won't believe what I have got arranged for us tonight!"

After organising the evening and planning prospective

outfits with Babsy, Cherry called Yam at his mum's.

"Yam? Listen, I'm not feeling too well, I think I've got food poisoning or something. Why don't you stay at your mum's tonight — 'cause I just wanna go to bed and sweat it out... No, no I don't need you to come by and mop my brow, I really just wanna be on my own... Okay, I'll speak to you tomorrow."

Yam thought it was too bad that Cherry had food poisoning, but he had to admit — in the nicest possible way of course — that the timing was perfect. This was because one of his DJ mates, Deadly Ringer, was playing at Subterania tonight and he'd been promising for weeks to go and check him out, but he'd always been in the studio, or at Cherry's and had never been able to make it. However, tonight he could finally catch up with him and actually put an end to all that ear bashing he had been receiving for 'neglecting his old mates'.

Mr. E left Josephine's in a jubilant mood, the only cloud in his silver lining being money — or rather, the lack of it. The deal was going great, but he felt that there was a chance it might not happen quickly enough. He knew how these things dragged on; even with the best possible scenario, it might take about three months of to-ing and fro-ing between lawyers before any cheques were going to be signed. *And he didn't have three months.* He wasn't even sure if he had three weeks.

If he didn't get some money fast, his whole company was going under, which meant that he was going to own jack-shit. Everybody at the studio, including Cherry, was signed to Black Knight Productions — so if the company went down, all his contracts with them weren't worth the paper they were written on. Which meant that everything he'd grafted so hard for would be worthless. He *had* to get some money — and fast. Which meant that he only had one option left.

Pulling out his mobile phone, he dialled a number and a middle-aged woman's voice answered, "Hello, Mr. Carrington's office, how may I help you?"

Mr. E's voice was gruff and to the point, "Put me through to Carrington."

"Can I ask who's calling?"

"Never mind who's calling, get me Carrington."

"I'm afraid Mr. Carrington's out of the country at the moment."

"Yeah? Well you tell him that if he doesn't call Mr. Knight — write that down: *Mr. Knight* — by Monday, all hell is gonna break loose! He knows the number."

He ended the call and cursed under his breath. That fucking secretary was lying like a bitch on heat. He wasn't a gambling man, but he'd put money on the fact that that muthafucka was sitting right there in his office right now. Nobody could be out of town that much — especially when you worked for the government. Well, he needed some money and he was going to get what was owed to him, even if it meant that he had to go round and personally kick it out of that out-of-town-muthafucka's ass.

Freddie Famous sat on the toilet in the bathroom of his hotel suite at the ultra-chic and trendy Lexon Hotel in Holland Park. The floor and walls were completely covered in huge white slabs of marble tiling, which were softly veined with different shades of grey and blue. In the corner was a huge pearly-white, semi-circular sunken jacuzzi-bath, flanked on two sides by mirrors, which covered the walls right up to the ceiling. Thick fluffy white towels, monogrammed with the Lexon Hotel initials were warming themselves on a Regency towel holder, plumping themselves in anticipation for the moment when our young superstar would wish to pat his famous skin dry.

The room itself was vast; in fact it was so spacious, you could move in an entire house-full of furniture and have a whole family living in it. Put this together with the incredibly high ceiling which towered over the room, with all its original ornate Victorian mouldings stretched around its lengthy border and clustered around the huge opulent glass chandelier that swung at its centre; and you will get some idea of the grandeur of a suite at the Lexon Hotel.

Unlike a lot of other megastars, who shall remain nameless, Freddie didn't hold with the idea that the rest of his entourage should be at a less expensive hotel than him. No, he liked to have his 'boyz' close by at all times, so he insisted his whole crew should live it up just as well as him, courtesy of B.U.L. Records and ultimately coming out of Freddie's royalty cheques. Whether or not Freddie was aware that he was eventually going to foot the bill for his 'boyz' extravagances, no-one knew, as no-one had cared to ask. The chances were however, that Freddie, even if he did know, would not have had it any other way because, like every other new megastar, having come into vast amounts of money and a seemingly open cheque book, Freddie thought that no matter how much he spent, he would never be poor again.

So, he was sat here on the john in one of the most expensive, and arguably the trendiest hotel in London, talking to his mother. Throughout his entire adult life, no matter where he was, he had always put in at least one call a day to his mother.

Freddie's mother was a strong independent Afro-American woman, who had more or less brought up her three sons single-handedly. Not that they'd wanted for a damn thing, because they weren't brought up on welfare or any other kind of state benefit — unlike some kids who were brought up by *two* parents. Most people seemed to assume that, because he and his brothers were raised by a single parent, they were underprivileged and impoverished. The reality was that his mother was an English Professor at

Yale in New Haven, Connecticut, and made a generous living from her teachings, not to mention the many lectures she delivered around the USA. And, like a lot of children in single parent families, Freddie had formed a close and unbreakable bond with his mother.

Of course, none of this was known to the general public. As Freddie's music was 'urban-contemporary', the publicity department had decided to make out that he'd grown up in 'the hood', belonging to a notorious gang that terrorised the East Coast, and had been in and out of jail several times. This, they argued, was vital for record sales, pointing out that you only had to look at 'Jack-knife', an infamous rap artist, who upon his release from jail after serving a sentence for double manslaughter, was enjoying the highest record sales of his entire career.

Of course, Freddie's mother was none too happy about this publicity, but the truth was that Freddie was a grown man now, and had every right to make his own decisions. Especially when those decisions just happened to be paying everyone's bills.

So here was our young superstar sitting on the john, bitterly complaining to his mother about the bathroom at the Lexon Hotel. His problem being that he hated the marble floor, as it felt like ice when he got out the bath. When his assistant, Latonya, had complained to the hotel, the staff were saying they didn't have any spare rugs to put down on the floor for him. Of course it was nuts — but what did you expect in a backward little island like England? So, he'd gotten one of his assistants to go over to the store — Harrods or something — and buy him a couple of rugs.

His mother agreed that it was disgraceful, and that he wouldn't have had that problem if he was 'back home', and after a couple of respective 'I love yous', their customary daily call was ended.

Freddie stood up and surveyed his butt-naked self from several angles in the double aspect mirrors above the bath. Yep, he was black and beautiful as ever! With his superstar lifestyle, he had a full-time personal trainer and worked out for a good four hours a day, which gave him the body of a god — or so the honeys liked to tell him. Regular visits from his personal beautician had gotten his skin clearer than a hot, sunny day and his nose-job — and we're not talking about the kind of regulation Doris Day nose-job that you used to get lumbered with in the eighties, oh no, we're talkin' about the kinda nineties nose-job that ensured that a brotha's African heritage stayed intact — made an almost-perfect face *absolutely* perfect. Of course, as his genre was 'urban contemporary', he then had to go and rough up his look, which meant shaving his head to a baldy, and sporting permanent facial hair, not to mention a couple of tattoos and a bit of body piercing (his left nipple). It might seem crazy to put in all that effort just to hide it but, as Freddie will tell you himself, all that rude boy stuff doesn't hang right if you ain't perfect underneath.

As usual his mind drifted onto the thought of pussy. He'd been living it up with his 'boyz' on this little trip to London and, as usual he'd been hittin' on a different honey every night. But the truth was he was bored.

He'd just about resigned himself to the fact that these English honeys weren't really saying it, and had made a mental note never to bother gracing these shores with his presence again, when he'd met Cherry.

Cherry... What a perfect name, 'cause this girl was more like a sweet, ripe juicy cherry than any other girl he had ever met, and he was just the nigga to bite on it. Well, he was going to have his chance tonight.

Freddie smiled to himself as he ran over the details of his tried and tested seduction routine. It was simple, all he had to do was dazzle her with a taste of his superstar lifestyle, get her to knock back a couple of glasses of Crystal, and that sweet, succulent Cherry would be his for the picking!

He got back on the phone. "Latonya? Send the limo to this address before it comes to pick up me and my boyz..."

The Date

YAM, MR, E, FINGERS AND D were congregated once again in the monitor room of Black Knight Productions for their late afternoon 'tea break'. As usual, the air was hazy with marijuana smoke, some half-eaten patties were on the smoked glass coffee table, and everyone's glass was filled with blackcurrant cordial, apart from Fingers who had his usual brandy and coke.

Mr. E was holding court. "So... after I told her how *large* we are as a corporation, I could tell by the way Ms. Nikki Stixx was looking at me with her sexy bedroom eyes, that she was thinkin' all kinds of dark and dangerous thoughts. She's probably plotting right now as we speak, how she can have her wicked way with me!"

D cut in, "Nah dread! Dat's *sexual harassment*, tell her dat she must deal with you on a business level, or not at all!"

"Wha'? And blow the deal!?" Mr. E adopted a martyr's stance. "If it's for the good of everybody and it's gonna put food into all of your starving bellies, then I'm prepared to *sacrifice* my beautiful body for the sake of the business. Many a powerful person has had to sleep their way to the top!"

Everybody fell about laughing at Mr. E's exaggerations. Still, they all suspected that there was a grain of truth in it somewhere. They thought it must be very cushy living it up in London's most exclusive restaurants, being wined and dined by beautiful young female record company executives, in order to cut a business deal. It certainly sounded a bit more inviting than sitting in a dark studio twenty-four hours a day, completely cut off from the rest of the world, trying to come up with number one records.

"So this Nikki Stixx really took to Cherry then, did she?" Yam was relieved that a woman was going to be handling the project, things might have got tricky if it had been a man. Not that he felt that he couldn't trust Cherry. He knew that she was devoted to him. It was all those sharks out there that he couldn't trust; and he didn't want some flashy record executive getting his slimy hands on his baby and turning her head with all kinds of promises about record deals.

Mr. E sighed in exaggerated frustration, and turned to Yam. "You always want to know 'bout Cherry! Don't ya know that it's not good to get too hung up on any one woman. *Yuh cyant trust 'em.* They'll act all sweet an' innocent wid a brotha, and then the minute his back is turned, they'll be carrying on the same way with a next man!"

Yam gave him a confident smile. "Not Cherry."

"How do you know? What do you really know about dis gal anyways — or where she comes from? It's just her prettiness that's got you acting all fool-fool, like some kind of madman. Don't ya know that *all* women have the same wet pum-pum on the inside? It's pure *packaging* you're killing yourself over!"

D chimed in, "Yeah, but dat's a package dat's *worth* killing yuhself over!"

Yam was beside himself. "Do you lot mind! That's *my woman* you're talking about and I'd thank you all to kindly talk about her with *respect*! Ya dyam *dogs*!!" He was really losing it. Who did these guys think they were talking to — a schoolboy? Where did they get off, talking about Cherry like she was some tart?

"If she's *your* woman, how come she's not with *you* tonight?"

"She happens to be *ill*, in bed with stomach ache."

Mr. E snorted, "So *dat's* what they're calling it now — *stomach ache...!* How do you know she's not foolin' around, dis very moment, with a next man?"

Yam got up, an expression of disgust on his face. "I've had enough of this, D, Fingers — I'll check ya later. Mr. E, I hope that next time we meet you will *not* be taking it upon yourself to be distressing me about my woman!" And with that, he stormed out of the studio.

D turned to Mr. E, "Why did you have to go an' give him such a hard time, man?"

Mr. E kept his eyes firmly fixed in front of him, and with a deadly serious tone said, "Sometimes, yuh haffe give someone a wake-up call. It's not good to be pining after just one woman, you're only settin' yourself up fe heartbreak."

Fingers and D looked at one another and shrugged their shoulders. Sometimes you just couldn't make any sense out of Mr. E. He was a law unto himself.

Babsy and Cherry were getting ready for their night out. Babsy was in the living room, piling on the make-up, listening to Cherry's beautiful voice, which wafted through the flat, as she sang to herself in the bathroom. She couldn't lie — Cherry really was incredibly talented. The only amazing thing about the recent train of events was that it had taken her so long to get a record deal.

As Cherry came out of the shower, Babsy mused, "You know Cherry, you've really got it. I can't believe you aren't at the top of the charts already!"

Cherry laughed wryly. "If only it were that easy! If there's one thing I've woken up to about the music business, Babsy, it's that being talented doesn't mean shit when it comes to being a success and riding the charts. I mean, there are a lot of very talented people out there who can just about make a living out of singing at weddings and in bars, and the charts are full of people who can't even sing in tune, never mind play an instrument! I tell ya, girl, I'd be a fool if I didn't admit that it's all about image and marketing and *who* you know within the industry. You don't have a hope in hell of making it as a singer unless you have the right contacts, and the right image — something that I never had before... But all that's changed now."

Babsy was perplexed. "I can't imagine how it could have been any harder for you to make contacts before than it is for you now!"

Cherry suddenly dropped her relaxed manner and looked guarded, saying, "Yeah, well, let's just say that I wasn't able to go for my career in the past like I can now — due to circumstances beyond my control."

Babsy bit her lip. She was dying to delve further, and find out what 'circumstances' beyond Cherry's control had prevented her from pursuing her career, but she knew that she was wasting her time. Whenever she asked her for any personal details, Cherry just acted like she was being persecuted or something and totally clammed up.

She decided to lighten the mood instead, "Well things definitely have changed now, because I can't imagine a better contact in the world than Freddie Famous! Tell me again what he said when he came up to you in the B.U.L. reception."

Cherry adopted a manly stance, imitating Freddie Famous. She swaggered over to Babsy and pretended to slip a note into her front pocket. In a low, masculine voice, she attempted an American accent and rasped, "You're cool baby."

The girls roared with laughter.

Babsy shot a sly look at Cherry and couldn't resist asking, "What did you tell Yam you were doing?"

"I told him I had a stomach ache." Cherry tried to look guilty, but it was no good and they started laughing again.

In an effort to justify her actions, she continued

"Anyway, it's not like we're *married* or anything. I'm just curious to see what an evening out with Freddie Famous is like. It's not every day an invite like this comes along — and, you never know, he might be able to help me with my career, which is a priority for me at this point in time. I can have a relationship at any time in my life, but this is something I have to do *now*."

Babsy stared at her friend, wondering why she always got so intense when she talked about her career. "Why is it so crucial to you, Cherry? I mean, I know that a career's important and everything, but you act like your life depends on it."

Cherry looked straight ahead, her features automatically arranged themselves into an expression of grim determination as she said, "That's because it does, Babsy. All I've ever wanted, my whole life, is to become a singer and to be successful. But people have always... got in the way of those dreams. Now for the first time ever, I feel like I'm in control of my own destiny. I've been through hell and back to get to this point, and this time I'm not gonna let anybody or anything fuck it all up." As she spoke, the air in the room seemed to gradually get colder under the seriousness she lent to her words.

Babsy tried to lighten the mood again. "Too right! And if by some chance you and Freddie don't make out, you can hand him over to me. I haven't had sex in so long, I'm wondering whether or not they've changed it!"

Cherry didn't smile however, she just kept staring ahead as if she was completely lost in her own thoughts.

Babsy's face grew serious again as she said, "I don't know how you do it, Cherry, you've only been here a couple of months and you've already hooked two slamming guys." She gave her friend another sly look from underneath her eyelashes. "Maybe if I threw myself at men the way you do, I could get a squeeze once in a while."

"You what?"

Cherry had to admit she wasn't really surprised. Recently, Babsy was always having little digs at her. It was like she just couldn't handle the fact that Cherry's life was starting to take a turn for the better.

Babsy continued, "Oh come on, Cherry, you're not shy when it comes to meeting men are ya?"

"What are you trying to say, Babsy?"

Babsy opened her eyes, so that her face was the picture of innocence. "Nothing. What I meant was, if I took a leaf out of your book, I might be able to find myself a decent man. You know that I'm sick of being single! I wanna be in a relationship. Or at least find a fling-down!"

Cherry laughed, she knew Babsy was full of shit, because she had so many men she was scared to answer her phone because it had gotten to the point where she couldn't tell one voice from another. And they didn't last long because she didn't want them to last long. But recently, all she seemed to be able to talk about was finding a 'good man' and getting into a 'serious' relationship. At the back of her mind she wondered, once again, if she'd told Babsy too much about herself. If there was one lesson that she'd learnt in life, it was that you never knew when people were going to stab you in the back.

She kept her mood light as she said, "Well there's gonna be plenty of talent comin' along tonight. Freddie told me that he's bringin' his crew, and I saw a photo of them all in the *Enquirer* and they are fly!"

Babsy rubbed her hands together with glee, "So, what are we waiting for? Let's get ready. Tonight I am gonna dress to kill!"

Once they were finished, the two girls looked deadly. Babsy was squeezed into a black PVC A-line mini skirt and an extra tight-and-tiny black PVC T-shirt with black, shiny knee-length moc-croc boots. Her red-brown corkscrew curls were fluffed out into a huge afro and she wore some glittery seventies make-up to match. Cherry had on a pair of chocolate-brown suede hipster bell-bottoms, with a tiny white vest. She was wearing chocolate-brown lipstick and had tied her hair in a scarf so that flowed freely at the back and hung in loose waves past her shoulders.

They were putting the final touches to their respective transformations when the phone rang. Cherry answered it, to discover that the chauffeur had arrived, and was waiting outside to pick them up. Babsy's eyes popped when they got downstairs to discover that a huge, white stretch limo had squeezed into Stockwell Park Estate and was waiting outside Byrant Court for them.

After the chauffeur ushered them into the back, they stretched out on either side, reclining along the soft leather seats.

The limo's intercom sounded. "If you ladies would like a drink, there's a bottle of Crystal to the right of the rear seat in the ice bucket. You'll find champagne glasses in the compartment next to the right-hand side door."

Unable to resist the offer, the girls dived in.

"Everybody gawps at you when you're in a limo, don't they?" Cherry remarked, as she noted all the enquiring faces, straining to get a peek inside as they cruised by.

"Yeah, well you better get used to this, girl, if you're going to become a star in your own right." Babsy couldn't hide the bitterness in her voice from either one of them, which caused both girls to fall silent, lost in their own private thoughts.

Their reverie was soon broken however, when the limo pulled up to the Lexon Hotel and Freddie and his 'boyz' piled into the car.

"LADIES! How ya doin'!" He reached over to give both of them a peck on the cheek. One of his 'boyz' clicked a CD into the car stereo and the sounds of Freddie's latest album pumped out of the speakers inside the interior.

He nodded at Babsy, "Wassup, money, I don't believe we've met…"

Babsy only just kept her voice from trembling as she said, "Oh, hello Mr. Famous, I'm Barbara."

Cherry raised a quizzical eyebrow and looked at Babsy, who was squirming with embarrassment. *Mr. Famous…? Barbara?* Where was she going with that dialogue? Cherry might have guessed that she was going to go all ga-ga when she came face-to-face with Freddie.

Freddie sat down next to Cherry and squeezed her knee. "How ya doin', baby-girl? Did ya miss me? I was thinking about ya today."

Cherry looked at him shyly from beneath her eyelashes.

"I was thinking about you too."

"Oh yeah? Nice thoughts?"

Cherry gave him a flirty look, "Maybe."

Freddie smiled his infamous smile, there was a wicked sparkle in Cherry's eyes that he liked. As he noted her voluptuous curves straining against the tight confines of her outfit, he felt Godzilla begin to rise. At that point nobody in the world could tell him anything other than the evening ahead was going to be a whole lotta fun.

They kept up their banter throughout the whole journey to Subterania. Babsy didn't mind — she was having a ball, enjoying all the attentions of Freddie's 'crew'.

When they got to the club, the crowd parted like the Red Sea, as Freddie and his entourage sauntered to the front of the queue. Babsy and Cherry walked with them and Babsy smiled triumphantly as she recognised some of her mates from the Queen of Sheba modelling agency in the crowd, their jaws dropping to the floor in shock at the sight of their colleague, living it up with the most famous black man on the planet.

Once in the club, they were given the VIP spot, and the manager sent over some Crystal, compliments of the house. It was pointless trying to attempt any kind of conversation over the roar of the music, so Freddie took hold of Cherry, and pulled her onto the dance floor, where he wrapped her hands, around his neck, and grabbed her firmly around the waist. They began to slowly wind and grind to the music, their bodies glued firmly together, entwining to become one, completely oblivious to all of the stares they were getting from their fellow ravers.

Yam was driving his Escort aimlessly through the streets of London. He was supposed to be at Subterania now, but he was too wound-up to be socialising. He was still majorly pissed off about what Mr. E had said about Cherry. Why did he have be all negative about his woman? Maybe the old man was just jealous because *he* didn't have a woman — probably hadn't had any pum-pum in years from what they could see at the studio.

Yam toyed with the idea of dropping by Cherry's to see how she was doing, but there was no point — she'd told him that she wanted to spend the evening alone — it would be selfish of him to just barge in on her at this time of night. He could imagine how she looked now, all tucked up, sweet and innocent, and sleeping like a baby... Oh, what the hell, Yam pointed his car in the direction of Subterania. He might as well go and see Deadly. He needed to take his mind off Mr. E's bullshit.

The evening was coming to a close, but both Cherry and Freddie Famous had a feeling that it had only just begun.

Freddie pulled her even closer and whispered into her ear, "Let's get out of here."

He was nursing a hard-on that had been getting stronger and stronger as the night had progressed. This honey was one of the sexiest he had ever met, the way she'd pressed and rubbed her ample curves against Godzilla on the dance floor in Subterania was driving him crazy. There was nothing he wanted more in the world at this moment than to get to know Cherry better. He had to get her back to his hotel, so that they could be alone.

As they slipped back into the limo, it was like they couldn't tear themselves apart.

Neither of them noticed the metallic-blue Ford Escort convertible that was waiting to pull into their parking space as they moved out.

Yam tried to get a good look in the stretch limo that was rolling out of the parking space. But his efforts were in vain, as all of the windows were totally blacked out. He couldn't imagine who it could be — it wasn't very often that you got limos at Subterania. Maybe some rich arab had lost his way.

He walked into the club to see his mate, Deadly, packing away his records into several cases.

"I see your time-keeping hasn't improved!" Deadly grinned from ear to ear, pleased as punch to see his old school friend.

Yam walked up and gave him a hearty slap on the back, "Awright Deadly. Long time no see! What's occurring?"

"Nothin' much. You've just missed the show. We've had Freddie Famous in here with his crew and two wicked-looking sistas! I recognised one of them, she's a model, I think I've seen her in 'Sister Girl' magazine."

"No shit! That must have been who was in the stretch limo then. It was pulling out of the parking lot as I was arriving."

Deadly laughed. "See how these supastars are stylin' it out now! What d'ya say we go and find a drink?"

Yam and Deadly sat at a table outside Bar Italia in Soho, sipping hot chocolates. It was past four in the morning, but the streets were a hive of activity, Bar Italia being a favourite after-club haunt for London's trendiest ravers. Deadly was pointing out the delights of a beautiful young girl who was sitting with a group of friends two tables away from them.

But Yam was disinterested, "Yeah she's okay, but she's got nothin' on Cherry, mate."

"Yam, all you keep talking about is this Cherry gyal. No wonder no-one's seen you for weeks — you're obsessed! When are we gonna meet the girl dat's turned London's number one Mr. Lover-Lover into Mr. Monogamous?"

"I don't know. I could bring her to the club, I suppose... It's just that we've been so busy lately, recording all the time, we haven't really gone out anywhere yet. I would have brought her with me tonight, but she's at her yard, laid up with food poisoning."

"Uh-oh, you haven't been cooking up some of your

chicken, rice and peas, have you?"

Yam laughed, and kissed his teeth in mock anger. It was great to be out with Deadly, just messing about, not a care in the world. Sometimes the studio could get on top of you. Especially when you had to deal with Mr. E and all his miserable lectures.

The limo was parked outside the Lexon Hotel. Babsy and the rest of Freddie's boyz were still having a party, screaming and shouting along to Freddie's latest album which was booming full volume from the car speakers. Freddie rolled his eyes around their sockets. His head was spinning from all the alcohol he had consumed throughout the night, and he felt hot and hungry with desire for Cherry.

He reached over and grabbed her thigh, "Let's go an' continue this party upstairs in ma room, an' then I can show ya the reason why bitches be goin' crazy over Daddy Freddie!"

As he leaned over and tried to thrust his tongue into her mouth, Cherry pushed him off in disgust. *He had to be joking!* What did he think she was, some kind of bimbo that would just jump into bed with him at the first opportunity?

"Wait a minute, Freddie! Don't think that you can treat me like one of your groupies! I think you're forgetting where you met me. I'm about to sign a deal with B.U.L. Records as well — I'm a talented artist in my own right! Don't think that I'm impressed by who you are — 'cause I don't care if you're Freddie Famous or *Freddie Flintstone!*"

He pulled back, and looked apologetic. "Oh baby, I know… Ya gotta forgive me, it's just that you look so fine, a nigga can't help but forget his manners… An' ya don't need to tell me that you're a talented artist in your own right — that's one of the reasons I wanted you to come out with me in the first place. I was hoping that maybe I could help you in some way… Look, I jus' wanna spend some more time with ya, baby. Me an' ma boyz are outta here in a couple of days, so I won't have much time to get to know you. Why don't you come up for a coffee? I *promise* I won't do anything you don't want me to."

Cherry hesitated and Freddie continued with an insistent, "*Please* baby, you're the most money I've seen in my entire life. Don't say I've fucked everything up 'cause I forgot ma manners for a second. C'mon… let me make it up to you!"

Cherry smiled. She had had every intention of going back to Freddie's room with him tonight anyway, but she'd just wanted to make him aware that she was the kind of woman that he was going to have to treat with respect. Now she'd made her point she felt like she could look forward to the rest of the evening. After all, she'd decided: he was going to fit very nicely into her plan.

When they entered Freddie's suite Cherry held her breath. She'd never seen anything quite like it. Every room in the Lexon Hotel had a different theme, and Freddie's suite was in the style of ancient Egypt. With all the masses of fabric that seemed to be billowed and draped and ruffled and swathed over… *everything*, Cherry had the feeling that she was in some sort of over-blown ancient Egyptian tent. It was breathtaking. And it was all softly-lit by flickering ivory candlelight and matching pairs of antique tarnished silver oil lamps.

After being momentarily taken aback by its endless exquisitely magnificent features, she deadpanned, "This is quite a room."

Freddie smiled, he'd known the bitch would be impressed. "Yeah, well I told ma people to get me something with a story, know what I'm sayin'?"

Cherry licked her lips, something told her that there was no point in playing any more waiting games with Freddie. She looked straight into his eyes and husked, "Yeah, well, why don't we get to work on the script?"

She grabbed the hem of her vest-top and slowly pulled it over her head, allowing her breasts to bounce into full view.

Freddie felt Godzilla instantly harden as her two golden globes jiggled in front of him. He longed to reach and cup each silky mound of shimmering flesh in turn and sink his teeth into each pert nipple. As far as he was concerned, she couldn't have played it better if he had walked up and told her what to do himself.

This proved it: Cherry was his kind of girl. The kind of girl that knew when it was time to fuck around, and when it was time to get to the point. The kind of girl that knew how to turn a man on. The kind of bitch that he could fuck all night and eat for breakfast the next morning. The kind of ho that he would only ever need to fuck once, before he went on to the next groupie-ho who was dying to get it on with Freddie Famous.

Needing no further invitation, he reached up and grabbed her roughly by the shoulders, throwing her down on the velvet *chaise longue* at the foot of the bed. He leaned over and pressed her soft, full lips against his. As their tongues intertwined he whispered, "Bitch, I'm gonna show you what you've been missin'."

Without warning, he thrust his hand between her legs. Cherry took a sharp intake of breath as she reeled from the sheer force he was using. He whispered hotly into her ear. "You like this? Huh, huh?"

Cherry's thoughts were that frankly, no, she didn't like it. Freddie was physically hurting her now and she began to fight him to stop, but the more she fought, the more excited Freddie became.

He grabbed a handful of her hair and growled in her ear, "I know you want this you fuckin' bitch. I know this is what you came here for you fuckin' ho…"

Cherry couldn't believe what was happening. Where was the sweet honey-tongued Freddie who had been so full of promises when they'd danced together in Subterania? In the space of a couple of minutes, the sexiest superstar alive had turned into a monster! And this monster was turning into the kind of freak that liked to rough up women before he had sex with them.

She let the reality of what was happening sink into her consciousness for a second longer, and then pulled her right hand out from under his dead-weight. With all the force that she could muster, she reached down and slapped Freddie as hard as she could across his left ear and the left side of his face. Freddie felt momentarily stunned as the sting from Cherry's slap reverberated around his eardrum. Before he had time to realise what was going on, she rammed the heel of her left palm against his forehead, right at the vulnerable point where his brow met his eye socket.

As Freddie reeled from the force of these two attacks, Cherry stood up. She stuck the steel tip of her boot against his chin and commanded, "Shut the fuck up, Freddie." Then she kicked his jaw with her stiletto.

Freddie felt a shock of pain seer through his skull, as her heel sunk into the soft flesh covering his jawbone.

Cherry didn't miss a beat. "I'm running this show now, you miserable piece of shit!" And before he could move, she took the silk scarf from her hair, and tied Freddie's hands tightly behind his head to the bottom bedpost.

Freddie lay stunned, unable to protest, never mind physically move. This was not how he'd expected the evening to go at all. His face was still stinging from her slap, and his jaw ached where she had kicked it. He could have sworn that she'd drawn blood. Much as he hated to admit it, Freddie was starting to feel a little scared. It was like the bitch had gone crazy, and before he could give her what she deserved for even *thinking* that she could disrespect him like that, she'd tied him to the fucking bedpost! And for the first time in his life, he felt out of control. He felt like he was entirely at her mercy...

Once she was sure he was firmly secured, Cherry stood astride him, and grabbed a handful of his hair, yanking his head back, so that he was staring up at her face, mouth ajar, wide-eyed and bewildered. Cherry couldn't resist a smile as she saw Freddie laid out helpless and confused across the *chaise-longue.*

"Now I'm gonna show you what *really* happens when you fuck a bitch!"

She let go of his hair and flung his head back against the bedpost, giving him a good crack against either side of his face for good measure as she did so. Freddie was about to come to his senses and give her a hefty kick with his legs, which were lying free and untied beneath her buttocks, when she grabbed hold of his penis.

Suddenly, he hardly knew what was happening to him. It was like his mind lost control, and he was being taken over by a flood of sensation that melted over his body. An indescribable surge of pleasure and pain had rushed throughout his entire being as Cherry sunk her Chanel Rouge-Noir fingernails along the length of his penis, pulling on his shaft as she did so. As moans of sheer ecstacy escaped involuntarily from his lips, she shoved a thumb into his mouth and to his surprise, Freddie found himself sucking on it like a baby. His face was flushed with excitement and he felt his whole body begin to ache with longing. His head was swimming in a delirious sea of confusion. Never before had he felt so totally helpless and out of control. Never before had he felt so much pain combined with such a bitter-sweet rush of pleasure.

He looked up at Cherry — still sitting astride him, her right hand working its evil magic as she squeezed Godzilla up and down against her firm, rounded buttocks — and he felt like he was hers to do with whatever she wanted.

As if she somehow knew what he was thinking, Cherry pushed her thumb hard against the roof of his mouth, until he felt like he was going to choke and snarled, "Do you like *this* muthafucka, huh? *Huh?* I'll show you what happens when you try an' mess with me!"

She leaned forward and slapped her firm, round breasts from side to side across his face, pushing further and further forward until Freddie thought that he was going to be suffocated by them. His mouth and nose became stuffed with what seemed like endless amounts of soft, silky meaty mahogany flesh. Wave upon wave of unbearable pleasure roared down to his groin until he felt like he was going to explode.

Cherry felt his growing excitement and slowly pulled away from him. She stood up and towered above him. Then, she kicked him on his side with the heel of her boot, and commanded, "Turn around fool."

Freddie did as she said, all the time wondering what was going to happen next. It was difficult to turn around as his hands were still tied to the bedpost and when he had assumed the position she wanted, with his chest down, buttocks in the air, his arms felt twisted with pain. He looked up expectantly at her.

"Now, I want you to tell me who's is it."

"What?" He wasn't sure what she meant.

Cherry lashed the back of her hand against his backside and screeched, "*Who's is it muthafucka?*"

She kept lashing harder and harder, her blows accentuating every syllable. "WHO'S IS IT YOU PA — THET — IC PIECE OF SHIT! WHO DOES THIS BE — LONG TO?"

Freddie got the point, and began to whimper "Yours, baby. It's all *yours!*" Each time her hand came into contact with his naked rump, a thrill of ecstacy raced to his groin. It was unbearable. Too caught up in the emotion of the moment to even begin to question it, Freddie began to moan and scream as he worked himself up into an uncontrollable frenzy. Freddie's need to ejaculate began to build like steam pushing at the lid of a pressure cooker, becoming more and more urgent. Until he felt like he was reaching the point of no return. Until he had reached the point where he could no longer hold back.

With a cry that he'd never heard, never mind used before, Freddie shot his load. And he kept shooting and shooting and shooting. And his orgasm went on and on and on. With a frazzled moan, he shuddered his last spasm and shot his last drop of juice onto the velvet beneath him, his belly squirming against his load. Weak and exhausted, Freddie lay motionless face down on the *chaise-longue*, and exhaled a long sigh of satisfaction.

He could hardly comprehend what had just happened to him, but in one night, it seemed as though his whole world had gone ape-shit. He felt lost... hardly knowing what was right and what was wrong anymore. All he knew was that he had just experienced the most incredible moment of his entire life. All he knew was that Cherry was quite unlike any girl he had ever met. And all he knew, the only thing that he was completely *convinced* of, was that at all costs, he wanted her to stick around. In fact he *needed* her to stick around.

When he finally found his voice, it came out as a weak, exhausted whisper. "Cherry, that was incredible, baby. You blew my mind. Listen... I didn't get a chance to discuss it with you earlier, but I think you're *very* talented... I'd like to help you with your career."

Cherry smiled to herself and walked over to untie his hands from the bedpost, saying, "Oh yeah... how?"

"Well, I've written some songs. I was gonna use 'em for my next album, but now I've met you, I think you should have 'em. They're just what you need to take you all the way to the number one spot."

He stretched out his newly freed arms, which were stiff and numb from being tied up for so long. When he turned his head to look at Cherry and saw that her face remained impassive, he felt himself panic a little. What if she wasn't interested? What if she never wanted to see him again? *What if he never again experienced the unbelievable amount of pleasure that he had just felt*?

In an effort to give her more of an incentive to stay, he said, "And of course, with me as a writing partner, you'll have no problem getting airplay and TV slots."

He kept his eyes on Cherry. She was still saying nothing, and was concentrating on smoothing out the wrinkles on her silk scarf — the same silk scarf that had bound him to so much pleasure just a few moments earlier. Freddie felt a lump rise to his throat. He thought at that moment that he would promise Cherry anything if she would stay, if she would take care of him forever, in the same way that she had tonight.

He tried to keep the desperation out of his voice, "Hell baby, we could even do a duet. Then you'd have *guaranteed* chart success. I haven't released one record that didn't reach the top ten in every single country in the world!"

Cherry knew she had him by the balls now, this fucked-up freak was ready to sell his mama for one more night of fun. She jumped into the lavish ivory folds of the Egyptian four poster and patted the space next to her, indicating that he should lie there, and said, "Great!"

As they snuggled under the bed covers, ready to go to sleep, Cherry replayed in her mind what had just happened between them. Freddie was more than a fool if he thought that she was going to accept being treated like a bitch and a whore in his bed… or any other bed for that matter. She knew *exactly* where he was coming from with all his perverted shit. Freddie was beginning to play a very dangerous game, but if that's what he wanted to do, then he had met his match — because Cherry had played every dangerous game in the book. And she was prepared to play this one to the max.

The Consequences

THE NEXT DAY YAM WOKE UP LATE. He'd stayed up until about six in the morning with Deadly, just chatting about the old days and laughing about all the trouble that they used to get into together. As it was Sunday, Earl and Monica were over with the kids, and they were running all over the place, making it sound like a madhouse underneath him. He sneaked downstairs to the hallway to get the phone. There was no way he could let the kids know that he was awake, or he wouldn't get a moment's peace.

Once safely ensconced back in his room, with the telephone in tow, Yam dialled Cherry's number. He needed to speak to his baby, he had missed cuddling up to her last night.

As the phone rang and rang, Yam looked at his watch — it was one o'clock in the afternoon. Maybe she was still asleep, or, even though it was unlike her, she could have gone out early. He tried hard to push them out of his mind, but Mr. E's words kept echoing around his head. A vivid picture of Cherry making love to another man danced before his eyes. God, what was happening to him? How could he think such thoughts about his baby?

He silently cursed Mr. E for filling up his head with so much foolishness, as he replaced the receiver. He had to get out of his room, otherwise he'd go mad thinking about it. His mouth was dry, and he felt like he had lead in his stomach.

With a heavy heart, Yam descended the stairs in order to join the rest of his family. Maybe some of his mum's ackee and saltfish would help take his mind off Cherry, and Mr. E's stupid lies.

For what seemed like the millionth time, Cherry gave herself a good all over scrub in the shower. She had to make sure that she was fresh and alert for the day ahead. Last night Freddie had promised her the world, and she was going to make sure that he wouldn't be able to renege on those promises.

It was all arranged, Freddie was putting her in the studio, and they were going to record five songs together. If the songs were anything near as good as the ones on his album, she would be instantly catapulted into megastardom. Freddie's current album had sold over twenty million copies, and it was still selling! If she could shift even a fraction of that amount she'd be up there. And then she could do whatever the hell she wanted to do. But to record those songs, she was going to have to spend time with the wanker himself. For the first time since she'd put the wheels of her plan into motion, Cherry wondered whether it was all worth it. But the thought of vengeance that filled her heart and tormented her every waking thought left her no choice. She had to go through with it. There was no way she could fuck this up.

Freddie Famous greeted her with a kiss as she walked into the room. "Listen, baby, my people have hooked me up with some interviews today, so I gotta split. I'm gonna get my assistant, Latonya — we all call her 'Miss Booty'; you'll love her — to take you shopping for some new clothes. That way you don't have to go home — 'cause I want you here when I get back. Now, I know it's Sunday, and ya whole country is closed down, but they've informed me that there's a ladies shop around the corner — Harvey Nichols? — and it's open all day today. So feel free to buy *whatever* you want. Okay money, be good. I'm outta here."

He gave her one more kiss before he left the room. He didn't even want to give her the chance to say good morning, never mind decline or accept his offer. That's why he'd arranged for Latonya to take care of Cherry today, he wanted to make sure that she didn't have a chance to leave the hotel. And, after last night, if he had his way she would never leave his side again.

As if on cue, Freddie's assistant burst into the room. Latonya Johnson was a beautiful young African-American sista in her mid-twenties. Her hair was a platinum blonde shoulder-length weave, and it had all been backcombed into a Mary J Blige style. She was wearing skin-tight leopard-skin print leggings and a tight, gold, v-necked tank top. Despite her attire, her one outstanding feature, the part that overshadowed everything else about her, and that you couldn't help but focus on, no matter how hard you tried, was her butt. No-one could deny that Latonya had quite a booty, and she was obviously *extremely* proud of her bounty, as she made no effort at all to lessen its overwhelming impact. It was a butt that seemed to break all the laws of nature itself — two round firm meaty globes of flesh that protruded almost at a right angle from her tiny waist. A bottom so high and so firm that you could rest a glass on there, or even lean on it.

She burst like a tornado into the room, her big butt swinging behind her, speaking loudly in a thick New York accent.

"Hey, girl! Wha-a-a-s-s u-u-urp! My, my, aren't we the beautiful one? No wonder Freddie's bugging over you! I ain't ever seen him trip like this over a chick!" She skidded to a stop, dead in front of Cherry, and gave her a huge pantomime wink. "You must have had quite a night last night!"

Cherry laughed — this girl was a trip. She couldn't stop herself from saying, "That's quite a booty you got there, girlfriend!"

Latonya laughed loudly back, she was used to people commenting on her butt and loved every minute of it. She gave her huge meaty rump a hearty smack, causing its two fleshy shanks to shimmy shimmer before Cherry's eyes, and exclaimed, "That's right, girlfriend! *Everyone* digs my butt!" She gave Cherry another huge pantomime wink and went on to say, "An' niggas be *lovin'* my butt. That's why they call me 'Miss Booty'!"

The introductions over and done with, the girls wasted no time in setting about shopping, and soon Latonya was running all over Harvey Nichols, barking out orders to a couple of harassed looking shop assistants.

"Do you guys have any Chanel? What? *No-o-o-o Chanel*? What kinda clothing store is this? What about *Gucci*? Oh well, at least you got *something*!"

Cherry was running in and out of the changing room, trying on what seemed like hundreds of different outfits. Every time she appeared wearing a new creation, the shop assistants would rush over to coo and fuss and exclaim how 'wonderful' she looked.

Latonya, however, was fully committed to giving her an 'honest' opinion saying stuff like — "No way girl, you look like Oprah Winfrey on a bad day!" And then —

"Oh no! Now you look like Oprah Winfrey's *husband* on a bad day! What are these *rags* you people keep throwing at us? I asked for *designer* clothes. Look at me! D-E-S-I-G-N-E-R clothes. Don't ya know you got Freddie Famous' woman standing right here?!"

Cherry smiled inwardly, Latonya took the word 'overpowering' to another dimension. However, nothing could change the fact that it was great being able to buy an unlimited amount of clothes — regardless of the price. She was beginning to feel like a little kid who'd been let loose in the candy store.

After they had chosen several outfits, Latonya grabbed Cherry's hand and led her up the escalators to the beachwear section.

Cherry was confused. "What are we doing here, Latonya? In case you hadn't noticed, London's nowhere near hot enough to start wearing bikinis."

"I know, but Miami is."

"*Miami*? What's that got to do with me?"

Latonya stopped in her tracks and looked incredulously at Cherry.

"Don't tell me Freddie hasn't filled you in? We're going

to Miami, girl! Freddie's doing a big concert out there and you're coming with us — in the B.U.L. private jet of course."

As this information sunk in, Cherry let Latonya help her choose some beach outfits. The whole thing was going so fast that it was hard to get a grip on what was really happening.

But there was one thing that she still had to confirm. "Latonya, did Freddie mention anything to you about getting some songs for me?"

"Yeah, this morning. I've arranged it so that you can preview them in Miami. Freddie's got a *slammin'* recording studio complex up on Ocean Drive. So, if ya like 'em, you can record 'em right there and then. I have to tell you, girl, I've heard them and they are *dope*! Mind-blowing. I couldn't believe it when Freddie said he wanted you to cut them. I don't know what kinda spell you've put on him, but let me tell ya, dis nigga is IN LOVE!"

Monday morning dawned. The sky was a clear blue, not a cloud in sight for once and Mr. E was feeling as happy as the birds that he could hear singing their songs of jubilation, through the persistent hum of traffic that clogged Stoke Newington High Street. He was cruising along in his Mercedes. Nikki Stixx had just called him on his mobile and she'd been all sweetness and light, laughing at all of his jokes, even cracking a few of her own. What a woman! She had everything — beauty, intelligence, class *and* a sense of humour. He started to drool at the thought of what it was going to be like when they hooked up this deal, and were together properly. Nikki had been telling him that she wanted the deal to move quickly, so she needed to know how soon they could be ready to go into the B.U.L. studios to master the tracks they'd been recording. Of course he told her that they were ready like yesterday, and that he'd call his team immediately and get them ready for some serious work.

After the message he'd left last week, he felt sure that Carrington was going to forward him the cash he needed to keep his company afloat. So basically, things were going okay, everything was hunky-dory.

Thus, it was with a light heart, that his fingers skipped over the digits that would dial Yam's number.

"Yam?"

"Yeah." Yam's voice sounded flat and lifeless — very unlike him.

"Are you okay? You don't sound too well? You haven't been overdoin' it with all those young gals have you?"

"Right."

Yam was feeling totally and utterly pissed off, the last thing he wanted to hear this morning was Mr. E and his stupid jokes.

Mr. E carried on, oblivious to Yam's obviously distressed state. "Well, you don't haffe feel so bad 'cause I've got some good news! Ms. Nikki Stixx has just called me, and she's *very* excited and eager about our kicking tunes — and as we are so wonderful and everyt'ing, she has decided to put us on the top of her lickle list. Which means that we can go straight into B.U.L. Studios and master up all our tracks! Now, I've already spoken to Fingers and D, and they are both ready and raring to go, so all I need you to do, is to get hold of your lovely lady, the *delightful* Miss Cherry, and get her to fix herself up *quick*, and be ready to run down to B.U.L. and blow 'pon some tunes today!"

"No can do."

"What?" Mr. E took his mobile phone away from his ear and tapped it. "I can't hear you right — my reception is cutting in and out."

"No... can... do," Yam repeated. "Cherry's not here, she left the country today."

Mr. E was confused. "What d'ya mean she 'left the country'...? Where she go?"

Yam sighed, he really wasn't in the mood to go over all this with Mr. E, he was still coming to terms with it himself.

87

"She called me from the airport and told me that she had to go to America, because she has some urgent family problems to attend to."

Mr. E tried to digest Yam's words. "Family problems?What *family*? She didn't mention anyt'ing 'bout havin' a family…! When is she coming back?"

"I don't know, her money ran out before she could say. Listen, I'm a bit busy right now, I'll call you back later."

Mr. E heard the line go dead — Yam had put the phone down on him!

He couldn't believe it. Cherry had left the country. He was just about to hook up a multi-million dollar deal with B.U.L. Records and this lickle roughneck rude gal was leaving the country! He raised his eyes to the heavens, convinced that he had been struck by some kind of evil curse. Damn that Cherry Drop, or whoever the fuck she was, he'd known she'd be nothing but trouble from the very first day she'd walked into the studio.

With a creeping feeling in his gut, he dialled Nikki's number. "Er, Nikki…? Yeah, er, I'm just calling to let you know that we'll have to postpone the studio dates for a while… No, no, nothing's wrong. It's just that Cherry's father in Mississippi — you know the one I was telling you about? Well, he's had a heart attack, and she's had to rush over there to wait by his deathbed in case he pops his cork… No, no I'm not sure when she'll be back exactly, it's all hangin' a bit indefinitely at the moment…"

Mr. E finished his call feeling completely deflated. His bubble was looking like it could well and truly burst at any minute. Now that Cherry was out of the country, the deal could be delayed for ever, which meant that he wasn't going to get that fat pay cheque that he had been looking forward to. Not in any hurry anyway. Which meant that the chances of him being able to pay off his debt with the money from the B.U.L. deal were slim at the very best. He didn't dare think about what he would do to that idiot gal, Cherry, if he could get his hands on her now. Anyway, he'd have to think about all that later. Right now he had to work out a way to get some money. And fast.

Mr. E's brow furrowed into deep lines of concentration as he sat and silently plotted.

Yam lay on his bed, looking up at his posters of Vanity and Whitney. Even they were beginning to lose their appeal. To hell with all women, they'd probably just run out on him as well, if they were here!

It still didn't seem real that Cherry had gone. He felt like the phone was going to ring at any minute, and he would hear her sweet voice, enquiring as to what time he was coming over, as she missed him. Once again, his thoughts turned to what Mr. E had said about her lovin' up a next man. Would she really do something like that? After all the good love they had made? Hadn't she told him that he was the best she'd ever had, that she loved him and that she wanted to be by his side forever?

As he thought about it, he realised she hadn't actually said anything like that at all — but it was besides the point, she had always acted like she was in love with him. However, the more he went over what had gone on between them, the more he realised that it had only been him who had been declaring his undying devotion and everlasting love. It hadn't mattered at the time, because he'd been so sure she felt the same way.

The Journey

A DENSE WALL OF HOT, dry and dusty air hit Cherry as she stepped off the private jet and into Miami. Freddie took hold of her hand, and they headed towards the terminal. They were both dressed, from head to toe in black designer clothes. He wore baggy, black leather Dolce and Gabbana trousers with nothing on top apart from a matching black leather Dolce and Gabbana waistcoat and a huge solid gold cross, that dangled on the end of a heavy gold chain and swayed from side to side at his every step. This served two purposes very well: one, he remained cool in the Miami heat, and two, it allowed him to have his well-toned biceps and shoulders on show. And Freddie welcomed any opportunity he could get to display his ample array of muscles. Lord knows, he'd worked hard enough for them.

As they made their way to the terminal, Latonya scurried along at their side, making a number of frenzied calls on her mobile phone, to ensure that their hotel suite was ready and that their journey through and from the airport would be without any complications. Behind them trailed a gaggle of Freddie's people, carrying a selection of Louis Vuitton suitcases and hold-alls.

Latonya finally tore herself away from the phone. "Freddie, we have a situation. The press are waiting for you at the airport."

"Shit." Freddie stopped in his tracks, causing the whole entourage to suddenly halt, and he turned to Cherry. "Listen, baby, there's going to be hundreds of photographers crawlin' all over the airport like cockroaches on an open trash can, so things are gonna get a bit scary. Why don't you walk along with Latonya and the rest of my people? I'm *sure* you don't wanna be harassed by these animals."

He took off his sunglasses and turned to his assistant. "Latonya, how's my skin?" Latonya rushed over with some face powder and a mascara wand and clucked and fussed over Freddie's face and hair, as the rest of the crew waited patiently, nonplussed by the comic scene that was unfolding in front of them. When she was satisfied that Freddie looked 'the *bomb* sweetie', she put her make-up away.

Freddie stood up straight and assumed the snarling, menacing bad-boy expression that his public had grown to know and love. Sucking in his six-pack, he swaggered over to the terminal alone. Cherry, having been relegated to the ranks, struggled along behind him with Latonya and the rest of Freddie's people. She could only wonder as she observed the scene that had been played out before her. She knew it already, but time and time again she was reminded that the whole of the music industry seemed to be built on nothing but a web of bullshit.

Things had moved at lightning speed since that first night she had stayed with Freddie. After she'd gone shopping with Latonya, she'd gone home to pack a few toiletries and her passport into her trusty old brown leather rucksack. She was beginning to wonder whether or not Freddie would have tried to stop her from going home if she hadn't needed to get her passport. Even then he had insisted on Latonya going with her. In the few short days that she'd known him, she had come to realise that he was obsessed with having her near him at all times — or, at the very worst, knowing her whereabouts. As far as she was concerned, no-one could own, or even act like they owned Cherry Drop. Not any more. But she realised it was a situation that would be made easier if she played along with it until she'd recorded the songs.

Latonya was chomping on Freddie's dick so hard it was beginning to get sore. Freddie was getting pissed — what was she trying to do, suck up the whole of Miami through his fucking dick? They'd been at it for about half an hour now, and there hadn't been so much as a flutter from

Godzilla. They were in her suite at Miami's ultra-trendy Taravala Hotel, which was decorated in a thirties art deco style. He had her chained to the bed, which had always been his favourite scenario and never failed to perk up the old pecker. In fact just one look at Latonya's glorious butt had been enough to get old Godzilla ready and raring to go before… Before Cherry. He looked at her face and realised that it was no good, nothing was going to give him a boner today.

In disgust — at the whole situation, and at himself for being so much into Cherry and her domination tactics that he couldn't even get a plain ole erection — Freddie pushed Latonya off his dick. He went in the bathroom to take a piss, leaving Latonya spreadeagled and still chained to the bed.

"Er… hello? *HE-LLO?*"

Shit, he'd forgotten that he'd left her chained up. Well, as far as he was concerned, the bitch could wait. Couldn't she see that a nigga had to take a piss. Maybe if she learned how to give head properly, he wouldn't have had to leave her there… But Freddie knew he was fooling himself. Latonya's fellatio skills had nothing to do with his failure to get a hard-on. Everyone knew that she was a world champion in that arena. Shit, that was why he had hired her. No, the real problem was that he was no longer able to get off unless Cherry was dominating him. And that pissed him off. He was even beginning to question his manhood. What kind of man must he be, if the only way he could get off was when a bitch was kicking his ass? Next thing you know he was going to turn into a fag or something.

Freddie's blood curdled. What had happened to him? How could he have reached a point where he was wondering whether or not he was a fucking fag? Shaking his dick off into the toilet, he stumbled back into the bedroom.

Latonya was looking vexed. "What the fuck do ya think ya doin'?"

"Shut the fuck up, Latonya." Freddie bent over to untie

her; he really wasn't in the mood for any of her shit.

Latonya sat up and rubbed her wrists. She felt like cussing him out for fuckin' with her like that, but she could see that he was pissed. And the last thing that you did when Freddie Famous was pissed, was start cursing him out. So she decided to get back at him in a more subtle way.

"So this chick has really got you fucked-up, huh Freddie?"

I don't know what the fuck you're talkin' about."

"Oh *come on*, Freddie, you ain't ever been able to resist me sucking on your lollipop before, but now 'Miss Cherry's about, seems the only thing you get a hard-on for is her!"

Freddie took a deep breath, he wanted to turn around and punch Latonya out. She was just about gettin' on his last nerve. Especially because she had the gall to be telling the truth. Cherry *was* the only thing on this earth that he seemed to be able to get an erection for now.

He sat on the edge of the bed and looked at Latonya. "I can't lie — you ain't talkin' 'bout nothin' but the truth, Miss Booty. I *have* only got eyes for Cherry. Who knows, maybe this nigga is in love."

Freddie felt pissed off almost as soon as he'd said it. Why had he gone and said some fucked-up shit like that for? And especially to a loudmouth like Latonya. Next thing you know, he was going to be reading about it in the *Enquirer*.

He got up and went to get himself a beer. "Get the fuck out Latonya. I need some space."

Latonya left the suite, muttering various obscenities under her breath, not least because he'd just kicked her out of her own room — Cherry was asleep in his.

Freddie sat down on the bed and swigged on his beer. Could that shit be true? Could what he was feeling for Cherry be love?

Well, if it was, it sure beat being a fag.

The expectant crowd in Florida's vast Orange Stadium area

was packed solid. Thirty thousand people were crushed together as they jostled for a better position, straining their necks to catch a glimpse of their idol. The lights went down, and as the stadium was cloaked in the black night, the sound of distant drums began to roll. A rich, throaty, velvet-toned voice emerged from the huge blocks of speakers that stood stacked high above each corner of the stadium. All of a sudden, a phat and nasty groove boomed out across the night sky and a single, white spotlight beamed on Freddie Famous, who was descending onto the stage in a gilded cage, which seemed to drop from the heavens. When he reached the ground, he burst out of the cage and a thousand footlights lit up to reveal a mass of dancers sprawled out behind him, all bumping and grinding to the rhythm of the drums. Freddie Famous snarled and grabbed his crotch, and the crowd roared in their appreciation.

Cherry watched it all from the VIP area and wanted to laugh. It seemed ridiculous to watch Freddie acting like the original rude boy, when she'd had him snivelling at her feet the night before. If only all those screaming teenage girls in the audience knew what a pathetic wretch their macho idol was. They didn't know how much better off they were with their dreams.

To take her mind off Freddie and his perversions, she thought of what had happened earlier that day. Latonya had played her the tracks and, for once, she hadn't been exaggerating — they were dope. Her heart made a little leap as she realised how much closer she was to completing her plan.

"He's somethin' else, ain't he." Latonya was standing behind her, and whispering in her ear. "You've gone and hooked yourself up with the most eligible black man on the planet, girl. And he told me today... he's *crazy* about you. If you play your cards right, you could have anything you want, and I mean *anything*. The whole world will be beggin' at your feet."

Cherry could see Latonya's point, but the truth of it was,

she really didn't give a shit who the hell Freddie Famous was. She was sure that she could be just as large, if not bigger than him anyway. The only thing she cared about was carrying out her plan.

She breathed back to Latonya, "Yeah, I feel very lucky."

Latonya leaned in closer. "Yeah, girl, I want ya to know that I love you, and that anytime you need a friend I'm here for you — twenty-four-seven, girl. America can be a lonely place, an' I know that you don't really know anyone over here, so feel free to call on me *anytime* you need me." Latonya squeezed her shoulder.

Cherry smiled. God, any minute now, Latonya was going to lean over and kiss her ass! But she knew that Latonya was only schmoozing her because she wanted to keep in with Freddie's woman.

She placed her hand over Latonya's, which was still squeezing her shoulder. "Thanks, girl, I really appreciate it. It's good to know that I've got a sista looking out for me over here."

Nikki sat in her office at B.U.L. Records. She rocked back in her burgundy leather swivel chair and twisted a pencil between her fingers, feeling very bewildered. When Mr. E had told her that story about Cherry growing up in Mississippi, she'd thought it was just bullshit. Not that she cared — the publicity department would lap it up, glad of a meaty article with which to feed the press. However, when he'd told her that Cherry had had to rush off to the States to wait by her father's deathbed, she was beginning to believe that there might be a grain of truth in it. Now, however she was really confused. She'd just gotten off the phone, after receiving a call from the New York office of B.U.L., asking her who a certain Cherry Drop was, and informing her that the aforementioned girl was about to start recording some tracks with Freddie Famous in Miami. She wondered what the hell was happening. Hadn't she just introduced Cherry to every member of her staff, presenting her as her *own* next big B.U.L. signing?

What was going on? Was Mr. E trying to hard-ball her with some kind of stupid game?

Angrily, she reached for the phone. "Denise? Put me through to Mr. E... Yes, I'm fine... Mr. E...? Listen, I need to know — exactly what kind of paperwork is there between you and Cherry Drop?"

Mr. E replaced the handset in a state of shock, what the *fuck* was going down? He had to get out of the office, because suddenly it felt like the walls were crashing in on him, ready to squeeze out his last breath.

As he drove off in his car, he fought hard to digest what Nikki Stixx had just told him. Could it be true that *his* artist — the same raggamuffin rude gal that he'd given weeks and weeks of free studio time to, the same miserable lickle wretch that he'd polished up and developed into a top flight recording artist, the same *ungrateful* gyal that he'd sweated buckets over in order to tie-up a multi-million dollar recording deal — had not only run off to America, but was also engaging herself in some underhand double-dealing bullshit!

Was she mad? Who the fuck did she think she was dealing with — *Mary Poppins?* Didn't she know that he had her ass tied tighter to a contract than a dying man holding onto his last straw? When he got hold of her, he was going to give her a very clear picture of exactly how t'ings were running. Even if he had to beat it into every single brain cell in her fool-fool head.

And if this wasn't enough, he still hadn't been able to get hold of that asshole Carrington. If things didn't start going his way soon, someone was going to get seriously hurt.

Feeling mad as hell, he dialled Yam's number. "Yam! What was all that *fuckries* you were going on with about Cherry the other day?!"

Yam clenched his fists. Mr. E's timing was beginning to get way off. He really didn't need to be hearing any of this bullshit right now.

But Mr. E didn't wait for an answer, instead he continued, "Nikki Stixx has just told me that she got a call from New York saying that Cherry's been holin' up with Freddie Famous!"

"I know. Babsy's just called me to say that she's seen a photograph of them together in the *Enquirer*, so I don't need to hear any of your *crap*!"

Yam slammed down the receiver. Mr. E forgot his anger for a split second, so taken aback was he by Yam's words. He'd never known Yam to lose his temper like that before. He hadn't known the boy had had it in him. Still, he had warned him. That was what happened to you when you got too hung up on a woman, especially a bitch like Cherry Drop.

His rage began to mount again at the thought of her and his insides smouldered and burned. He felt like he needed to hurt somebody.

Suddenly his phone rang again, piercing through his thoughts like a tiny musical drill.

He picked it up and snapped, "Yeah — who the fuck is this?"

A calm voice, seemingly unperturbed by this greeting, drawled, "E."

As Mr. E recognised the tones his angry heart began to pound, but this time it was beating to the drum of fear. It was Mr. Ice, one of Big Red's cronies. He desperately willed himself to calm down and forced his voice to sound light and jovial as he said, "Yo! What's up Mr. Ice! I thought you were Warner Records — they've been hassling me 'cause they wanna sign up one of the kicking acts on my roster! You know what these suits are like once they start sniffin' millions!"

"So business is good then?"

"Couldn't be better."

"Cool, 'cause Red wants you to know that he'll be callin' in that debt soon."

Mr. E felt himself go cold. He slipped a perspiring finger underneath the collar of his Yves St. Laurent shirt. A mental picture of a noose hanging loosely around his neck flashed involuntarily into his mind. He forced out a casual laugh and, acting like Mr. Ice had just invited him around to his mother's house for Christmas, he replied, "Cool. Whenever Big Red is ready... He knows that."

Mr. Ice put down the phone, and Mr. E sat frozen in his seat listening to the resultant dead tone for what seemed like an eternity. There was no point in trying to play Big Red for time when it came to paying back the hundred grand. If they so much as sniffed any sign that he might not be able to come up with the cash, they'd have him in their club so fast it would make a brotha's head spin. No, he had done the right thing. Frontin' like he could come up with cash no problem should at least give him a little time to play with.

He sank back into the soft, luxurious upholstery of his car seat. The sound of his own breathing was so loud it was going to give him a headache, and his heart was banging like the clappers. He had to rest for a minute... Hearing Nikki's bad news and having Mr. Ice calling him at the same time, it was enough to give him a cardiac arrest.

As he sat there trying to calm his nerves, he pictured his whole world, the empire that he'd built from scratch, his goldmine that was finally looking like it was going to pay off to the tune of *millions*, crash and crumble all around him in slow motion. It all seemed to be going wrong. Faster than the speed of light, events were galloping by one after another and he had no idea how to slow them all down, never mind turn everything around. So far, he'd just been holding on to the seat of his pants, riding the waves and just trying to keep his head above water. *And the noose was tightening*.

If he didn't get this cash soon, not only was he going to lose Black Knight Productions and all its affiliated companies, Big Red was going to squeeze that noose so tight that he wasn't ever going to come back up for air. No, the more time passed and events continued, the more he realised that he only had one option. There was only one situation that could get him out of this whole stinking mess that he was wading through.

Mr. E turned his car around and stepped on the gas. He was about to pay somebody a visit.

Yam sat and stared at the photograph of Cherry snuggling up to Freddie Famous in the *Enquirer*. The headline read 'FREDDIE'S MYSTERY LADY'. Well it was no 'mystery' to him, he knew *exactly* who the 'mystery lady' was — his so-called girlfriend. Now that Babsy had enlightened him as to how Cherry had been bragging to her about lying to Yam so she could go on her first date with Freddie Famous, he was starting to feel angry. Especially when Babsy had told him that Cherry had targeted him from day one, and her only intention had been to use him in order to get some studio time. The more Babsy said it, the more it seemed to be true — Cherry had taken him for a mug.

He was devastated. There had even been a moment during Babsy's phone call when he'd thought he was going to cry; especially when she'd told him how he'd taken their car parking space outside Subterania that night. It was unbelievable. If he had arrived just five minutes earlier, maybe none of this would have happened.

So, of course, when Babsy had told him to come right over it had seemed like the right thing to do. He was getting himself into such a state that he really needed someone to talk to. And Babsy was the only one who knew Cherry as well as he did — which, when they'd talked about it, turned out to be not very well at all.

Yam cradled the glass of warm brandy that Babsy had poured for him, feeling like he was going to collapse.

Like a zombie he said in a flat, lifeless voice, "I still can't believe it, Babsy. I keep thinking that it's all a nightmare and I'm gonna wake up and find that everyt'ing is just how it used to be." He stared at the floor and shook his head, saying, almost to himself, "The whole thing just doesn't make sense."

Babsy sat next to him on the edge of her bed. "Yeah, tell me about it."

Yam bit back the tears. "But there must be some sort of explanation. How can me and Cherry be so in love one minute, and the next minute she's running off to America?"

Babsy sympathetically rubbed his shoulder and said, "Well I tell you what, Yam, I don't believe that story about having 'family problems' for one minute. Cherry doesn't have any family. If she did, we would have heard something about them by now. Or at least seen a photograph or something."

Yam stared at his boots. "I know, Babsy, I don't believe that either now. But I still don't know why she wouldn't have told me the truth. There's *got* to be a really good reason for all of this."

Babsy's features arranged themselves into the kind of expression you would have if you were about to tell someone some awful truth, like you were a convicted murderer or something, "Look, Yam, I know what you're saying, but you might as well face it — Cherry is nothing but a lying bitch!" She put a comforting hand on his knee. "You're not gonna like this, but I think you're gonna have to try and forget all about her. I know I have."

In his horror at her suggestion, Yam looked up. For the first time since he had entered her room, he noticed Babsy's appearance. She was wearing a very tight pair of red gym shorts and a low-cut, skimpy vest top. As she leaned forward to talk to him, he could not help but notice the gentle curve of her honey-coloured breasts. Tears pricked his eyes when he thought of forgetting about Cherry. If only he could. If only he could stop the painful turmoil he'd found himself in since she had told him she was leaving for the States. In that moment, Yam felt that he would never feel happy and carefree again; he felt that he'd been sentenced to a life of heartache and misery. It was all too much.

Overcome with emotion, he buried his head in his hands, "I-I just feel so *stupid*, Babsy. I don't know how I could have let her fool me like that. And… and I just think of her all the time, and everything we used to do together. I mean, we couldn't bear to be apart. And then I keep picturing her with another man and it just drives me *crazy*. I-I feel like I'm going to go mad!"

Babsy pulled Yam close, and he sobbed into the soft warm comfort of her bosom.

Freddie Famous took at long hard look at Cherry as she emerged dripping wet from the pool at the Taravala Hotel on Miami's Ocean Drive in South Beach. She looked like she had been dipped in a cup of steaming hot coffee. As she came out of the cool, turquoise-blue water, she ran her fingers through her long, jet black hair, which was hanging in thick, wet waves all the way down her back. She was *all* money!

They had been in his studio until the early hours of the morning, laying down vocals on his songs. He had almost forgotten what a dope voice she possessed; the girl was nothing short of mind-blowin'. Even Latonya couldn't believe it. He knew she had pegged Cherry as being one of those bitches who said she was a 'singer' or an 'actress', but was really just prowling the streets looking for a rich man. Well, there was no way that he, Freddie Famous, the biggest megastar on the planet, was going to hang with some gold digging bimbo. No, he had himself a *lady* with beauty, talent and class.

He smiled as he thought to himself that, not only did Cherry give him the best sex he'd ever had in his life, she was also going to make him a lot of money. Which was exactly how a bitch should be hookin' a nigga up.

He gave Cherry a hearty slap on the rump as she came to join him on the recliner next to the pool and cracked, "Who's is it, money?!"

Cherry gave him a sideways look from underneath her eyelashes, and without missing a beat she replied, "All yours, baby."

He was sucking on a blunt, and started waxing lyrical about how wonderful he was, which seemed to be his favourite subject — his *only* subject in fact. "So when me and ma boyz did the Letterman gig, the whole place just exploded! Dave let me know *personally* that they had *never* had a phatter jam kicking up his show. Me an' ma niggas *tore* the house down! And the dialogue between us was electric. I mean, ON FIRE! I was playing with him like he was just one big, wide-open wet and warm pussy!"

Cherry squinted, the thick black smoke that was curling back into her face from Freddie's blunt was making her eyes water. She felt a sudden urge to get as far away from him as possible, so she said, "Freddie, can you pass me the mobile, I'm gonna call Latonya so that we can go shopping."

"Good idea sweet *thang*. Make sure that you buy something hot too, 'cause we're goin' out tonight with ma crew and we're gonna have ourselves a par*tay* to celebrate the show goin' down so well. We gotta prove that Freddie Famous can rock Miami both in *and* out of the stadium!"

Later on that evening, Cherry had a dilemma. She could not decide between the seemingly hundreds of outfits that she and Latonya had bought earlier. In a couple of hours, they were all going to 'The Cave', Miami's number one R & B hotspot, and she wanted to make sure that she looked extra special.

This was because she was still finding it hard to get used to the way women would just throw themselves at Freddie. It was crazy how many girls called their hotel suite. Lord knows how they got the room number, because Freddie was checked in under a pseudonym, and the hotel operator had been told to carefully screen all their calls. And these girls had no problem coming on to him right in front of her face either. Some of them got real sexual too, not even bothering to hide the photographs of themselves — usually lying butt naked stretched into the most unbelievable positions — before they handed them over to Freddie, together with their phone numbers.

Freddie said that he hated it, and that he felt offended that these 'hos' would think he was the kind of brotha that would be interested in any kind of nastiness like that, but added that he had grown to accept it as just being one of the many downfalls of a life in the public eye. Not that he'd needed to bother to explain his feelings on the subject, because Cherry didn't give a shit. As far as she was concerned, they were all *more* than welcome to Freddie and his sick perverted self once she had finished recording the tracks.

But for now, she'd decided to make sure she looked extra good, so Freddie's mind would be on her and making the music, and not on running all over town looking for pussy.

"What's up, money? How come you ain't ready yet? Ya know we gotta be outta here in an hour."

Freddie took a break from the sofa where Rhonda, his personal beautician, was buffing up his fingernails, as a prelude to giving him a pedicure.

"I can't decide which outfit is gonna be right for The Cave."

"Make sure it's something hot, babe. Just pick out the smallest and skimpiest thing you got."

You couldn't get any simpler than that — the smallest and the skimpiest. That was Freddie's special talent — to always come up with the simplest of things, not to mention the smallest and the skimpiest.

When they were all finally ready to go, because, of course, everyone was on B.M.T. and had ran a bit late, the whole crew piled into a couple of limos that were waiting for them at the back entrance of the hotel (there were too many fans waiting outside the front). Once safely inside,

Freddie poured everyone a glass of ice-cold champagne and pulled out a packet of white powder from a compartment in the limo side-door, exclaiming, "Okay people, we are gonna get H-I-G-H tonight!" This was greeted by much cheering and whooping from the rest of his crew. Everyone took turns to arrange lines of white powder on the back of a magazine that was being passed around, each of them hoovering up a couple of rows through a metal straw.

When it came to Cherry's turn she waved it on and shook her head. In disbelief at her social *faux pas* everyone stopped what they were doing and turned their heads to stare at her. As fate would have it, the CD that had been playing reached the end of its last track, so the car fell into an eerie silence at the same time.

Latonya took it upon herself to break that silence. In a loud, sneering voice she said, "What's up, girl? Ain't you ever done powder before?"

Cherry felt herself go red and she cursed Latonya under her breath. She held onto her seat in an effort to resist reaching over and giving her smug face a good hard slap. Trust Latonya to go and open her big fat mouth.

Freddie chipped in, "Course she has. Don't ya know ma bitch is a woman of the world! From *London* no less! She won't let ole Daddy Freddie down and ruin the party!"

He slapped Cherry's thigh. "Don't worry, baby, we ain't with the po-lice!"

They all fell about laughing except Cherry who felt like she was caught between a rock and a hard place. She didn't want to do the lines, but there seemed to be no way of getting round it without losing face in front of Freddie and his crew. Of course, she could tell them where to go, but her tracks weren't finished yet and she didn't want anything to rock the boat. So far, she'd been going along with them and all their stupidness, but this was one game that she didn't feel like participating in.

The seconds dragged by and no-one said a word as she deliberated what to do. The way they were acting, it was like it was turning into some kind of fucking test. Cherry sighed inwardly... What could a few lines really hurt?

She felt their eyes burning into her skull as she slowly arranged three neat lines of coke on the back of the magazine. As she bent over to do her first line the whole crew leant in *en masse* to take a closer look, with the same type of fascination that you watch a dying boxer drawing his last breath as he lies beaten and immobile in the ring.

When she had finished hoovering up the light, powdery substance, they all started cheering and slapping hi-fives. Anyone would think that she had just cured cancer from the way they were acting. Some new sounds were put into the CD player and everybody was happy in the knowledge that *nothing* was going to stop them from having a great party.

Cherry sank back into her seat. She didn't feel anything yet, but she knew that in about ten seconds, her nose would start to tingle, her eyes would throb, her head would begin spinning and her heart would pump blood around her body faster than a Ferrari on a racetrack.

The Cave was a huge underground maze of rooms, decorated in a neon-lit, futuristic style. There were two main dance floors, each playing different sounds. The larger one did R & B, hip-hop and soul, and the smaller one played jungle and garage. There was also a chill-out room and a VIP room — which was where Freddie was ushered straight away, together with Cherry, Latonya and his 'boyz'.

The first thing Freddie did was go to the bathroom. And he kept running there throughout the night, with different members of his crew, to snort more and more coke. He was getting higher than the Statue of Liberty. And getting progressively louder — and, if it was possible, even more arrogant.

In the club, the music was pumping and everybody was looking finer than a midsummer's day. Miami, being one of the modelling centres of America, was packed with beautiful faces from the pages of all the leading fashion magazines. It seemed like they were all hangin' at The Cave tonight. The supermodels were there in droves — Tyra Banks, Veronica Webb, Naomi Campbell, Tyson. You name them, and they were there. A lot of celebrities had flown in too — just to see Freddie. And *everybody* wanted to check out his new babe. Rumour had it between insiders in the industry that she was Freddie's latest protégé, and that she going to be bigger than Whitney Houston, Toni Braxton and Mary J. Blige put together.

Cherry tried to keep a low profile, which wasn't easy with those few lines pumping the blood through her veins faster than the speed of light. The last thing she wanted to do was get caught up in bullshit conversations with a bunch of bullshit people. Luckily, Freddie was busy havin' a ball, gettin' high and being congratulated on his fabulousness by every famous person on the planet. A couple of the supermodels were throwing themselves all over him and running off to the toilets, giggling at the thought of being able to hoover up a few lines with Freddie Famous. When one of them shot a smug look at Cherry, as if to say 'watch out, girl, I'm gonna take your man, Cherry wanted to laugh out loud.

When her demos were cut, 'Miss Thing' could do what she wanted with him. Cherry only hoped, for her sake, that she would be able to do it right.

When they eventually got back to the hotel, Freddie disappeared into the walk-in closet. His eyes were like bulging flying saucers, and he was way past hyperactive. Cherry was still feeling pretty energised herself from the lines that she had done, but it was a sick, nervous energy that gripped her intestines with the white hand of fear.

Freddie came back out of the closet, stripped down to his black Ralph Lauren boxer shorts and holding a small box wrapped in black tissue paper all tied up with a silky black ribbon. He held it out toward Cherry, "I got you a present baby."

Intrigued, Cherry took the box. Normally she would have been excited at the thought of a present, but there was something different about Freddie's manner tonight. And that something made her tremble slightly, as she peeled off the tissue paper. She lifted the lid of the box to reveal four pairs of golden handcuffs, set into the soft, black velvet lining.

Freddie licked his lips, as he watched for her reaction. Cherry's brow creased as she squinted back at him. Why had Freddie bought *her* a set of handcuffs? The only person that got chained up in their bed was him. She thought he knew that.

"Now be a good girl and get on the bed, and lie on your back with your hands and legs apart. I've been looking forward to this for a long time."

"What?" For the first time, Cherry felt a little scared about what Freddie had in mind. It was obvious that he wanted to chain her up, and she didn't feel quite sure that tonight she could turn that shit around. Of course, they had played this game before. They sometimes role played that Freddie was going to humiliate Cherry in some way, and then she would turn round and kick his ass for being so 'insolent'. Yet tonight it felt different. Tonight it felt like Freddie didn't intend to get his ass kicked — on the contrary, it felt like he wanted to go all the way with the humiliation shit. And that was something Cherry *definitely* wasn't in the mood for. Especially when he was so high.

She felt her throat, which was already dry, go even dryer. Her heart began to stab at her ribcage. Freddie took hold of the handcuffs and moved towards Cherry. He grabbed the neckline of her dress and in one smooth action ripped it from her body.

"You little bitch! You've been asking for this ever since I met you!"

Without giving him time to think, Cherry grabbed one of

107

the handcuffs and cracked him with it on the side of his head. As he staggered back, stunned, she pushed him to the ground so that he was on his knees in front of her. As he looked up dazed and off his head she snapped, "You piece of shit! Who the *fuck* do you think you are? Coming at me with handcuffs!"

Freddie looked up at her helplessly. In less than an instant, he felt the blood rush to his groin and Godzilla sprang into action. He knew it was over. She had won again.

Tears sprang to his eyes as he bit his lip and surrendered. "You're a bitch, Cherry Drop... I swear, you ain't nothin' but a fuckin' bitch."

Cherry looked back at him, feeling well and truly relieved, and fully in control again. How could she ever have been scared by a wretch like Freddie? As the cocaine raced around her system, she threw her head back and laughed. "You're damn right I'm a bitch, the biggest fucking bitch that you're *ever* gonna see in your whole goddamn life!" And then she let out a roar of laughter, and kept on laughing like it was the funniest shit she had ever heard.

Blackmail

TEN IN THE MORNING, AND YAM stretched his arms out, and sat up in bed. The curtains in the room were tightly closed so, even though it was daylight outside, his room was cloaked in darkness. He yawned and reached for the remote, which controlled the portable TV that sat at the foot of the bed. As the television winked on, he saw a middle-aged, distinguished-looking black man appear on the screen. He was conservatively dressed, wearing a well-cut dark charcoal grey suit, with a plain white and blue striped shirt, and a subtly patterned navy blue tie.

A newscaster read: "Delroy Carrington could well become Britain's first black Prime Minister. After winning the die-hard Tory seat in the London borough of Westminster with a strong majority, he has been virtually unstoppable in building upon his success and winning over the hearts of the entire nation. Dubbed 'Britain's most likable MP', because of his down-to-earth nature, Mr. Carrington has the quality to lead Britain toward a brighter future. Since Paddy Ashdown stepped down from the leadership last Monday, Delroy Carrington has decided to make a bid for the leadership of the Liberal Democrat Party. The bookies have him tipped as the hot favourite, with the odds at two-to-one. We'll join him now, in Westminster, where Mr. Carrington is holding a press conference at his constituency..."

The camera cut back to a shot of Carrington addressing the press. Yam turned round to make a comment on this momentous occasion to Babsy, who was lying naked beside him, her legs entwined about his. But there was no point, as she was fast asleep, snug as a bug in a rug.

That evening, Delroy Carrington sat at the long mahogany dining table that stood in the centre of the huge dining room at his home in Kensington, and ate dinner with his family. Tiffany lamps lit the room with a gentle glow and the cool jazz sounds of John Coltrane played in the background. They ate off a pearl-white porcelain Wedgewood dinner set, edged with gold, and dabbed the corners of their mouths with freshly laundered, crisp white linen table napkins. The menu consisted of baby quails with shallots and a white wine sauce to start, red mullet with a basil and olive crust on a warm tomato coulis served with boiled new baby potatoes in their skins, asparagus spears and sautéed baby carrots as the main course, and desert was to be lemon tart served on a tangy raspberry coulis with clotted cream on the side. To drink with the main course there was a lovely, full-bodied Chateau Lafitte, and they were served Laffayette Blanc as the desert wine — a particular favourite of Delroy's. Port or brandy would be available at the end of the meal, and to round it all off, there were a selection of biscuits and cheeses and fresh gourmet coffee or herbal tea. The catering people had arrived that afternoon, and they were doing an excellent job.

Delroy sat at the head of the table. His wife and her parents sat to his right, whilst his mother and his brother and sister-in-law sat on his left. His father sat at the other end.

The mood at the table was jubilant, as everyone was celebrating Delroy's bid to become the leader of the Liberal Democrat Party. Delroy's wife, Bernice, was in particularly high spirits and was throwing herself wholeheartedly into her role as hostess. The table was so busy with jokes and family chit-chat, that no-one seemed to notice that Delroy had hardly said a word all evening.

Delroy's heart had sunk to his boots earlier that morning when his secretary, Charlotte, had informed him that a certain 'Mr. Knight' had been at his office the day before, asking for him. She had described Mr. Knight as being a 'well-dressed gentleman, but with a coarse manner and rough way about him'. When she had informed him that

Delroy was not in the building, he had become very angry and had started to shout and swear at her. She confided that she had begun to feel a little afraid that Mr. Knight would become violent at this point, and was about to call security, when he had left. But not before saying that she should be sure to tell Mr. Carrington that Mr. Knight was 'not a happy man,' and that he had been 'messed about for far too long,' and should 'prepare himself for the consequences'.

Delroy had been able to think of nothing else all day. He had no idea how he'd managed to get through the various press conferences and meetings he'd had to attend. The timing could not have been any worse if somebody had planned it. Not only did he have a campaign to mount, but he now had to deal with this man, Knight, as well.

Delroy looked at his wife. Bernice was a very attractive, immaculately groomed, Nigerian woman. At forty-nine, she was two years older than her husband. And she was the daughter of a diplomat. Marrying her had been a big step up for Delroy, and her top-class pedigree hadn't gone unnoticed by his voters either. She was the perfect trophy wife. Like him she'd studied law, and had only recently given up practising, in order to support Delroy's political career. They had two daughters, aged twelve and fourteen respectively. Delroy was completely devoted to his family. He loved his wife and children.

Although he still found Bernice attractive, they'd stopped having sex years ago, because she no longer enjoyed it and, being a gentleman, he didn't want to force her into doing anything she didn't like. It had happened gradually; at first they were both so busy raising two young children and pursuing their respective careers, that they just didn't seem to have time. Their marriage seemed to go the way a lot of marriages do, when both parents are high achievers — it had become more of a friendship and a meeting of minds. Delroy still loved Bernice more than any other woman in the world. He had never met another woman with her level of intelligence, her tenacity, or her vivaciousness. When you had a relationship that was as special as theirs, the sex wasn't really that important. So they, quite simply, didn't do it... It was about that time when he had first met Knight.

At the thought of Mr. Knight, Delroy bit his lip. There was no way he was prepared to jeopardise his career, not to mention his wife and family — not after everything they'd been through together. Not when they were so close to reaching the goal they had all been working so hard to achieve. There was nothing else for it, he was going to have to do something about this man, Knight.

It had been a week now since Yam and Babsy had become more than just good friends. He was walking back from the corner shop where Babsy had sent him to buy a bottle of milk, and she was on his mind.

He had to admit that he'd never imagined in his wildest dreams that he and Babsy were going to get together. It had all seemed to happen without them knowing really. At first, they'd both just needed someone to talk to about Cherry and what she'd done to them. Then, with all the time that they were spending together, they had started to become close. Yam began to sleep over — because it didn't make any sense for him to have to drive all the way back to Hackney from Stockwell late at night — and one thing had led to another, until here they were in what seemed to be growing into a fully-fledged relationship.

Of course, it didn't hurt when Babsy had told him that she'd always fancied him and that, when Cherry had first met him, she'd felt more than a little jealous. Not only because it seemed like he was taking away her best friend, but also because Yam seemed to be such a great catch: good-looking, successful, exciting, attentive... *and* Cherry had confided to her that he was great in bed. This, Yam proudly noted to himself, she had said she could now verify.

Babsy had argued that it really hadn't seemed fair that

Cherry should have both Freddie Famous *and* Yam. Maybe Cherry's escape to Miami wasn't so bad after all, she'd suggest, as it would enable the bond that was growing between Yam and herself to become stronger.

For his part, Yam wasn't so sure. He felt he would never be able to get over Cherry or to find another love that even came close to what they had had together. But he had to admit that it was very comforting to be with Babsy right now. She'd been quite right when she'd pointed out to him that he really couldn't handle it all alone, and that if it wasn't for her, he might have had a nervous breakdown, or even topped himself.

When he arrived back at her room, Babsy greeted him with a huge kiss. "What took you so long, babe? I missed you."

Yam's brain went into automatic as he held her in his arms and replied, "I missed you too."

Delroy Carrington clicked off the phone. He was working late, and everyone else had gone home, so he'd decided to take advantage of his solitude and return Mr. Knight's call. Now he sat and thought back to that fateful night, the night when all his troubles had begun. The night that had changed his life forever.

It had happened five years ago. Delroy had been seeing a pretty young girl who'd told him that he should call her Tootsie — obviously not her real name. About once or twice a week, for several months, he'd visit her flat in Knightsbridge from where she worked. When he arrived, she would fix him a drink and they would indulge in a few minutes of casual chit-chat, and then they would engage in thirty minutes or so of straight sex — nothing kinky. After his hour was up, he would pay her a sum of two hundred pounds and then be on his way, usually home. He'd never really spoken to her at any great length, but Tootsie seemed to be a pleasant enough girl and always seemed to be extremely pleased to see him — but then of course that was what she was being paid for.

It had been Mr. Knight who had introduced him to Tootsie. One cold October evening, after a long, hard day's work at his office, he had stopped off for a nightcap at his private drinking club on Pall Mall, where he often went to wind down before going home. He'd been sitting alone, browsing through a selection of the daily papers, when Mr. Knight had approached his table and asked whether he minded if he joined him. Of course Delroy had had no objections. He'd seen Mr. Knight at the club a couple of times before and, although he hadn't spoken to him, he looked like a decent enough chap. Besides, it was good to see another black man at his club, as it was so rare. They chatted away a few pleasantries and, like men sometimes do, had eventually got onto the subject of sex. Carrington couldn't remember exactly what he had said, but he knew he'd made some sort of joke about no longer getting any from his wife. When Knight had told him about a beautiful young girl in Knightsbridge with whom, for a small fee and no emotional involvement, he could enjoy some wonderful and discreet love-making, Delroy had looked upon it as a very kind gesture. He'd presumed that, like himself, Mr. Knight was a successful businessman who needed to have sex from time to time, without the complications of being in a relationship. He'd also thought that Knight was probably a family man too.

It was only later that he discovered that Mr. Knight was Tootsie's pimp.

Well, introductions were made, and after several months things were working out fine. Delroy partook in regular visits to Tootsie's, making the payments with his company credit card for expenses — in case his wife got suspicious. It was all going so well, that he felt like he was forever indebted to Mr. Knight... Until that fateful evening.

Delroy felt the bile rise to his throat as he thought about the last time he had gone to visit Tootsie. Just like in the movies, it had been a bitterly cold, wet and windy February evening. As Delroy ran from his taxi to buzz the intercom, there'd been no escaping the rain, which was relentlessly pouring down from the heavens, onto the filthy streets of London. In his haste to escape the miserable weather, he didn't stop to think that no voice from the intercom had welcomed him into the large Victorian mansion house.

He'd climbed the two flights of stairs to find the door to Tootsie's flat ajar. That wasn't unusual, as she often left the door off the latch after buzzing the front door open. So Delroy walked straight in.

He'd only begun to think that something could be wrong when he realised that all the lights were off, the flat lit solely by a dull yellow glow from the street lamps outside the windows. Feeling a little worried, he'd called out Tootsie's name, and that was when he had stumbled over something lying on the floor. To his horror, he discovered that he had tripped over a body And that body had belonged to Tootsie. The hairs bristled on the back of his neck and terror struck to his very core, and his only thought was to get out of there as quickly as possible.

As he scrambled to get up, his left hand touched something hard and cold, he lifted the object in front of him to find that it was a gun. As he'd registered the murder weapon, a brilliant flash had blinded him and all the lights in the room were suddenly turned on. He'd opened his eyes to see Mr. Knight standing in front of him with one of his cronies, a big brute of a man who was holding a camera. As he stared at them both, the stranger continued taking photographs, walking all around Delroy and Tootsie's limp and lifeless body, making sure that he was capturing the moment from every angle.

Understandably shaken, Delroy had demanded to be told what was going on. Mr. Knight had then taken the gun from him, with a hand coated in a rubber surgical glove, and slipped it into a plastic bag, proclaiming that it would be needed as 'evidence'. He'd gone on to explain that Tootsie had been murdered earlier that evening and that they were going to have to pin it on him. He had openly gloated as he'd declared that it was going to be an open-and-shut case for the police, now that they had Delroy's fingerprints on the gun, not to mention a selection of photographs of the murderer kneeling over the dead body and holding the murder weapon at the scene of the crime. Mr. Knight had added that he might even get some kind of reward for his heroic capture of the murderer, and for assisting the police by finding so much indisputable evidence. He had told Delroy to look upon it as an insurance deal, saying that it was going to be 'a lickle bit of cash' he could grow to depend upon in his old age.

Delroy sat and shuddered; when he thought of how that poor girl had looked, he wanted to retch. Tootsie had been lying across the floor in one of her see-thru outfits, on her back, in the centre of the living room. She had been shot in the head, right between the eyes, and once in her heart. There was blood everywhere — all over her negligée, coming out of her mouth, lying in a pool on the carpet — and her face had turned a ghastly, greyish white. And her expression... Never, as long as he lived would he be able to forget the look of sheer terror that was in that poor girl's eyes as they stared up unblinkingly at the ceiling. And the way her mouth had contorted and froze into an ugly expression of fear, probably as she was crying for help at the moment of death. The ghostly image of Tootsie's dead body had haunted him ever since, stealing into his thoughts during the day, and floating through his dreams at night.

So there it was. Mr. Knight had him backed into a tight corner, and had been blackmailing him ever since. Of course, he could have probably put an end to it if he had attempted to fight him in court. It certainly wouldn't have been too hard to prove that Knight was an unsavoury character who had been blackmailing him, and if they'd performed an autopsy on the body, they could easily have established that he hadn't been there at the time of her death. But there was no way he could have taken the publicity. It would have raised too many awkward questions and become very, very messy. His career would have ended; he would have lost his wife, his children and everything he had ever worked for. So, Delroy had decided to run with it for a while and see exactly what Mr. Knight had planned.

Knight started to hassle him for lump sums of money from time to time, but nothing too drastic, and the sums seemed to get less and less each time. As the months unfolded into years, it seemed to become harder and harder to think about ways of trying to get rid of him. Delroy was so consumed with his blossoming political career. Tootsie's dead body had long been buried, and Mr. Knight had become no more than a pesky fly that he had to get rid of from time to time. So, he resigned himself to a lifetime of trying to dodge Mr. Knight's calls and handing over the occasional payment whenever Knight managed to catch up with him.

But now Knight's timing was off — every spare bit of cash Delroy had was tied up in his election campaign. And this time Knight had seemed desperate, telling him that he wanted a hundred thousand pounds in a week's time at the latest, otherwise he was going to the press.

What Delroy didn't know was that, after he had left the scene of the crime, Tootsie's 'dead body' had come back to life, and she'd proceeded to have a drink with Mr. Knight — alias Mr. E — and his crony. The whole thing had been a ruse. Mr. E had tried the same thing several times before on some of his more affluent clients. Of course, it didn't work every time — sometimes their potential victim would realise that Tootsie wasn't dead, or they would get all heavy themselves and refused to pay out any cash — but Delroy Carrington had been perfect. Because of his position as a leading politician, he couldn't afford to be linked to anything as controversial as a murder case. And the fact that he had been sleeping with a prostitute might have destroyed his career, not to mention his marriage. Even if the murder charge was dropped, Delroy had way too much to lose if Mr. E went public.

Which, of course, was exactly what Mr. E had now threatened to do.

Tootsie had been the perfect foil for Carrington, because, out of all of his girls, Tootsie was his very favourite. This was because she always played her part so well. Having studied drama, she knew how to be a convincing corpse.

As Mr. E got out of pimping, and moved more and more into the music business (some would say that there wasn't much difference between the two) he'd left all his old acquaintances, like Tootsie, behind. Delroy Carrington was the only person he still kept in contact with who had anything to do with that world. For the most part he had left him alone — he'd been far to busy running his empire to go chasing after Delroy for money.

But now he was desperate. Real desperate. If he didn't get some money like yesterday, his whole empire was going down and he was going right down with it.

The next day, Mr. E was still feeling a little better now that Carrington had called him. He knew the fool would come round once he started to put the frighteners on. He had that guy by the balls for life. Carrington was an idiot if he ever thought that he was going to get away from Mr. E.

So, he was in a more positive frame of mind as he sat with Nikki Stixx in the Attco coffee shop in Soho, which was decorated in a funky style.

Nikki was being very business-like, and to the point. "So, have you brought the contracts?"

Mr. E patted his briefcase, "Yep, I've got the copies right here, signed, sealed and delivered."

"Any idea what Cherry's doing in Miami?"

"Yeah, well, she's just living it up that's all — you know what these kids are like. Her father made a quick recovery, so she decided to go and let her hair down for a bit to help her get over the shock of it all." He leaned forward to make sure that Nikki realised that she was about to hear some confidential information. "I didn't mention it before, 'cause I didn't think it was important, but I know all about the Freddie Famous situation. I was with her when she first met him in your reception area at B.U.L. They've been together ever since then."

This was something Nikki didn't know, and she couldn't help exclaiming, "They met in *my* reception area? What do you mean? What are they doing, exactly?"

Mr. E was pleased with himself, he'd hoped that little bit of information would throw Nikki off balance. Feeling cocky, he joked, "I don't t'ink I have to describe to you what de yout' dem get up to behind closed doors, Nikki." He gave her a theatrical wink.

Nikki smiled back, maybe she'd been underestimating Mr. E's involvement in all this after all, so she asked, "Do you know if they're gonna do any recording?"

Mr. E was incredulous. "What? Freddie Famous? *Record* with Cherry? He doesn't drop it like that! As I said before, their business is of an entirely *sexual* nature. And even if, by some *miracle,* they did t'row down a tune, nobody can move without my say so, 'cause as you will read in the contract, *I own Cherry Drop* — lock, stock and barrel, right down to every last strand of hair on her head!"

"Do you know when she's coming back to England?"

"Er, well, we haven't worked out an exact date as yet, but it will be soon. Very soon. Definitely within the next couple of weeks."

Nikki leaned back, for a moment there she wasn't sure, but now she was quite certain that Mr. E hadn't got the slightest clue about what was really going on. Her associates in New York had informed her last week that Cherry was working on five songs with Freddie at his recording studio in Miami. Still, if Mr. E's contract was as tight as he said it was, then he didn't have anything to worry about — which was good for her, because she needed Cherry to sign the deal to B.U.L. in England. If she signed in the States, Nikki wouldn't get any points on the album, which meant no royalty cheques, no independent label, no glory, no Audi convertible, no nothing. Just one hideous burgundy Saab.

Nikki had to work out a way to get Cherry back to England. And she needed to do it fast, before things started to get out of hand.

Her voice was brusque as she concluded their meeting. "Mr. E, I'll take this copy of your contract with me, and I'll get our lawyers to send you the first draft of our contract so that we can get this ball rolling. Call me the minute you find out when Cherry will be back in London." She stood up and slipped the contract into her bag, and shook his hand.

"Call me when you know what date she's coming back."

Mr. E watched Nikki's well-shaped behind sashay out onto the street and felt that all hope was walking out with her. Suddenly he didn't feel so happy any more. It seemed like he and Nikki were drifting apart; she'd even gone back to calling him Mr. E. He'd much preferred it when she had just called him E — it was more intimate.

Even though he had been frontin' to Nikki that he had everything under control, nothing could be further from the truth. He had no way of getting hold of Cherry. He couldn't even find out whether or not she had called Yam again, because even Yam seemed to have disappeared off the face of the earth. He started to feel panicky, it was like his whole team was falling apart. He *had* to find Cherry, he needed to have the deal signed so that he could pocket the two hundred and fifty thousand pounds advance that he'd negotiated with Nikki in Josephine's.

But first he was going to deal with Delroy Carrington.

Confrontation

CHERRY HELD HER LAST NOTE and let her voice tremble slightly, milking the emotion of the moment for all it was worth. Freddie, Latonya, the two engineers and the tape op all sat in the air-conditioned monitor room of Freddie's Miami studio, completely silent. Cherry's voice had that effect on them, it was like it just took their breath away.

As she stepped out of the vocal booth, they all rushed up to give her a hug.

Freddie slapped her rear end, declaring, "Yo ma bitch. Yo ma bitch!"

Latonya loudly exclaimed, "Girl, you are gonna be a major, *major* S — T — A — R!"

After two crazy weeks in Miami, Cherry had finally finished recording five songs with Freddie. Even she had to admit they were slammin'. It felt like she'd been there a lifetime, with the endless merry-go-round of partying, doing drugs, shopping, sunbathing and recording. Two weeks in the sunshine had Cherry looking better than ever and with Freddie's songs in the bag, she felt incredible. Invincible.

She turned to them, "Okay you guys, I'm gonna catch some sleep now. It's a wrap, I'm completely exhausted."

"That's cool hotlips, you go right ahead, I'm gonna stay here and finish mixing the tracks. We're all really proud of you — ya kicked some ass today, money!" Freddie cocked his head. "Make sure you keep the bed warm for me now."

Inwardly grimacing, because she knew what 'keep the bed warm' meant, Cherry smiled, blew him a kiss and turned to go.

"Wait up, girl! I'll walk you back to the hotel. We gotta make sure our new superstar gets there safely!"

As they took the colourful walk along the bustle of activity that was Miami's Ocean Drive, Latonya tried to keep cool, but she could barely contain her excitement as she said, "Ya know I been waitin' for an opportunity to tell you, Cherry — I've been in touch with B.U.L. in New York, and they are *hyped* about the tracks. I played 'em a couple of samples of what to expect, and the whole building went *nuts!* I spoke to Dick Francis — he's the head of the whole company — and he wants to sign you personally. I know that I can get a lot of *serious advance* money for you over here." She paused for dramatic effect, "*I'm talkin' six figures girl*! When can we discuss this in more detail? I need to sit down with you and find out exactly what you want, so that I can go in there and pitch it to Dick."

Cherry chewed over Latonya's words. It was all happening so fast, she hardly knew what to think.

As they arrived back at the entrance to her hotel, Cherry turned back to Latonya and said, "That sounds great. Why don't we meet tomorrow?"

"Sure! How about I meet you for lunch at The Dealano's Water Salon, say around two o'clock?"

"See you then."

As Cherry wearily climbed the pale limestone steps that led into the foyer of the Taravala Hotel, she felt pure elation through her tiredness as she realised that, with the demos finished, she was one more step closer to completing her plan.

She was looking forward to seeing the back of Freddie. All she had to do was figure out a way to get rid of him. Maybe she could pass him on to one of those model bimbos that hung around his tired ass like the sun shone out of it. Hell, since everything had turned out so well, she might even kick his butt one last time — just to say thank you!

Back in their hotel suite, she walked like a zombie over to the huge triple king-sized bed and, letting her clothes fall into a crumpled heap on the floor, she sunk into the haven of the cool, pale-blue silk bedsheets.

Freddie laid out a couple of white lines on the mixing desk.

As he started to get high, he began barking out orders to the engineers and the tape op: "What the fuck are you fools doin' with the bass? Don't you know that the bass is supposed to *PUMP* through the track? Have you got that? You waste-a-time muthafuckas have got it soundin' like a *fuckin' acoustic guitar*! Don't MAKE me have to come and slap some sense into yo stupid heads!"

The other guys took Freddie's ranting and raving in their stride. He always got like this when he was high; it was just the drugs talking, the endless pressures of stardom and all that, so there was no point in taking it personally As usual, they ignored him. After all, the only thing they were interested in was gettin' paid at the end of the week — and Freddie was renowned for his generosity. So if the nigga needed to get flighty once in a while it was not up to them to make it their business. Unruffled, and taking their time, they put some more low EQ on the bass.

It was about eight o'clock in England and Nikki Stixx sat in her office. She had finally got hold of the number for Cherry and Freddie's hotel suite in Miami, from the B.U.L. office in New York. She couldn't believe the hassle she'd had to go through to get it. The New York staff always seemed to think that the British branch of the company was totally unimportant — something that never ceased to amaze her. It wasn't like she was based in the North Pole or something... and Cherry just happened to be *her* discovery!

By-passing her secretary, she dialled the number, and a sleepy girl's voice answered.

"Oh hello. Could I speak to Cherry Drop?"

The voice croaked a barely audible, "Speaking."

Nikki was taken aback; she had hardly recognised her, "Cherry? Are you okay? You sound terrible."

Cherry was starting to come out of the deep coma she'd been in. Freddie hadn't returned to their suite yet, so she presumed he was still mixing the tracks. She tried to prise open her eyelids. "I'm fine, I was just sleeping… Who is this anyway?"

"It's Nikki Stixx calling you from B.U.L. Records in London."

"Oh." Cherry sat up and rubbed her eyes, she yawned and continued, "How are you?"

"I'm fine, now that I've finally been able to locate you. We've all been very worried, Mr. E is beside himself. Anyway, it's good to actually hear your voice. How are the tracks with Freddie going?"

Cherry was a little taken aback. How did Nikki Stixx know about the tracks with Freddie? You couldn't keep anything a secret these days.

Nikki didn't wait long for an answer. "We wanted to know when you are planning to return to England, darling."

Cherry wasn't about to report her every move to Nikki Stixx, or to anyone, so she said, "Listen, Nikki, I'm really tired at the moment. Can I call you back tomorrow to discuss this?"

"Sure."

Nikki clicked off the speakerphone, feeling a little deflated. The conversation hadn't gone quite the way she had wanted it to — she was still none the wiser with regards to Cherry's movements — and now there was no option but to wait in limbo until tomorrow before she could get any kind of idea as to what Cherry was up to.

Mr. E was driving back to the office with mixed feelings. On one hand, he had finally spoken to Carrington and was going to get the money to stop Black Knight Productions from going under. And pay back Big Red. But on the other hand, the B.U.L. deal with Nikki was standing on decidedly shaky ground. With Carrington sorted, he had to think of some sort of plan to get Cherry back over to England.

As various possible plans for this came into his mind, he couldn't help but wonder whether Freddie Famous slept with prostitutes. More than likely. And he had yet to find a man who could resist the indisputable charms of the lovely Tootsie. Still, if he pulled one of his murder scams on Freddie, it would probably do nothing but help his career. Nowadays, it seemed that any mention of scandal seemed to help a celebrity's career rather than hinder it. Mr. E thanked his lucky stars that politician's weren't at that point yet.

With all this running through his mind, he arrived back at the office of Black Knight Productions to find Denise packing away her computer.

"What are you doing?"

Denise jumped, startled at the sound of his voice. She turned round to face him, a dangerous glint in her eye, and picked up an official-looking piece of paper.

She thrust it into his hands. "I'm handing in my resignation. You haven't paid me in six weeks and I can't afford to take this craziness any more. I'm a *professional* person, with bills to pay — something for which you have *no* respect — so I've gone out and found myself a decent job, working for a *legitimate* company. Now, if you'll move aside, I'll be on my way. And don't worry, I won't ask you for any of the severance pay that I'm entitled to, because I know you don't have it."

Mr. E couldn't believe his ears, he'd never heard such foolishness. "Now, wait just one minute Denise, don't think that you can walk out on me dat easily. You're my woman!"

Anger flashed in Denise's eyes as she shot back at him, "Oh no I'm not, not any longer! I've found myself a *decent* man, who treats me with love and respect and is *there when I wake up in the morning!*"

"Wha'? You've been rubbing up to a next man!?" Mr. E was beside himself now. "Woman, I should *lick* you down, right yah soh!"

Denise looked Mr. E straight in the eye and with a low, steady voice, she hissed, "Don't you dare even *think* about laying a finger on me. I'll have the police around here so fast, it'll make your head spin! They'd have a field day in this office, with all the dodgy dealings you've been up to.

"I've slaved over all your paperwork and kept my bed warm for you for too long. And what did I get in return? Nothing! Not even a thank you. The only thing I ever got from you were lies and deceit and broken promises. You've used me as a work slave and for sex. If you could call it sex which, by the way, was absolutely *crap*!! So, let me tell you, Mr. E, Mr. Knight or whoever the hell you are — I'm not going to be treated like shit by you or any other wanker on this planet. I am going to live the life I deserve, and be with a *good* man who loves and cherishes me in the way that I ought to be loved and cherished. Now get out of my way!" And with that, Denise went up to him and gave him a good, hard shove, and strode out of the office, taking her computer with her.

Mr. E looked on in horror and disbelief, could Denise really have spoken to him like that? Was he dreaming, or did she actually attack him with physical force just now? How could she turn on him like that, say all those nasty things and make all those wild threats and accusations? The girl was delirious, making that ridiculous comment about his sexual prowess — as if he hadn't been the best lover that she'd ever had! After everything he had done for her!

He slumped into the receptionist's chair, flabbergasted. Sometimes he just couldn't understand women. Cherry had disappeared in Miami, Nikki Stixx was acting like an ice maiden and now, to top it all off, Denise had deserted him in the final hour.

Cherry woke to the feeling of something cold and hard slide across her skin, breaking her out of the deep sleep that she'd fallen back into on the king-sized bed in Freddie's suite at the Taravala Hotel. She wondered if she was still dreaming as she felt one of her arms being pulled over her head, and soft warm velvet crush against her wrists and ankles. A dark shape leaned over her naked body and breathed hot air against her cheeks. As she slowly regained consciousness, she made out the outline of Freddie's face, as he reached out to handcuff her arms and legs to the posts at the four corners of the bed.

When he had finished, he stood up to admire his handiwork, smiled into Cherry's eyes and whispered, "I'm back, baby."

Cherry's heart filled with dread as she realised what a state Freddie was in. His bloodshot eyes were bulging out of their sockets, and his brow was oozing salty beads of sweat. He was seriously coked out of his head.

He reached down and squeezed her breast, saying, "Now you've finished the songs, we can *really* celebrate. First, I'm gonna show ya what happens to very very bad girls who think they can mess with li'l ole Daddy Freddie."

Freddie stepped over to the walk-in closet and came out butt naked, apart from his customary black silk Ralph Lauren boxer shorts. He carried a small golden suitcase in his right hand. Cherry looked on, helpless and vulnerable, as Freddie rested the suitcase on the dressing table and flicked open the locks. Smacking his lips together in anticipation, he pulled out a long black leather whip, similar to the kind a lion tamer might use in a circus ring.

He walked back over to the bed and towered over Cherry's naked body. "Now... tell me what a bad girl you've been."

Cherry felt a slight stirring of alarm. Even though Freddie had tried to use the handcuffs on her before, she had never seen the golden suitcase. And she had never ever seen the whip. Her voice wavered as she began to say, "Look, Freddie—"

"Ssshhhh!" Freddie trailed the tail-end of the whip along the length of Cherry's naked, trembling body. "Just answer ma question, baby, an' everything mo be all right."

Sheer terror slowly took a hold of Cherry's heart. Freddie looked really high — higher than she had ever known him to be — and she had a horrible feeling that he was so off his head he didn't even know what he was doing. Now he had her helplessly chained to the bed and was standing over her with the whip, only God knew what he was going to do.

She tried to remain calm as she pleaded, "Look, Freddie baby — I think you've been overdoing it at the studio, why don't we—"

Freddie's features darkened with anger, "Shut the fuck up, bitch!!" He flicked the tip of the whip across her bared thighs. As he saw her wince, a rush of power shot through his consciousness. Finally, he had got this bitch where he wanted her. And this time, there was no way she was going to be able to turn this shit around. Now he was going to see exactly how much 'love' he felt when he kicked *her* ass. Now he was finally going to have the chance to prove that he was a man after all and not some fuckin' fag acting like a bitch over some pussy.

He bared his teeth. "Now, answer my question, before I start to lose my temper!"

Cherry screwed her eyes tightly shut in an effort to hold back the hot angry tears that were threatening to cascade down her cheeks. Damn Freddie and his cocaine-fuelled perversions! For the first time ever, she felt completely at his mercy. She wondered how she could have been so tired that she didn't wake up before he'd started locking on the handcuffs. Just when she thought she was going to be able to finally walk away from all this shit, she had to find herself in the midst of the worst scenario yet.

At that moment, Yam's face flashed in front of her. He would never have treated her like this. Cherry suddenly felt herself longing to have him hold her in his arms, and to be safely back in England. For the first time since she'd arrived in Miami, she found herself actually missing Yam and the life they'd had together. What the hell was she putting herself through? And all for the sake of revenge. Why couldn't she just have gotten on with her life, had a normal relationship, everyday problems and goals — like she could have done with Yam? She wondered if he still cared about her, and what he was doing back in England... while she awaited her fate at the hands of Freddie Famous.

It was a hot and sunny Sunday afternoon in central London's Hyde Park. Its wide stretches of freshly cut grass were peppered with colourful patches of sweet-smelling flower beds and cool clusters of green leafed trees, their long branches forming areas of shade against the golden sun. Rollerbladers glided over the maze of walkways that ran like a web across the park's length and breadth. Assorted groups of people played lazy games of softball and tennis. Lovers kissed and cuddled on beach towels, and tourists strolled arm-in-arm, taking in the park's infinite varieties of sights and sounds. Yam was stretched out, his head resting on his hands, basking in the warm sunlight. Babsy lay across him, her head on his lap. He played with her red-brown corkscrew curls as she read an article from *The News* out loud.

" 'There was plenty of party fun to be had at Miami's number one naughty nightspot, The Cave, on Friday night. America's top celebrities turned out in droves to whoop it up with everyone's favourite soul singer, Freddie Famous.

"No expense was spared for the lavish do, which insiders say must have cost multi-millionaire Freddie tens of thousands of pounds. Although there to celebrate Freddie's sell-out concerts at Miami's Rose bowl, the hot topic of conversation was Cherry Drop, the beautiful 'mystery lady' who has caused Freddie to give up his playboy lifestyle and get ready to settle down.

"Rumour has it that they might have already done just that, and that the couple flew off to Las Vegas last week for a quickie wedding.

"*The News* can reveal exclusively today that sexy stunner Cherry Drop is one of our very own and comes from somewhere in south London. However, she still remains very much a mystery, which is why she is so talked about in the American press…"

Yam felt his heart fall like a dead weight to his boots as he listened to Babsy's words. Surely it couldn't be true. *Surely Cherry hadn't married Freddie Famous.*

Babsy ran her finger to the end of the article and went on to read: " 'Do *you* know Cherry Drop's real story, before she became Freddie's 'mystery lady'? We'll pay for any information or any photographs that we use. Phone us any day, between ten a.m. and six p.m'." She took a break from reading to look up at Yam, and enthused, "We should call them. One of the girls from my agency had an affair with Les Ferdinand and *The News* paid her *twenty grand* for her story. It really helped her modelling career; she gets loads of jobs now. What we know about Cherry has got to be worth a mint, Freddie Famous is *much* more famous than Les Ferdinand!"

Yam stopped playing with Babsy's curls and looked at her in horror. "Are you saying dat we should sell Cherry's story to the papers?"

Babsy was defensive. "Well, why not? We're not friends any more. She's run off and left you for a pop star. We don't owe Cherry anything."

Yam was incredulous. "But we don't even know anyt'ing about her to tell the papers! All they want to write about is pure sex and nastiness."

"Well, how do we know that Cherry didn't get up to any nastiness? You've just admitted we hardly knew anything about her. She could be anyone. I mean, as far as we know, she could be the nastiest girl on the planet."

Yam started to feel angry. Although they had split up, he still didn't like to hear a bad word being said about Cherry — at least, not until she came back to London and told him the truth. "You're not suggesting we just make something up, are you? That would be bang out of order, Babsy!"

But Babsy was having none of it. She reached into her bag to get her One to One mobile phone, and dialled the number that was in *The News* at the bottom of Cherry's article. An electronic voice said, "You have reached *The News*..." It was an answering machine. Babsy clicked off her phone, she had no idea what to say as a message.

Yam was relieved. "See? That was a sign! Look Babsy, I know you're not the type of girl who would go dishing the dirt to sleazy tabloids. All we have to do is wait until Cherry comes back, then we'll get the real explanation."

Babsy however, was deep in thought, and Yam's words were just background music. Surely he couldn't still be pining after Cherry? Not now. Not now they'd got together. Not after Cherry had dumped him for someone else.

She turned to him, determined to give him a piece of her mind. "I would say you've had all the explanation you need after the way she dumped you and ran off with Freddie Famous! Don't you get it, Yam? Cherry *used* you the whole time. The only reason she got together with you in the first place was because she thought you would help her get into the music business. She used to laugh at you behind your back! How much longer are you going to go on defending her? I mean, I thought *I* was your woman now. Aren't *I* the one who was there for you when you were upset over Cherry? Without me you would have had a nervous breakdown!"

Yam felt dejected. "I don't know Babsy... Maybe you're right, maybe I am only fooling myself."

"That's *exactly* what you're doing and you better be careful, 'cause if you don't stop moping around after Cherry pretty soon, I'm gonna have to break up with you. You can't expect me to stick around, if all you're gonna do is pine after some other girl who treated you like shit. You're a good guy, Yam. You deserve better than that."

She huddled close to his chest and said in a soft voice, "I thought you were over all that now. I mean, don't you love me?"

She was looking directly up at him, and as Yam looked back into her eyes, he felt himself sigh inwardly. It was always like this; Babsy constantly reminded him what a fool he'd been over Cherry and made him feel guilty because she had helped him cope with the loss that he had suffered. Sometimes he didn't know what was worse — Babsy's digs, or the thought of living without Cherry. All he really knew was that he needed time to get over it — after all, you can't get over true love in a couple of weeks.

That's why he felt certain — how he just *knew* — that Cherry couldn't just have left him like that. There had to be some sort of explanation. But, he was also aware that he owed Babsy an awful lot, and it was true that she *was* there for him, and Cherry *was* running around Miami with that sleazeball Freddie Famous.

He gave Babsy a sincere look and said, "Of course I love you."

She smiled, comforted by his words. "Good. Because I love you, Yam. And, unlike Cherry, I'll always be here for you." She squeezed his hand, "We've got to stick together on this. I mean, we *deserve* to make some money out of Cherry after the way she's just used us. Anyways, I'm not planning to say anything bad about her. I mean, she was my best friend. I also have a few feelings left for her, no matter what she's done." She kept on squeezing his hand, "I just think we should fill in a few blanks for the general public, that's all. And why shouldn't we make a bit of change out of it? She's not exactly hard-up now she's running round with Freddie Famous! Have you seen the outfit she's got on in this photo?" Babsy waved *The News* in his face. "That dress is Gucci — it must have cost over a grand! I just don't see why we should scrimp and save over here, while she's rolling around in the lap of luxury in Miami!"

Yam still wasn't sure, but even he had to admit that Babsy had a point. Resignedly, he stuffed the newspaper and mobile phone back into her bag. Taking her hand, he said, "I don't know Babsy, maybe you're right. Anyways, I'm sick of all this talk about Cherry and Freddie Famous. Let's go for a walk through the park and talk about you and me for a change."

And with that, they both set off, hand in hand, to take in the delights of the day.

Bernice and Delroy Carrington were in bed. It was around ten-thirty in the evening, and they were sitting up, supported by an assortment of plumped pillows, their prospective reading lamps on. Delroy was deeply absorbed in Nelson Mandela's biography 'Long Walk To Freedom', and Bernice was reading the *Guardian*.

She wagged a finger at the article she was reading. "It says here that Wright is going to resign after that scandal."

Jonathon Wright was a tory backbencher who had recently been under the endless scrutiny of the British press. This was because a certain lady from south London — 'Madame (Se)X' — had informed the British public that a member of their parliament had been visiting her for almost ten years in order to dress up in his old school uniform (Eton) and receive a good hard spanking, not to mention full 'sexual favours', every Tuesday and Friday. It had given the papers something to write about for a few weeks. Wright was expected to ride the storm, take a break from his responsibilities and return when all the noise had died down. However, his wife had cracked under the pressure and, finding it hard to cope with the public humiliation, had decided to leave him, taking their teenage son with her. Distraught, and unable to continue with his work, Wright had resigned from the Tory party, of which he had been a member for the past twenty-four years.

Delroy felt uncomfortable, the last thing he wanted to hear about was a politician resigning because of a sex scandal.

Bernice, of course, was completely unaware of this. "Apparently, the final nail in his coffin was when his wife left him... I guess it was all too much for her. I wonder what was the hardest to cope with — her husband's strange sexual preferences, or the fact that he was unfaithful. What do you think, Delroy?"

Delroy's face remained impassive, but his insides had turned to jelly. Why should Bernice be so interested in Wright's wife's feelings? *Had she heard something?*

He cleared his throat, "I should have thought that *both* scenarios would have been uncomfortable for her."

"Uncomfortable! Her husband's name is being bandied around the papers in some lurid sex scandal and you'd only think she'd be *uncomfortable?* Is that how you feel about adultery, Delroy?"

Delroy felt himself go hot under his blue and white pinstriped pyjamas. Why was Bernice getting on to the subject of adultery? Had one of the secretaries from his office been spreading tales about Knight's visit? *Had she found out anything?*

Cautiously, he said, "Well no, of course not. I mean it's dreadful — but sometimes these things can get blown out of proportion, I really don't like to comment about anything like this, until I'm aware of all of the facts."

Bernice turned on her side to face him, her thick cotton nightdress silhouetted against her reading light and said quietly, "It's just that we've never really discussed the subject of adultery and I wondered how you felt about it."

Delroy was really starting to feel nervous now. Why should Bernice ask him about adultery all of a sudden? His voice faltered as he struggled to answer her question.

"Well, I er... don't know, I would imagine that it would depend on the circumstances and the various parties that were involved." He could stand it no more. If Bernice knew or suspected anything, he wanted her to come out with it there and then. All this beating around the bush felt like torture. "Look Bernice, why all this sudden talk about adultery?"

His wife looked uncomfortable, "Oh, no reason really, it's just that we haven't... I mean we don't... well, you know. And... and I was just wondering if you ever... well, felt that—"

"Look Bernice, unless there's a point to all this nonsense, I'm not in the mood to continue with this kind of conversation. You know I'm completely tied up in the election, and I haven't got time to be wondering about Wright and his various adulteries."

He paused before softly asking, "Well... *is* there a point?"

Bernice turned away to resume lying on her back. "No, not really. I was just wondering that's all. But you're quite right, darling, this isn't really the time to be exploring those issues."

As they both turned off their reading lamps, Delroy felt his heart race. This was no good. If he carried on like this, he was going to have problems with his already higher-than-average blood pressure. He was going to have to take care of Mr. Knight once and for all.

'This isn't really the time to be exploring those issues', Delroy wondered what Bernice meant by that. She could be a funny woman sometimes. He had been married to her for almost twenty years, but sometimes he'd swear that he hardly knew her. And why was she being so nice after he'd just about bitten her head off? It wasn't like Bernice to play the meek and humble wife. Well, if she did suspect something, she obviously wasn't completely sure about it, otherwise she wouldn't have beaten around the bush like that. He felt himself start to relax a little bit, relieved that at least she had decided to stop her awful line of questioning. And with that small crumb of comfort, Delroy sank into a restless night's sleep.

Freddie sat on the purple crushed-velvet sofa in his suite at the Taravala Hotel. He had flicked on the Playboy channel, and the tape of the latest mixes of Cherry's songs was booming out of the stereo. He was trying to focus on scooping up a spoonful of powder from the huge mounds of cocaine that were on the glass coffee table in front of him. He tipped the contents of the spoon into the bowl of his pipe and his hand wavered as he made an effort to light his spoils, his head swaying uncontrollably as he leant over to inhale the thick white smoke that collected in the stem of the pipe and was curling towards his lips.

He drew back his head as he scored another hit. In the space of a second, the Special K went straight to his brain, and he felt a heady rush shoot through his entire consciousness.

Cherry lay aching on the bed. She could only thank God that Freddie hadn't gone mad with the whip earlier and she had, so far, escaped a beating, but she was feeling as stiff as a board on the bed. This was unsurprising, considering that it had been five hours since Freddie had first arrived back in the room, and she'd been chained up in the same goddamn position ever since. And those five hours of stretching felt more like a hundred. And, worse of all, she was dying to pee. So now she was in purgatory. Even though Freddie had finally left her alone, content to watch the TV and dabble with a little freebasing, she needed him to uncuff her so she could go to the bathroom. But she didn't know if she dared risk asking him to uncuff her, because he might use it as an excuse to resume torturing her — or, even worse, resume torturing her *and* refuse to let her go to the bathroom.

Freddie grunted as he blew his nose — a little blood was coming out of it now. This happened to him from time to time, on the occasions when he got really fucked-up. He shook his head as he tried to get his blurred vision into focus.

Cherry was in agony. It was no good — she *had* to go to the bathroom. And, as unpleasant as her predicament was, she was in no doubt that wallowing in her own pee would make it even worse. She tried to sound confident, but she had to stop herself from cursing her voice as it came out as a weak and frightened whisper.

"Freddie."

No answer.

She tried again, this time a little louder: "Freddie?"

No answer.

After several more attempts, getting progressively louder, Freddie had still not heard her above the beat of the music, Cherry felt like she was going to explode. Any minute now, her dam was going to flood the bedclothes. In a last, desperate attempt she screeched at the top of her lungs, "*FREDDIE!!!*"

"Huh?" Freddie turned round and clicked off the DAT tape with the remote control.

Cherry, now in a turmoil, was oblivious to the new silence, she could only feel her own urgent need, and went on screeching, "FREDDIE! GET YOUR ASS OVER HERE NOW!!"

Freddie rushed over to the bed — well, as much as anyone can rush when they're completely off their head. "What the fuck is up with you, bitch? D'ya wanna wake up the whole goddamn hotel?"

If only, Cherry thought. She said, "You *gotta* unhook me, I need to pee real bad."

Freddie took what seemed like an eternity to register her sentence. "Oh yeah…? Ya not trying to get clever on me, are ya?"

Cherry reasoned with him, "For God's sake, I've been here for five hours! If you don't let me go to the bathroom right now, I'm gonna pee all over the bed."

Freddie grimaced, "Ugh. Don't go gettin' all nasty on me now. I'll take ya to the bathroom. But be warned — you make one false move and I'll kick your butt!" He started to recite the lyrics to one of the raps he had written for his last album: "*Bitch don't make me lose ma muthafuckin' rag,*
 'Cause you'll find yo tired ass sittin' up in a body bag…"

Cherry didn't know whether to laugh or cry. Here she was, strapped to a… a *crazy* man's bed, about to drown in her own piss if she didn't get to the bathroom, and this muthafucka's acting like he's on MTV! "Yeah, cool, *nice* performance — that was one of my favourites, Freddie. *I get the message.* Look, I'm not gonna do anything silly, baby. *Please*, just unhook me!"

Freddie was still unsure. He'd been in this situation with Cherry before — there was no way that he was going to let her turn the shit around this time. He had yet to prove to her, and to himself, that he was a man. And that he was the kind of man who would not tolerate being fucked with. Not by her, or any other bitch. He reached out and cuffed Cherry across the side of her head.

Cherry bit her lip as the pain reverberated throughout her skull. She knew he had only hit her lightly. But it still hurt like hell. All those daily workout sessions meant that Freddie could box like a world heavyweight. A shudder ran through her being, when she realised the pain he could cause if he used all of his strength.

"That's jus' a warnin', Cherry. An' I swear to God, if you so much as say one word out of line, *I mo kick the shit outta ya.* You got that bitch?"

Cherry got it. Only too well. She gulped back the tears that had the nerve to be pricking at her eyeballs and said, "Yes, Freddie."

Freddie smiled. Now this was more like it. Finally she was beginning to talk to him with respect. Like a real man should be spoken too. If he wasn't so fucked-up, he would have gotten Godzilla to drive his point home — right there and then.

As if in slow motion, he unhooked her arms and legs. Then he re-cuffed her hands behind her back so she couldn't do anything with them, and grabbed hold of the back of her neck as he led her to the bathroom, standing guard over his prisoner while she did what she had to do.

When Cherry was once again strapped to the king-sized bed, having been escorted to and from it by the ever-present Freddie, she stared up at the ceiling and it was as if a thousand memories were playing across it like a movie screen. The feel of the cold hard steel of the handcuffs against her wrists brought back the memory of the first time that she had been led into her cell at Holloway. Before that moment it would have been impossible for her to imagine just how helpless that bit of steel could make you feel. Not to mention how... worthless. It wasn't just the fact she was rendered helplessly in the control of her jailer. It was more than that. They made her feel less than human. With one simple click of the lock they took away her humanity along with her liberty. Somehow, she felt that she would always have their impression indented on her wrists, that she would be forever branded with their steely ring of shame. That was maybe the worse part. The complete and utter *shame* of it.

She thought back to the countless journeys to and from court in the police van and the cuffs burning into her wrists. She remembered the open-mouthed stares from the public gallery, the grim faces watching over the proceedings like a hungry chat show audience drooling in anticipation for the next juicy titbit of scandal to tantalise their greedy palates. Safe and smug in their liberty, gleefully waving their unblemished records as good citizens, ready to judge the already damned, joyful at being able to toy with the life of the criminal that stood before them. Balancing her future in their hands.... She felt as though the imprint of those handcuffs and all that they had meant would be forever tattooed on her consciousness.

And all for a crime that she did not commit.

Which was why she felt that her only chance of truly finding liberty, the only way she could rid herself of the weight of the... *injustice*... was revenge. And how very bitter was the irony that the path of revenge should have led her straight back into the handcuffs that she was yearning so much to free herself from. To think that her future was now in the hands of a nut like Freddie Famous.

As her mind drifted back to Freddie, the cold hand of fear slid its icy fingers around her intestines. He was really high. Higher than she had ever seen anyone get. And she had seen some extreme cases. She tried to block out the feeling that he was capable of anything. And that she was completely at his mercy.

As the various monstrosities that Freddie was capable of reared their ugly heads before Cherry's eyes, she desperately racked her brain for a plan. A way for her to get the hell out of her predicament before Freddie did something that they might both regret.

But she didn't have long to think, because now he seemed to have made up his mind. Totally psyched up after hours of doing lines and freebasing, Freddie was once again standing over Cherry's naked, helpless form.

"So, are you ready to admit that ya been a bad girl to li'l ole Daddy Freddie then?"

Cherry decided to play along, and replied meekly, "Yes I am, Freddie."

"Good. 'Cause I mo give ya jus' what you deserve. You ain't acted like nothin' but a *bitch* since the day I met ya — an' now it's payback time. An' don' think that I mo spare ya — 'cause I ain't. I been lookin' forward to this moment for a very long time, an' now I mo show ya what happens when bitches like you try an' fuck with a man like Daddy Freddie!"

Cherry bit her tongue. She longed to tell him where to go, but knew she was in no position to do that. Yet. So she kept her tone sweet and said, "Thank you."

Freddie smiled a triumphant smile, confident that he had finally got her to behave how he wanted. "Yes Cherry, you've been a very very bad girl and you need to be *severely* punished. So I mo gonna piss all over you, you li'l bitch, an' then you can suck my dick 'til it's clean."

He put his hand to her throat and hissed, "An' you better make sure you drink up every last drop, or else I'm gonna really whip yo ass!"

The Interview

YAM AND BABSY SAT IN SILENCE at the cheap and cheerful orange formica table in Le Café Anglais, an egg and chips type restaurant in London's East End. They were both deeply engrossed in thought, as they stared into their respective mugs of luke-warm hot chocolate, and waited for Dave Armstrong to arrive.

Fortunately, they didn't have long to wait before a plump white man in his late thirties approached their table. He was wearing a dark-blue suit that fitted snugly over his well-rounded beer belly. His liverish skin had a sallow, uneven tone, and was marred with pock marks — the unfortunate remains of teenage acne. And he had a slight, supposedly 'designer' stubble on his large jutting chin. The whole vision was framed by some lank, longish dark-blonde hair which was loosely greased back over his skull, its sparse strands clumped together, so that they had separated to reveal the odd patch of flaky scalp.

He gave them both a wide, lurid grin and extended his hand. "Barbara?"

Babsy shook his clammy hand and smiled and nodded a 'yes', and he extended his hand again to Yam. "And you must be... Dan, is it?"

"Yam." Yam corrected the reporter and kept his eyes on his hot chocolate, his expression sullen.

Dave seemed unperturbed by this unwelcoming reception and kept his cockney tones jolly. "Well, let's get straight to it shall we? As you both know, my name's Dave, and I'm a reporter for *The News*. Now you're both very lucky that they sent me along for this job, 'cause I always cover the biggies. I was the one who uncovered the Jonathon Wright sex scandal!"

He sat back and beamed at them, pausing to let the magnitude of what he had just said sink in.

Yam piped up. "You're not gonna put any nastiness like

that in our story, are you?"

Dave looked genuinely offended. "Of course not —
unless you decide to tell me nasty things! We only ever put
the *truth* in our newspaper. We have to, otherwise we'd get
sued by everyone we wrote about and then we wouldn't
make any money!" He stretched his dry, cracked lips over
his yellow teeth once more as he eyed the two of them,
beaming, "And that wouldn't do *anyone* any good, now
would it?"

Yam didn't believe him for one second, "Yeah, well don't
go making anyt'ing up, I heard it's just pure lies they put in
your paper."

He reassured them, "Nah mate, you've got it all wrong.
Honest. Look I know that Freddie's mystery lady — I mean
Cherry Drop — is a good friend of yours and I respect that.
Actually, I'm hoping to do a sensitive little piece with this
one, maybe a rags-to-riches story, you know the type —
local girl makes good an' all that."

"That sounds great, Dave." Babsy nodded
enthusiastically, glad to get a word in edgeways. She shot a
dirty look at Yam. Why did he always have to act like such
an idiot? Hadn't she told him that Dave had said their story
was worth about eighty thousand pounds? That was forty
grand apiece. If Yam didn't get his act together sharpish, she
had a good mind to do the interview herself and keep all of
the money.

Dave responded to her words of encouragement, and
gleefully skinned his teeth at Babsy. "Good! I'm pleased
that's all settled. You didn't tell me that you were *so
beautiful*, are you a model, love?"

Babsy beamed back at him, and said, "Yeah, I'm with the
Queen Of Sheba modelling agency."

"Never heard of it. With your face and your figure you
should be working with one of the top agents, like Yvonne
Paul. Would you be prepared to do a photo spread with this
article?"

Babsy glowed and said coyly, "I might do."

Dave could sense that she was game, and went in for the kill. "It'll really help your career, love. Did you know that *Baywatch* are looking for a coloured girl? David Hasslehoff told me personally, when I interviewed him last week, that he reads our newspaper religiously every Sunday — we're always givin' his girls a few column inches — no pun intended!" He cackled at his own joke and, after seeing their blank expressions, continued, "So, there's every chance that he could spot your photograph and want to audition you for his show. It's happened before — we were the ones who got Catherine Zeta Jones out of TV and into Hollywood films!"

"Oh really?"

"Yeah, maybe we could approach the article from a me-and-my-best-friend type of angle. That way we could feature you a lot more."

Babsy was starting to feel excited, she hadn't even thought that the article would give *her* some sort of notoriety. With all the exposure she would receive as Cherry's 'best friend', she might well become an actress — or at the very least, a supermodel. And a part on Baywatch sounded wicked.

She gave Dave another bright smile and said, "Great!"

The reporter reached for his tape recorder, he could see that he had Babsy all fired up now.

Yam, however, was still sulking into his hot chocolate. There was something about this reporter that he just didn't trust.

Dave carried on regardless. "Now, tell me all about how you met Cherry Drop."

Babsy and Yam launched into their prospective stories — Babsy going into every detail of how she and Cherry had connected on a spiritual level at the gym and Yam reluctantly going over the bare bones of the relationship that he had had with Cherry.

Dave licked a furry tongue over his dry lips and stretched them into another yellow-toothed smile. "So, let me get this right, Mr. Yam — you and Cherry Drop were about to get married before she fell in love with... I mean *met* Freddie Famous."

Yam scowled. He knew that this reporter was going to twist everything they said. *"No*, I was just saying that I was hoping that we would *eventually* make our relationship legal."

Dave nodded, as if Yam had confirmed what he had just said. "Right. And Babsy — you say that Cherry used to work with you in this West End nightclub — Touchdown was it?

"No, Dave, what I said was that she used to *meet* me up there, and we just used to hang out."

Dave gave Babsy a saucy wink, "What, getting up to mischief, were you?"

Babsy laughed, "No, we were just hangin' out, you know, doing girly things."

Dave gave her another playful wink, "Yeah. Well we all know what that means, don't we darlin'?" He roared with laughter at his own innuendo, and Babsy giggled along with him.

Yam felt sick. Somehow, he had a very bad feeling about this guy Dave Armstrong; he had to put an end to this before Babsy went and told Dave that Cherry was the leader of a vice-ring or something. "Listen, I should think that you've got your story now. Me and Babsy had better get going."

Babsy looked daggers at him. Why did he always have to spoil the fun?

She smiled back at Dave, "Oh, I think we could stay and chat for a little while longer."

But Dave clicked off his tape recorder, "No, no, I've taken up enough of your time already. I've got more than enough for a good story on our 'mystery lady'. Now, why don't you call me tomorrow and we'll arrange a time for the photo session with you and Yam. We'll give you the cheque for the money we agreed upon at the end of that. Oh, and make sure you bring some kind of identification, just so we know that you haven't been telling porky pies about who you are. And, while you're at it, why don't you bring along those photos Cherry did for your recording studio, Yam.

"Right then, you two love birds — don't worry about the bill, I'll take care of it. And Barbara, make sure that you stay beautiful for the photo session, we want to make sure you look absolutely gorgeous."

As they got up, Dave shook Yam's hand and puckered his lips to give Babsy a sloppy kiss on the cheek, depositing a liberal amount of cold, saliva as he did so. Once they were out of the restaurant, Babsy gave her face a hearty rub with the sleeve of her jumper. She liked Dave, but she hated the feel of his wet saliva drying on her skin.

Still feeling angry, she turned to Yam. "Why did you have to embarrass me like that in there?"

Yam was surprised at her sudden attack. "What d'ya mean?"

"You were so rude to Dave. You nearly blew that article!"

"Don't be stupid Babsy, that guy was a snake."

Her voice dripped with sarcasm, "Oh that's rich, *you* calling me stupid."

"Well you must be stupid if you can't see what he was doing in there. He's gonna make up pure lies for that article."

Babsy kissed her teeth, "How can he? You heard the man, if they print any untruths, they get sued."

"Yeah, dat's if the victim's got the money to do that. He's nothing more than a bullshitter! And what was all that about a photo session…? I'm not letting him put my boat-race to his sleazy story."

Babsy put her nose in the air and flicked her coppery corkscrew curls over her shoulder, "Oh don't worry about that Yam, I'm sure he was only saying it to be nice. *I* was the one he got all excited about and called 'beautiful'. Didn't he say he was gonna take a 'me-and-my-best-friend' angle on this one? I wouldn't be surprised if he didn't even mention you, never mind use your photo."

"Good. I hope they keep me well and truly out of it."

Babsy was fuming, why did Yam always have to be so difficult? Trying to explain even the simplest things to him was like discussing philosophy with a retard. He was probably still secretly moping around over Cherry. Which only went to prove just how stupid he actually was. The whole world knew that she was riding Freddie Famous; he'd read it in black in white in all the newspapers for Christ's sake. Yet he was still running around holding his little torch for her, convinced that when she came back, she'd have this miraculous 'explanation' that was going to make him understand why she'd just run off and left him! Ha! What a wally. Well, he'd better not mess up *The News* article because she had eighty grand riding on it, not to mention international stardom.

Yam was probably just jealous because Dave Armstrong had said she had what it takes to get to the top, and had practically ignored him the whole time they were doing the interview. She had a good mind to keep all the money herself — why should Yam earn out of her story? He could go and ask his precious Cherry for some cash; she'd soon knock him back.

Yam noted for what seemed like the billionth time, that he and Babsy were always bickering like this. It was as if they couldn't agree on anything. He hadn't noticed until recently just how bossy she could be. Once again, his thoughts turned to Cherry, and he thought of how happy they were, and how much fun they'd had together. He prayed that she would come back to London soon, so that they could sort out their relationship once and for all. Even though she'd run off with Freddie Famous, he refused to believe that they'd really split up. Not until he heard it from Cherry herself. And as for the thing that he had with Babsy... well, they didn't really get along did they? It was hard to believe she even liked him sometimes, the way she treated him. Yam felt that the only reason he was with her was because he wanted to be with someone who'd been close to Cherry. Until she got back.

Suddenly he had a horrifying thought. Maybe, with all the stuff that Babsy had blabbed to this *The News* sleazeball, Cherry wouldn't even want to speak to him when she came back, never mind entertain the idea of resuming their relationship. Yam felt a cold chill melt over his consciousness as the magnitude of what they were about to do sank in.

Panic stricken, he turned to Babsy. "Listen, I think we should knock the whole thing on the head. I mean, Cherry was your *friend*. Have you any idea the damage that this article could cause to that friendship?"

Babsy stared goggle-eyed at Yam like he was a crazy man. Had he really just said that he didn't want to go through with the article? Was he *really* suggesting that she should kiss goodbye to eighty grand? "That's right, Yam, she *was* my friend. And if you think for one second that I'm gonna give up an opportunity like this for a two-faced cow like Cherry, you can think again! Don't fuck with me, Yam. If you even *think* about jeopardising this article, I'll make sure you regret it for the rest of your life!"

Yam stared at her as if he was seeing her for the first time. And he didn't like what he saw. What a bitch! More than ever he felt like he had to find a way to stop Dave from trashing Cherry in *The News*. Before it was all too late. Before he lost Cherry — the *only* love of his life — forever.

The Aftermath

CHERRY COULD NOT BELIEVE what she was hearing; this had to be a very, very bad dream.

Unfortunately, the feel of Freddie's hand clutching at her throat, and the pain that ached through her body from being stretched out on the bed for so long was very real. Not only did she feel sure that he was going to carry out his threat and make her drink his... his *urine*... she knew that while she was trapped in the handcuffs there wasn't a damn thing she could do about it.

It was official: Freddie was a truly sick muthafucka. This latest idea of his made his former behaviour seem positively angelic in comparison. She always knew he was a perverted bastard, but she hadn't realised that he was the devil incarnate. And, worst of all, she felt like this latest turn of events was only the beginning.

Cherry suddenly felt an overwhelming urge to cry, to... *beg* him to just let her go. But she knew that he would only get even more excited, so she bit back her tears and played along, saying, "Oh... I will baby — every last drop."

Freddie looked a little disappointed that she was going along with him so easily. He'd expected a fight. "That's very good. I like it when you talk to me with respect!" His tone became hopeful, "I was thinkin' that I was gonna have to beat some respect into ya..."

Cherry summoned up all her strength and opened up her huge amber eyes. "Oh no, baby, you know that I'll always do anything you say... Do you want me to help you?"

Freddie smiled like a cat that had just got the cream — now he was *sure* he was in control. He nodded eagerly, "Yeah."

"Well you're gonna have to uncuff my hands, so that I can do it properly."

Freddie hesitated — was she trying to trick him? "You're

not thinkin' about playing games with me now?"

Cherry fluttered her eyelashes until she looked like what she hoped was the picture of innocence and answered, "How could I do that baby? There's not much that a little girl like me could do to someone as big and strong as you. You've shown me that *you THE MAN*, an' I'd be a fool to think any different. I'm never gonna mess with you again, Freddie. Not now you've taught me that I have to treat you with respect."

She narrowed her eyes in an effort to stop the memories of every other time she'd been humiliated come flooding back. Once again, scenes from the prison fought their way into her mind. Scenes from Holloway, when... when...

It was unbearable. She longed to tell this wanker where to go. And she longed to tell her cursed memories where they could go too. If she'd had access to a gun she would have fired a bullet straight through his eyeballs there and then. For him and every other fucka who had ever tried to mess with her... But that was just wishful thinking. The reality was that she had to get out of the predicament that she was in. And her only chance was that Freddie was high enough, and stupid enough to fall for her lines, so she pleaded her case even further.

"Come and unhook me, baby. I've been so horny lying here all this time... just waiting for you. Don't you want me to satisfy you?"

Freddie hovered, still uncertain.

Cherry laid it on thick. She *had* to get herself out of there before Freddie got completely crazy. Her plan wasn't very ingenious, but then neither was Freddie, so she could only pray that he would fall for it.

She writhed about in her chains and moaned, "Oh *please*, baby!"

Freddie needed no more persuading. Now that she was begging — just like a bitch should — he was convinced. He slurred, "Yeah, yeah." His eyes began to glaze over, and his head started to throb. He could have sworn he could even hear the sound of his own blood coursing through his veins.

Staggering over to the golden suitcase, he picked up the key, and just about made it back over to the bed to get his prize. Swaying uncontrollably, he leant over to release Cherry's right arm. As he reached across her naked body to uncuff her other one, Cherry slowly stretched out her newly freed hand until it rested on the bronze, art deco telephone that she had clocked earlier. For a moment she had second thoughts. What if her plan backfired? If Freddie realised that she had been fucking with him, there was no telling just how angry he would get... And he was in a bad mood already. What if...?

But it was only a momentary hesitation, Cherry knew it was her only chance; if she wanted to have a hope of it working she had to act fast. She lifted the phone, and in one smooth movement, crashed it down with all her strength onto Freddie's skull.

He responded with a loud grunt. She felt his body slump and go limp and heavy on top of her... Could he have finally passed out?

She silently prayed for deliverance.

After what seemed like a lifetime, but was actually only a matter of seconds, she dared to speak.

"Freddie."

No reply.

"Freddie." ·

Nothing. Slowly she slid her hand from underneath Freddie's bulk. Carefully, she pulled the key out of his grasp. Once her left arm was free, Cherry shook out her wrists in an effort to get the blood flowing through them again. They felt numb with all the hours of being fettered above her head.

Now there was the question of what she should do with Freddie. She was almost too scared to move him in case he came round... That was if he ever came round again. His form was so lifeless, she couldn't help but wonder if she had actually killed him... *Was Freddie dead*? Part of her hoped he was dead... but the last thing that she needed right now was to get mixed up in a murder case. Furtively, she checked his pulse... it was still there. With all the drugs and drink that he'd downed, he probably hadn't even felt the blow, which she thought was a pity. She wanted the muthafucka to have felt the pain.

Satisfied that Freddie was alive, but completely knocked out, she pushed his limp, lifeless form off her and got to work on the ankle cuffs.

Cherry's heart kept pummelling against her ribcage. What now? He could come round at any minute. *What if Freddie came round before she got out of there?* She needed to get back to England, fast. But she had no cash, no credit cards, no nothing. Her brow furrowed in concentration, as her brain tried to come up with some sort of solution.

Nikki Stixx! Nikki Stixx had called earlier and had sounded like she was *dying* to get Cherry back to London.

Hastily, Cherry searched for the number that she had scribbled down the day before and then dialled the digits.

"Good morning, B.U.L. Records."

"Can you put me through to Nikki Stixx?"

"Who's calling please?"

"Tell her it's Cherry Drop, and that it's an *emergency*."

The cockney receptionist remembered Cherry from the time she had met Freddie Famous in the B.U.L. Reception area. She adopted a cheerful, friendly tone. "Oh *hi* babes, how are you?"

Cherry, didn't really have time for pleasantries. Her voice was brusque, "I'm fine, is Nikki there?"

But the receptionist was having none of it, like the rest of the world, she had read all about the romance between Cherry and Freddie Famous, and she was dying to know more. Of course, it would have been her jetting off with Freddie, if Cherry hadn't thrown herself at him like that, but that was what these singers were like: a bunch of tarts... Anyway, that was all water under the bridge now, and she was very excited to have Cherry sitting on the other end of the telephone line, calling all the way from her love nest with Freddie in Miami. What would all her mates say if she got some inside information on them straight from the horse's mouth.

She adopted an ingratiating tone of voice, "Oh yeah, Nikki got in bright and early this morning, she's been absolutely up to her eyes in it recently. Anyway, forget about us in boring old England — how are you doing in Miami?"

Cherry couldn't believe that the receptionist was trying to get all friendly with her now, just when she was trying to escape the clutches of a violent lunatic. *What if Freddie came round?* She willed herself to remain calm, "Look, I don't really have time to chat at the moment, I'm in the middle of an *emergency* here."

The receptionist was offended — just because Cherry was shacked up with Freddie Famous, didn't mean that she could put on airs and graces and think that she was better than everyone else. "Oh, I see. Well don't mind me, I was only trying to be *nice*. If you'll just hold, I'll find out whether or not Ms. Stixx is available to take your call."

Great. Now the fucking receptionist was probably going to keep her on hold for half an hour. Cherry sighed, with some people, you just couldn't win for losing. She squeezed her eyelids together in an effort to hold back the panic. *What if…?*

However, she wasn't kept waiting for long, in a matter of seconds, Nikki Stixx's voice sounded on the other end of the line.

"Cherry! Good to hear from you!" Nikki was genuinely pleased. She took it as an extremely good sign that Cherry had returned her call so quickly.

"Hi Nikki, listen I don't have much time to talk, but I need to ask you a favour. It's urgent."

Nikki was intrigued. "Fire away."

"I need to get a plane ticket from here to return to London, and I need to leave today."

"Why? What's happened? Have you and Freddie fallen

out?"

Cherry felt herself growing more and more anxious. She didn't have time for questions. *What if Freddie came round?* "I can't discuss that at the moment. All I've got to say is that, if you're still interested, I'm ready to sign the deal with you when I get back to London."

These were the words that Nikki had been waiting for. "Of *course* I'm still interested! I'll organise that plane ticket right now. Can you call me back in five minutes to get the details?"

"I'm on my way to the airport now, so I'll call you when I get there."

Cherry jumped off the bed, she searched around for her bag. She *had* to get out of there, and fast — before this moron woke up, or one of his cronies tried to stop her. She found her old rucksack — the only case in the room that was actually hers, and threw in her passport and the DAT tape of her finished songs. Then she quickly pulled on some clothes walked away from the Taravala Hotel and Freddie Famous and his entourage and all the clothes and all the jewellery he had bought her forever.

Once outside, she found the limo that was permanently on stand-by, in case Freddie needed to go anywhere. She tried to keep the panic out of her voice as she called to the driver. "Hey Frank, I need to go to the airport."

The Italian-American chauffeur was hesitant, "The airport? Freddie didn't tell me that you were going anywhere."

Cherry couldn't believe it, what was she — a prisoner, who was only allowed to do things if Freddie said it was okay? What if Frank wouldn't drive her without speaking to his boss first? What if he went to look for Freddie in the hotel suite and discovered what had happened? *What if she couldn't get out of there?*

She fought back her rising hysteria, and adopted a casual, friendly tone in an effort to reassure him. "Of course I'm not going anywhere, could you imagine me travelling with only this itty-bitty bag?" Cherry forced a laugh and held up her battered rucksack as evidence. "I'm going to pick my girlfriend up, she's comin' over from London."

"Oh really? Is she as pretty as you?"

Cherry smiled to herself. Sometimes it seemed that was the only thing men were interested in — how attractive you were. "Oh yeah, Frank, she's much, *much* prettier than I am. She makes me look like a dog!"

"Oh yeah? Well what are we waiting for?"

And with that he put his foot on the gas and headed off to the airport, double speed.

Mr. E was in the shower when he had got the call. Of course, he always answered his phone, whether he was in the shower, asleep, having a shit — anything. You never knew who could be on the end of the line, and he wasn't about to miss out on a business deal because he hadn't picked up his own damn phone.

But for the past week or so, every time it had rung, his heart had flown to his mouth in case one of Big Red's cronies was on the other end of the line. He had considered turning it off, but he knew that that would do him no favours — it would only make Big Red suspicious. And the next thing you knew, all of the equipment would go missing out of his studio, and Big Red would be on his way to find him. And there wasn't anybody Big Red couldn't find if he wanted to. He'd swear the muthafucka even had spies in Sainsbury's.

He had decided to keep running his shit as normal, hoping he could come up with the readies before Big Red called him in. Now, every time the phone rang, he was scared shitless that that day had come.

And he was in the shower when his fears finally became reality.

It was Mr. Ice again. "Red wants to see you tomorrow, four o'clock at the club. Don't come empty-handed."

"Oh Ice — good to hear from ya, man! Er, I'm not sure I can make tomorrow, Warners have arranged a... a... Ice?"

It was no good, Mr. E was talking to a dead dial-tone. He knew it was a futile excuse anyway. When Big Red summoned you to the club, you went to the club. Especially when you owed his ass some money. Mr. E's naked body began to look like it was crying black tears as the water from the shower mixed with the streams of salty sweat that began to ooze from his every pore. He slid down against the wall, and slumped to a heap on the floor.

What the fuck was he going to do?

Cherry woke up to see a clear blue sky. It was a beautiful, hot and sunny day in London. She had been back in her flat for almost twenty-four hours now, and had pretty much been sleeping the whole time. Although she felt refreshed and invigorated, she was still tired. Tired of the whole *pantomime* of it all. She couldn't wait until it was over. Until she could finish what she'd come here for. She *had* to complete her plan. Fast.

After having a quick wash, she made herself some coffee and sat down on the sofa in her living room, which faced the panoramic view she had of London. Slowly sipping her drink, she thought long and hard about her future.

Her mind raced through the endless possibilities in her quest for a record deal. She was certain that her best move would be to sign to B.U.L. Records direct. But would Nikki still want to sign her if she didn't bring her songs with Mr. E or Freddie Famous to the table? Cherry most certainly hoped so. Because if Nikki didn't want to sign her, she was right back to where she started — no demos, no money and just a whole lot of bad experiences behind her.

Desperate but hopeful, she dialled B.U.L. Records.

Freddie Famous felt like shit. As he slowly peeled open

his encrusted eyelids he realised that he was lying almost butt naked, face-down on the bed in his suite at the Taravala Hotel in Miami. His face had been resting in a small, soggy pool of blood, as his nose had been bleeding slightly throughout the night, like it sometimes did when he got really fucked-up. But the one thing that overshadowed everything else was the fact that his head hurt like hell. Waves of pain hammered at the inside of his skull and he was in agony. Still half-asleep, he raised his hand to his head, to feel a bump the size of the Trump Tower. What had happened to him?

His voice was weak and hoarse as he called, "Cherry!"

Freddie winced, as the noise of his own voice reverberated around his head, causing it to hurt even more. Where was that bitch?

He braved the pain, and called again, *"Cherry!"*

No answer.

With great difficulty, Freddie pulled himself into a sitting position. He yawned, and wiped away the beads of sweat that had accumulated on his brow during the night. Where was Cherry? He needed her to get some aspirin for his head. Wasn't that just like a woman? Never there when ya need 'em.

As he stretched out again, Freddie noticed one of his golden handcuffs, dangling from a bedpost. Quickly he turned to see that the other three posts also had a cuff locked to them. They acted like golden triggers. As fragments of what had happened last night came trickling back to him, Freddie struggled to recall how it had all ended. The last thing he remembered was bending over Cherry... and then his mind was a blank.

But it didn't take him long, even in his state, to put two and two together.

Freddie found his conclusion hard to believe — *surely she hadn't knocked him out*? She couldn't have. He knew that he'd been giving her a hard time last night, but it was only because he was a little high. *Surely* she hadn't been able to turn everything around again, and had ended up kicking his ass so hard that it had rendered him unconscious...? But the pain throbbing in his head was proof to the contrary. It was quite obvious that Cherry had brutalised him with some sort of heavy object.

As Freddie digested his train of thought, he looked around the room... So where was she now?

He picked up the phone and dialled Latonya's room, and croaked, "Latonya? It's me. Listen, I can't find Cherry. Has she been with you today."

Latonya sounded pissed off, "No, I was gonna ask you the same question. Me an' Cherry were supposed to meet for lunch at the Water Salon. I waited for three hours this afternoon and she didn't show up, not even a phone call!"

"Oh... 'Cause we... er, we had a kinda argument last night, and she seems to have disappeared." Freddie winced, the pain in his head was getting worse. "Get over here and bring me some aspirin. I got a hangover."

When Freddie and Latonya discovered Cherry's missing passport, they both thought the worse.

Freddie shook his aching head, "I can't believe she'd run out on me like that."

Latonya looked around at the state of the room, taking in the golden suitcase, the whip, and the handcuffs. She could definitely believe that Cherry had run out on him like that. Lord knows what he was doing to her last night. The room looked like a fuckin' torture chamber. Trust Freddie to go and get himself all messed up and frighten the bitch off. Just when she was hooking up a deal with B.U.L. in New York.

She put a comforting arm around her boss. "Look, don't worry. My guess is that Cherry's gone back to London. What you should do is give her a few days to calm down, and then we can both talk to her and smooth things over. I'm sure that, with a little careful handling, we can work this out."

Freddie felt better with Latonya by his side. But the truth was, he'd really begun to feel he was in love with Cherry. She was the only woman he'd ever met who'd truly understood him and his 'special needs'. Everyone tended to think that the life of a megastar was all fun and games, bright lights and big cities. But the reality was that life on the road could be very lonely — completely cut off from your family and all of your real friends. Just surrounded by the bullshit, twenty-four-seven. Now that she had gone, Freddie was starting to realise how great it had been to have Cherry around, always there whenever he needed her. And she hadn't been one of those hanger-on bimbos just looking for a free ride. No. Cherry was in the business and she had understood all the pressure he was under. The truth of it was that Freddie was getting tired of sleeping with a different girl every night of the week; he wanted some kind of emotional connection, to form a genuine bond with someone. Kinda like the thing that he had goin' on with Cherry. He felt himself starting to feel desperate. He didn't want his life to go back to the way it was before she was around.

There was nothing else for it — he had to get Cherry back.

His face wore a steely expression of determination when he turned back to Latonya and said, "Okay, if you think it's better to wait until Cherry calms down, I'll wait. But I gotta tell ya, this nigga ain't mo be happy until she's back by his side. I don't care what you have to do… just make sure that you do *whatever it takes* to get Cherry back over here!"

The Record Deal

NIKKI STIXX FELT LIKE SHE WAS FINALLY BACK where she belonged — in the driving seat. And she wasn't yanking the gears on no crappy burgundy Saab either. Oh no, she was on automatic cruise control all the way to a brand new convertible Audi and her own record label.

Last week she'd seen the whole deal slipping away from her, but now it was a completely different story. She hadn't been sure when Cherry had asked her to pay for that ticket out of Miami, but now all her fears were laid to rest. Cherry was dying to sign the deal. In fact, she had almost sounded desperate. Nikki was certain that she had Cherry exactly where she wanted her — right in the palm of her hand. And in just under half an hour, the meeting to sign the contract was scheduled to begin.

And she was totally prepared.

She dialled reception, "Hi, it's Nikki. When Cherry Drop arrives, show her straight into my room. I don't want to be disturbed for the rest of the day. No visits, no calls, nothing. Nobody can be allowed to interrupt this meeting — and when I say nobody, I mean *nobody*. Even if the head of B.U.L. himself calls and says it's urgent, I don't want you to put him through. Say I'm not in the building or something."

The receptionist chewed on the fresh piece of gum she had just put into her mouth and squeaked, "Yeah, no problem Nikki, no-one but Cherry is allowed to see or speak to you for the rest of the day."

Nikki felt slightly annoyed, why was it that whenever people came to work for a record company, they would get all slapdash? Once she had her own label, there would be no way that the receptionist would be allowed to chew gum whilst talking on the phone.

Cherry arrived at B.U.L feeling a little nervous and

apprehensive. She entered the reception and replayed the moment she first met Freddie Famous in her mind's eye, smiling to herself as she remembered how desperate Mr. E had been to see what was on the note he'd handed her. So much had happened since then. And she would stake her life on the fact that, if Mr. E had any idea of what was about to happen next, he would be ready to kill somebody. Cherry had to stop herself from laughing out loud. That was the funniest shit that she had thought about in a long time. Who'd have thought that in the space of a few weeks, she'd be sitting here again, without Freddie or Mr. E, ready to sign the deal with Nikki direct?

Or so she hoped.

Cherry mentally checked herself. She had to stay positive. She wanted this deal more than she'd ever wanted anything in her life. And if she messed up, her entire plan would be fucked.

Nikki was all smiles as she rose to greet her, brushing her lips against both of Cherry's cheeks. "Babes! It's great to see you again!" She stepped back to get a full view. "I see Miami has treated you well, girl, that's a wicked tan you've got!"

"Thanks. You look very well yourself." Cherry was glad that Nikki looked so pleased to see her, but she wondered if her smile would be quite so wide once she knew that Mr. E and Freddie Famous were no longer in the frame.

They sat facing each other. Nikki leant back in her chair and casually swivelled from side to side behind her desk, as she asked in a cheerful tone, "So, what's happening? Why the sudden rush to get back to London?"

Cherry began to weave her story, "Well, I'd finished my demos with Freddie and couldn't see much point in staying on in Miami..."

Nikki wasn't going to be fobbed off so easily. She knew Cherry had been frantic to get out of Miami, "Oh, but the way you called me the other day made it seem so urgent. I have to tell you, Cherry, I've been very worried about you... I thought you were in some sort of trouble out there!"

Cherry laughed, "Really? I don't know why you got that impression. Of *course* I wasn't in trouble! No, the truth of it is…" She leant forward to indicate to Nikki that she was about to impart some confidential information. Ms. Stixx, eager to get the inside story, echoed her movements. Cherry adopted a dramatic expression as she dropped her bombshell. "The truth of it is… Freddie and I have split up! It was all getting too serious too soon. I felt that I couldn't really commit, because I want to devote my time and energy to my career, rather than to a relationship. As you probably know, it's hard to make a relationship work when both of the people involved have demanding careers. I wasn't prepared to sacrifice my dreams, and there was *no chance* of Freddie giving up what he does for me. So, once I'd decided it wasn't working out between us, I wanted to get out of Miami as quickly as possible without him knowing, so as to avoid any arguments. Which was why I asked you to send me a ticket. I know that it might have come as a surprise, but it was a very last minute decision."

Nikki was finding the whole story hard to believe. "You and Freddie are *over*? But you've only just met… Are you sure that you've thought it through properly, Cherry? I mean, what about the songs you were recording with him?"

Cherry gave Nikki her most confident smile, "Fuck Freddie's songs. I'm a talented artist in my own right. I don't need them — especially now that I've become a household name myself. I'm not working with Black Knight Productions either. I don't want a character like Mr. E to be involved with my album. That's why I scheduled this meeting to happen between just you and I."

She took a deep breath and silently prayed that Nikki would go for her offer. "I want to sign the deal directly with you and B.U.L. With nobody else involved."

Cherry tried to look relaxed and confident, but inside her nerves had started to jump and spin. Nikki had looked seriously pissed off when she'd told her that she wouldn't be using Freddie's songs. She'd got up and walked to the window, where she stood with her back to Cherry, looking out at the grimy Soho streets. She had anticipated an awkward reception to this new turn of events, but she hadn't expected Nikki to become so upset.

Nikki turned round to face her, with a grave expression on her face. "You know, Cherry, every year B.U.L. gives me a budget to develop new talent. Within that budget, I set aside a substantial sum with which to sign a priority artist. That is, someone who I believe has got what it takes to be a major superstar, to become a creative *tour de force* within the recording industry. That particular artist has to have *everything* — talent, charisma, the right kind of material and stunning good looks. Someone who could be up there and compete with Whitney or Michael. Someone with the potential to sell millions and millions of albums..."

"Right," Cherry wondered what Nikki was getting at. She felt apprehensive as she watched her walk over to the state of-the-art hi-fi system, and click in a DAT tape, saying, "Now, I want you to listen to this..."

She turned her back and looked out of the window again, Cherry listened to the tape. An incredible voice — a latter-day Patti Labelle — soared out of the speakers. The song was good too — a Whitney Houston-type ballad, like 'The Greatest Love Of All' or 'I Will Always Love You'.

When it had finished, Nikki clicked off the hi-fi, sat down in her chair, and explained, "That was a new artist. Came in last week looking for a deal. What do you think?"

Cherry thought that the demo was incredible, but there was no way she was going to admit that to Nikki, so she shrugged her shoulders and said, "It wasn't bad. I know loads of backing singers who can sing like that. However, like you said earlier Nikki, in this business you've got to have the whole package."

Nikki reached into her drawer and brought out a large envelope and pulled out a huge colour photograph, and handed it to Cherry, "Her name is Diamond Charmer. She's just turned eighteen years old. The song you've just heard was one of the hundreds she's already written, and the rest are just as good if not better."

Cherry looked at the photograph. A huge close-up of a beautiful white girl with long blonde hair smiled back at her. Her perfect ivory teeth caught a gleam of light from the camera flash, and her bright blue eyes shone out of the picture. She looked like a fucking Colgate ad.

Cherry could hardly believe it, saying, "But... she sounded like a black singer on the demo."

Nikki grinned, "Yeah, I know, isn't it incredible? We're *very* excited about this one!"

Cherry's hammering heart sunk to her boots. She could see everything slipping away from her. In the space of the last five minutes, all her hopes and dreams had been dashed to the ground. *Her plan was being destroyed.* This girl was a record company's wet dream — a beautiful white girl who could sing like a black woman.

Nikki's voice sliced through her nightmare. "So you see Cherry, things aren't exactly as simple as before." She held her hands up in the air and looked genuinely distressed, "I'm in a dilemma! I've now got two amazingly talented and beautiful young women who are looking to sign with me, but I only have the funds to give one of them a deal."

She moved around her desk and perched on the side that was closest to Cherry. "But I have to say — talent and looks aren't the only important things here."

"No?" Cherry looked up at her.

Nikki shook her head. "No. Making an album — turning raw talent into a superstar with a long career of record sales in front of her — is an enormous commitment. It's vital that I have a very good relationship with the artist. Making records is incredibly hard work and emotions tend to run high. It helps a lot if the artist can have, shall we say, a 'friend', within the record company. A link between them and the suits that write the cheques. Someone who understands music and will be in their corner... someone with whom they can form a strong and unbreakable bond."

She reached over and took Diamond's photograph from Cherry's lap, casually brushing her thighs as she did so, "The very first day you walked into this office, I knew you were special. You've really got what it takes, Cherry, and I want to be the one who makes all your dreams come true."

She took Cherry's hand in hers and looked deep into her eyes. "I think that you and I could become... *close*."

Cherry looked back into Nikki's eyes, which were sparkling like black diamonds in oval-shaped pearls, and tried to believe what she was hearing. She might have guessed she would turn out to be a fucking dyke. The entertainment industry was crawling with them. She needed this deal to happen more than she needed life itself, and Nikki Stixx had made it quite clear that if she wanted the deal, then she was going to have to get her rocks off. Whaddaya know — the bitch was hard-balling her!

Slowly, she took in Nikki's full, Maybelline mouth, and the outline of her small pert breasts against her white shirt and thought... why not? Shit, she even *felt* like some pussy — at the very worse it had to be an improvement on what she'd had with Freddie Famous...

Latonya sat in her room, silently cursing into her mobile phone. The fucking receptionist had put her on hold again. After a careful bit of detective work, she'd discovered that the last call made by Cherry from Freddie's room had been made to B.U.L. Records in London. When she had investigated the matter further, she'd found out that Cherry had been about to sign a deal with a certain Ms. Nikki Stixx, who was head of A & R there, before she came to Miami. So, the first thing Latonya decided to do was to call Ms. Stixx and see what was up. She had to find out whether or not Cherry was trying to go ahead with the deal, if only because if she did, it would mess up her own deal that she was trying to hook up for Cherry in New York. But also because her job was on the line if she couldn't get Cherry back with

Freddie. Freddie had made that crystal clear earlier on.

She'd been calling London since five a.m., and the fucking receptionist kept telling her that Ms. Stixx was in a meeting. Now she had been put on hold, and had been waiting for almost twenty minutes.

"I'm sorry, Nikki is still in that meeting…"

Latonya had had enough. "Look, do you know who I am? I'm *Latonya Johnson*, personal secretary to *Freddie Famous* — who only happens to be the *biggest fuckin' act on B.U.L.* right now! And I'm making this call, which as I have already told you is very urgent, *on his behalf!*"

The receptionist was enjoying herself. It wasn't very often she could tell someone as important as Freddie Famous' PA where to go. There was no way Nikki could complain about this, she had distinctly told her not to let any calls through while she was in her meeting with Cherry.

She shot back at Latonya. "I don't care if you're God's personal assistant, I'm *not* putting your call through."

Latonya was getting really pissed off, didn't these English bitches know that they couldn't fuck with a New Yorker like this? "Listen, sweetie, what's your name? I'm not gonna be treated like this by a fucking receptionist!"

But the receptionist wasn't falling for that old chestnut, "I'm sorry? I didn't quite catch that — your line's breaking up. Oh, I've got another call coming through, I'll have to put you on hold again." She adopted a high-pitched cheerful tone of voice and ended the conversation, "Thank you!"

Latonya listened to the line go dead and seethed. She played a thousand scenarios in her mind of the receptionist meeting a slow and painful death. But it was no good, getting mad wasn't going to get Cherry back. She'd call Nikki later, then she'd deal with that bitch of a receptionist.

Later that day, Nikki Stixx sat in her office, looking like the cat who had just got the cream. It had been a very successful meeting. She had taken a chance, playing her old — 'I've got a white girl I might sign' — trick on an artist as important to her as Cherry was. But she just hadn't been able to resist it. Cherry had been so desperate for the deal to happen there and then, she'd had her dancing like a puppet on a string...

She had wanted her ever since she had first laid eyes on her. Of course it had been a risk — she could have blown the whole deal — but having so much at stake only added to the fun of it. And it had been a gamble that had paid off royally. Nikki reached in her drawer and pulled out the photograph of 'Diamond Charmer" who was really a model 'friend' of hers who went by the name of Sally. The photo was quite something. It had been taken for a toothpaste campaign. And the tape that she'd played to Cherry had just been a demo of a song that had been sung by a session singer.

Nikki had done the same thing many times before. You'd get an artist to the point where they were just about to sign the deal, usually after months and months of negotiations. Then, in the final hour, you'd hard-ball 'em with the old "Diamond Charmer" routine. It worked every time. The poor artist was usually at the point where all they wanted to do was sign the deal so that they could go ahead and record their albums and get on with their careers. Rather than swinging back and forth between lawyers for the rest of their lives. With 'Diamond Charmer' threatening to put them back to square one, they were usually more than willing to make a few concessions on their recording contracts. Of course, as a rule, she only did it to minor signings, so as to keep everything well within her budget, so to speak. But there was something about Cherry that she just hadn't been able to resist. And with Mr. E and Freddie out of the picture, she'd been the perfect target for Nikki's hard-ball tactics.

Still smiling, she locked her little secret back in her desk, and prepared to go home.

The Meeting

IT WAS THREE-THIRTY A.M., and Mr. E was leaning against the wall of the Harlequin Club in Notting Hill Gate, pulling on a cigarette like his life depended on it. He'd given up smoking years ago, but tonight he needed something to calm his nerves... Anything to help him him cope with the next couple of hours. Mr. E almost felt the noose flap against his neck as he thought to himself that they could well be the last couple of hours of his life.

A little voice told him that he should just get the hell out. Leave all this shit behind and start afresh. Somewhere where there was no Black Knight Productions, no out-of-town muthafuckas like Delroy Carrington, no Nikki Stixx and B.U.L. Records, and no double-dealing whores like Cherry Drop. Or whoever the fuck that bitch was. *And no Big Red.* But he knew that it was no damn good. Wherever he went Big Red would track him down eventually. And then he would kill him — no questions asked. No time for an explanation. Not even time for a last cigarette.

He could hear the hyperactive sounds of the latest jungle track being pumped from the club. The ground was trembling with every rumble of the bass. Mr. E wondered what type of sound system Big Red must have that was so powerful he could feel it on the street. He must have racked the walls of the whole fuckin' club to get that kind of volume. Still he could afford it. Big Red could afford to do anything he wanted. Unlike himself.

He looked at his watch. Ten to four. *Shit!* That must have been the quickest twenty minutes he'd spent in his whole goddamn life. Well there was nothing for it, he had to go and meet his fate. There was no point in pissing off Big Red by being late as well as not coming up with his money.

Grinding his cigarette into the pavement, he made his way over to the club... *and further into the noose.*

As he entered, a wall of sound hit him through the hot

smoky air. Big Red sure was pumpin' it tonight. Maybe he didn't want anyone to hear the screams of his debtors... Mr. E shuddered, and dragged his feet through the clusters of scantily dressed revellers and over to the bar, which was lit by a glow of orange and red lights. As red was Big Red's favourite colour, all the decor and furnishings were in various shades of red as well. Mr. E thought — as he did every time he stepped into the Harlequin — that this must be what hell looked like. It was as if the club had been decorated by the devil himself. Some would say that it had...

"What's up, E?" Alfred, the resident barman, had stepped up to where he was leaning on the counter.

"I'm here to see Red."

"Cool, he's been expecting you. Wanna drink before you go in?"

"No thanks mate." *'He's been expecting you'*. Mr. E felt the noose itch against his throat.

Within a matter of minutes a tall, white guy with a shaved head and a carefully trimmed black beard emerged from the door behind the bar. The large silver hoop earing dangling from his ear, together with a black and white bandanna around his skull, and a charcoal tailored suit and tie, made him look like some bizarre cross between an investment banker and an eighteenth century pirate. Mr. E, as always, thought that he looked ridiculous — the schmuck always dressed like he was auditioning for a fuckin' Michael Jackson video or something.

It was Mr. Ice.

Mr. Ice nodded a greeting and flipped up the part of the bar counter that would allow Mr. E through to the back, saying, "The boss is ready for you now."

Mr. E hesitated for a split second. Once he was in there, there was no turning back. He suddenly had an overwhelming urge to turn on his heels and run. Get the fuck out of the Harlequin and London and England — forever. He wanted to jump off the world. Anything to avoid the fate that awaited him at the hands of Big Red.

He turned to Mr. Ice, smiled and said, "Cool." and followed him through the door behind the bar.

When they'd wound through the maze of blood-red corridors that led to the office, Mr. Ice ushered Mr. E in ahead of him. As he stooped to go into the door — one short muthafucka must have built the building that housed the Harlequin — he was hit with the stench of petroleum.

Two guys were sitting at a small makeshift table in the centre of the room, about to play a game of cards. A bottle of brandy and four glasses were on the table. Three of the glasses were full. One was empty.

To their right, an oriental man was hunched up in the corner, his knees pressed flat to his chest, his chin was jutting over them. The position sure looked uncomfortable. But there was nothing he could do about it, as a thick, nylon rope had been knotted and tied tightly around his body, leaving him no room to move. A balled-up cotton rag had been stuffed into his mouth and it was dripping with petrol that was also dripping from his clothes and hair.

Out of everybody in the room, Big Red was by far the most imposing figure. He was large — almost six foot five inches tall — and of mixed race. Mr. E presumed that his black parent must have been Jamaican because, as with a lot of Jamaican Londoners, he would occasionally break into patois. Usually this only happened when he was cracking a joke, or when he was pissed off. He had pale yellow, almost white skin and strong features, which comprised of a broad flat nose and full thick crimson lips. Now that it was summer he had a liberal dose of browny-red freckles sprinkled over his face. His hair lived up to his name. It was a thick wiry bush of bright red curls, which mushroomed into a carefully fluffed afro-puff. The tiny room was roasting hot and condensation was crying tears of blood down its red walls. Big Red was suitably dressed for the overwhelming heat in a white wide-mesh vest and white Nike tracksuit bottoms. Around his neck dangled several thick heavy chains of gold, which matched the chains that twisted around both of his wrists and the huge gold rings that bulged from his fingers. His tall, lean physique was rippling with a full set of well-defined muscles and, as he dealt the cards, they bulged and popped, flexing and unflexing beneath his vest and along his arms; and his bracelets and necklaces clunked and jangled against each other. He rolled the big fat blunt around his mouth, and thick plumes of black smoke curled up from his lips, as he puffed and chewed.

Sitting next to him was his right-hand man — Stevie-Jack-Shit — a small thick-set, dark-skinned man, who was so black he was almost purple. He had the appearance, and sometimes the mannerisms, of an angry bulldog and everybody knew that he would give his life for Big Red — such was his devotion.

Mr. E waited at the doorway with Mr. Ice, until Big Red dealt his hand and found fit to acknowledge him. They always kept him hanging at the door. He guessed it was a power trip — Big Red wanted to make sure that nobody moved unless he said so. Until he gave the nod, everybody who entered the room had to wait until they were told to sit — just like Fido the fuckin' dog.

It was Stevie-Jack-Shit who broke the silence. "Mr. E! What's up!"

As always Mr. E, fought the urge to laugh. Not only did he have the most ridiculous name a brotha had ever heard, but little Stevie-Jack-Shit also spoke in a high and squeaky falsetto. He must have have been the only man on the planet over the age of thirty who's voice had yet to break.

Big Red chose that moment to lift his head, and he gestured toward the table. "Pull up a chair my bredrin, an' 'ave a brandy on me." His voice sounded like somebody walking across gravel.

In response to the invite, Mr. E found himself grinning like a fool and trotting up to Big Red's table like he was going to collect a prize on *Come On Down*. He completely ignored the oriental guy in the corner because, as far as he was concerned, none of that shit was even happening.

Big Red rolled his cigar over to the other corner of his mouth and simultaneously sucked and chewed it, whilst at the same time blowing large, trembling smoke rings. Mr. E couldn't help but stare. He was very impressed — Big Red had major lip control. That was the first time he'd seen anyone pull a stunt like that.

Big Red, unaware of his amazing talent, calmly went on to say, "So wha'ppen? Ice tells me that you've got all the major record companies knocking at your door."

Mr. E smiled coyly like Big Red had just paid him a huge compliment, and he was embarrassed, and overcome with modesty at his own brilliance. "Yeah. No big t'ing really — as you know we've been firin' out some shit-hot product for about a year now. So, of course all the suits at the record companies have been sniffin' millions, and they all wanna piece."

"Is dat so?"

"Yeah." Mr. E felt nervous as hell sitting up in the devil's parlour, with nothing to look at apart from some oriental schmuck all trussed up like a Christmas Turkey, dripping with petrol and a rag shoved into his mouth... He tried not to think that *it could be him next*. The longer he could stall talkin' about the money he owed the better. Music was his business so, since Big Red had asked, he launched into a huge monologue about how well the studio was doing and how famous and successful they all were. When he'd finished he was pleased to note that Big Red was with him all the way, nodding as he said, "Yeah, one of my yout's dem was playin' this phat remix that you guys did for that white guy Egg-Head the other day. I couldn't believe that it was you, man — yuh made that bitch sound like a nigga! It's about time one of my bredrin was kickin' up a lickle noise on de streets!"

Mr. E grinned so hard he could have sworn the corners of his mouth stretched past his ears. And Big Red and his boys were leering right back at him, displaying a startling array of dentistry. Never in his life had Mr. E seen such a selection of gold teeth and precious stone insets.

Then, right in the middle of his moment of glory, the oriental guy shifted and moaned. Ice, who was standing right next to him, dropped his smile and gave the oriental a good hard kick in the ribs, snarling, "Shut the fuck up!"

Big Red nodded to the oriental as if indicating a bag of groceries in the corner. He rolled his cigar around his mouth and did his trick with the smoke rings again, saying, "Some of that Triad fuckries, man. His boys 'ave been leanin' on some of my bredrin up in Soho, so we haffe make an example of 'im. Y'understand?"

Mr. E made an effort to look like he was sympathising with the weight of responsibility that Big Red had to deal with. He nodded sagely like he'd had to cope with the same kind of thing himself only last week. And all the while he could feel sweat begin to ooze slowly out of every pore, as the noose tightened and he thought, me next... me next...

Big Red continued, "Yeah, so we'd like you to join us for this game of blackjack." He grinned as he delivered his punchline. "Whoever loses gets to light the match!"

The oriental guy moaned again when he heard this and Big Red and his cronies started cackling. For some reason, Shakespeare sprang to Mr. E's mind, and he thought of when the three witches met in Macbeth, and huddled around their cauldron cackling, 'When shall we three meet again...' He sure as hell felt like Macbeth now, winging his way to a slow and inexorable destruction. The armpits of his shirt soaked through with fearful perspiration as he forced himself to laugh along.

The three witches nodded their heads up and down to their communal mirth, until...

Mr. Ice took his cue and sat down at the table. He picked up one of the cards that Big Red had dealt for him earlier. Big Red obviously played the game casino-style, as he had dealt two cards to each player, one of which lay face down on the table, and the other was face up for your opponents to see.

Mr. E's upturned card was the five of clubs. Gingerly, he lifted the top of the card that faced downwards — it was the seven of hearts. A total of twelve, which was nowhere near the twenty-one he needed to come out of the game unscathed. He was going to have to risk twisting for another card. It was not a good start.

Beads of sweat began to slowly collect like black pearls on his forehead, and the growing panic in his stomach tightened its grip on his intestines, as he started to wonder if the whole thing was a set-up. Big Red had been dealing the cards as he had entered the room. *Had he fixed it so that he, Mr. E, was going to lose?* Surely *he* wasn't going to have to light the match that was going to burn the oriental guy to a cinder?

Big Red turned to Mr. Ice. "Pour E a drink."

As Mr. Ice poured the brandy into the one empty glass on the table, Big Red picked up his pair of cards and kept talking,. "Anyway, as I was saying before I was so rudely interrupted..." He shot a piercing look at the moaning oriental, who now had vomit on his chin. No doubt the fumes from the petroleum had made him throw up. Mr. E was amazed that he hadn't choked. Instead the thick orange vomit had soaked through the rag in his mouth, and was foaming down his chin, and trickling lumpy gobules onto his knees. "My yout' was checkin' big time for that remix you did for Egg-Head. Y'member my oldest boy, Ashton?"

Mr. E nodded yes, although he couldn't really recall the boy. Big Red had so many baby mothers, he probably had a different child for every day of the year.

"Well he keeps bendin' my ear about you guys, saying how mad up your music is and everyt'ing." Big Red grinned at Mr. E and then, in the same tone you might use if you were about to give someone a million pounds, said, "I thought you might want him in the studio."

Mr. E tried to keep from choking on his drink. Why

would Big Red want his son to be up at Black Knight Productions? Was it his way of trying to muscle in on his business, now that everything looked like it was firing? He stretched his mouth into a benign smile, the kind of smile that says you're open to any suggestion. "Yeah?"

Big Red nodded, and poised with the remaining stack of undealt cards in his hands. Stevie-Jack-Shit wanted another card. Mr. E had another card — it was the four of clubs, which took the total of his hand to sixteen. He gulped back his fear as he realised that it still wasn't enough to make him a contender in the game. He was going to have to twist for another card. Maybe this card was going to bust his hand. *Maybe he would have to light the oriental…*

Big Red continued talking. "Yeah. He's got together with some of his spars an' they play in a band — they write some nice nice tunes, y'know. When I told him that the Black Knight Sound System was run by a bredrin of mine, he went mad-up. An' he's been beggin' an' pleading with me to get you guys to record with him ever since!"

Mr. E felt a pin prick of hope pierce his wall of fear. This was the best news he'd heard all day. Although the last thing he wanted was Big Red and his devil's spawn crawling all over the studio, it was definitely preferable to being burnt to a cinder for a piddly hundred grand… *The hundred grand…* Mr. E's joyful heart began to sink as he realised Big Red hadn't even asked him about the money that he owed. Would he still be so amenable when he discovered that Mr. E wasn't able to pay him back? Maybe this recording session for his son was so important to him that he would give him a little leeway with regards to repayment.

He decided to lay it on thick. "Sounds like a *great* idea Big Red! We can *most definitely* hook young Ashton up! I haven't mentioned this to you before, 'cause I didn't realise dat you had, er, *interests* in the music business, but we're about to sign one of our artists to a mega multi-million dollar deal with B.U.L. Records!"

Big Red looked impressed, and nodded his acknowledgement, his huge red afro swaying, its oily sheen glistening in the light. "Isn't that the label that Freddie Famous is signed to?"

Mr. E laughed, as if Big Red had imparted some great piece of wisdom, and he was just bowled away by how clever he was. "That's right! I can see you're familiar with the music business then!" He leaned across the table, "Between you an' me, I'm very tight with a sista up there — Nikki Stixx. She's one of the heads of A & R. And she'll just about do anyt'ing I ask her to." He winked at Big Red, "If yuh know what I mean."

"Yeah, I understan'. I wouldn't mind a bit of that record company pussy myself bredrin!" Big Red's muscle-bound shoulders heaved as he started cackling again, and everyone joined in with him, laughing and bouncing their heads with abandon. "Okay, anybody else for a twist?"

Mr. E nodded. As his cards only added up to sixteen: he had to risk another to get him closer to twenty-one.

Big Red hesitated. "Are you sure, bredrin? You've had one twist already, y'know." He grinned at his cronies, "I think Mr. E's tryin' to fix it so he gets to light the match!"

Mr. E attempted to laugh, but he could only manage to curve his lips into a feeble half-smile. What was Big Red tryin' to say? Was this card going to bust his hand? Unable to think of a witty rejoinder, he just nodded at Big Red to twist him another card. He had no choice. If he just stuck at sixteen he was going to lose anyway. His only option was to take a chance.

Big Red stopped laughing and silently did his bidding sliding his final card, *the card that was going to decide whether or not he had to light the oriental,* across the table, face down. "Okay my brothas, time to show our hands. Let's see who's gonna be lucky enough to put an end to this fool's misery."

Everyone turned in their hand... Mr. E felt his body become drenched with perspiration. He peeked at his final card and almost screamed out loud when he saw the King of Spades leering back at him. His hand was well and truly busted. The King, the four the five and the seven brought his hand up to twenty-six.

He looked wildly around at the other guys and then toward the door. He had to get out of the room. Would he be able to escape? *He had to escape.* There was no way he could go through with setting fire to Mr. Wong. Even if he did, Red was going to discover that he couldn't pay back the money that he owed him. And it would be him next. And they'd probably do him, just like they were going to do the oriental guy. If not worse. And, if by some miracle, he did escape a painful death, he'd be up for a murder rap for the Oriental. Big Red would have him by the balls for life...

The sounds of the other three cackling and whooping cut through his thoughts. They were all slapping Stevie-Jack-Shit on the back and hitting high-fives. Mr. E struggled to make sense of their merriment.

Mr. Ice cleared his confusion. "You never could resist lightin' a fire could you, Stevie!"

It was only then that Mr. E realised that they were congratulating Stevie-Jack-Shit because he had the worst hand. Which meant that he, Mr. E, hadn't lost. The extra card that Stevie-Jack-Shit had been twisted had taken his hand to thirty. Which meant that the sick fuck must have planned to lose all along. The other two were laughing and congratulating him like he had just made the cleverest manoeuvre in the world. And the muthafucka actually looked happy that he was going to be able to set light to the oriental! It all seemed too good to be true, Mr. E still felt sick with fear. *Maybe they were just playing with him.* He checked Stevie-Jack-Shit's cards again, and, sure enough, there it was for the whole world to see — a grand *glorious* total of thirty... Mr. E wasn't a religious man, but at that moment he felt like throwing himself to the ground and praising the Lord for sparing him.

But Big Red suddenly halted the proceedings. "Hol' on a minute. We've been so caught up in all this talk of fame an' fortune, that we forgot to clear up de business of the hundred grand." He looked Mr. E dead in the eye. "I trust you've brought the cash."

Mr. E's mouth opened and closed like a fish that had been slung out of water. "I er... I er..."

"Yes or no, E? Y'have my dollars? Yes or no."

Mr. E gasped for air; he suddenly felt like all the life was being squeezed out of his body. "Well, I er... I, er."

Big Red's voice was low and quiet, a bass drum being rolled across gravel. "Don't tell me that you came here to fuck with me."

Mr. E started babbling. How could everything have been so nice one minute and then have turned so nasty the next? "Look, Big Red, you know that I would never even *think* about fuckin' with you! It's just that this deal I was tellin' you about — you know the one with B.U.L. Records? Well I-I got all my money tied up in that, and I'm just waiting for the paperwork to be finalised an' then I can pay you back in full." He tried to keep the desperation out of his voice as he added. "With interest, of course."

Big Red leant back in his chair and slammed his drink down on the table. "So you *have* come here to fuck with me!"

"No! NO WAY, man!" Tears were starting to prick at Mr. E's eyeballs as he forgot all his pride and began to openly plead. He wondered if the oriental had done the same thing, before Big Red had had him all tied up ready to be turned into a human fireball.

Mr. Ice jumped up and squeezed his hands around Mr. E's throat, snarling, "You little fucking piece of shit! Nobody — but *nobody* — fucks with Big Red! D'you want me to do him now, boss?"

Mr. E spluttered and gasped for breath, as he cried, "No! NO!"

Big Red looked at him in disgust. "Ease off, Ice. I promised my boy that he was gonna record with de Black Knight Sound System, so for now, I need this cunt to be alive. Put him down."

Mr. Ice threw Mr. E into a dishevelled heap at Big Red's feet.

"Mr. E," Big Red told him, "you have exactly seven days. In those seven days you an' your crew haffe record my yout' Ashton and his group. When the seven days are up, you'd better have all the money you owe me, plus fifty per cent interest, or you're gonna wish that you could be in dis little oriental fucka's shoes today. 'Cause, believe me, what I'll have for you will be a lot worse. An' if Ashton's shit doesn't come out correct... I'll kill you anyway."

Mr. E stood up and clasped Big Red's hand in his. "*Thanks*, man. I won't let you down. You have my word, man."

He turned to get out of there, he couldn't wait to leave the hot sweaty confines of the torture chamber. Elation raced through his being. He was free! By a glorious stroke of sheer... *brilliance*.... he'd made it through, without so much as a hair out of place! It was enough to make a grown man wanna throw himself down and give up his life to Jesus!

Then Big Red said, "Where the fuck d'you t'ink you're going?"

Mr. E turned back, bewildered. The noose had been slung back around his neck, and Big Red was firmly holding the rope and reeling him back in. "Er... I thought it was all settled?"

Big Red gestured to his left, "What about Mr. Wong here?"

Mr. E looked confused. *What was Big Red talking about?*

Big Red answered his question by handing Mr. E his blunt and saying, "Light him."

Mr. E looked back at him in horror. What was this bullshit? He hadn't lost the poker game. Stevie-Jack-Shit was supposed to be lighting the oriental. "But... but... the whole room'll go up in flames!"

Big Red laughed. "Oh no it won't."

He gestured towards Mr. Ice, who was holding a fire extinguisher, "We're jus' gonna heat him up a lickle. An' den

Ice is gonna cool 'im down so that the fun can really start, seen?" He threw his head back and laughed again.

Mr. E's blood curdled. Red had to be the sickest muthafucka he had ever met. He and his cronies were actually enjoying this.

The big man's brow knitted together, and he tensed his amazing array of muscles underneath his vest. His voice was low and serious as he turned toward Mr. E and growled, "Light it, muthafucka."

Mr. E turned toward the oriental. His heart was in his mouth. He was caught between a rock and a hard place. If he refused to light him, Big Red would kill him. Yet if he lit the match he would have committed murder. With three witnesses. He grew ice-cold as he realised that, if he ever wanted to get out of there alive, he had no choice.

Gulping back the fear, which had risen like bile to his palate, he took hold of the blunt and threw it at the oriental. In less than a split second, the guy burst into a mass of flames, and the heat from his screaming body was an intense wall of fire. Big Red and his cronies whooped and cheered and roared with laughter.

When they'd had enough of the show, and as the oriental guy rolled around the floor, howling in agony, Mr. Ice rushed forward and blasted him with the fire extinguisher.

That was the last thing Mr. E saw. He ran from Big Red's room of torture as if the devil was at his coat-tails. He tore through the maze of bloody hallways and out of the back door, and into the street. Blind to everything around him, Mr. E raced towards his car which he had parked several streets away. What had he done? *He had to get himself out of this nightmare.* No matter what it took. Or who he had to hurt.

The Bombshell

CHERRY WAS BACK IN HER FLAT, on the seventeenth floor of Byrant Court. She'd been at meetings with her lawyer all week, and her contract was finally ready to go. Her lawyer had said that, in all his twenty-five years of practicing, he'd never seen a record company so anxious to have a contract signed. Cherry knew this was because of Nikki. Her lawyer had suggested that she should see other record companies about a deal, as she was obviously *extremely* talented — otherwise B.U.L. wouldn't be so keen. But Cherry had decided against that. She was starting to build a very good relationship with Nikki, and felt confident that her career was in safe hands. Besides, B.U.L. were offering her a really good deal — one of the best deals of the decade according to her lawyer. So, so far the negotiations had gone very smoothly indeed.

She sat down in her living room with a cup of coffee, and pondered what had happened. Events had occurred at breakneck speed over last few months, and despite the occasional setback, she was relieved to see that things were still going to plan *And she could finish what she had started*.

Somehow her mind wandered onto Yam. She still hadn't called him, and there was no way she was going to, until she'd signed the deal with B.U.L. She didn't want Mr. E finding out that she was back in London and coming round and making trouble. Not yet. She had, however, tried to get hold of Babsy, but to no avail. She was never in. Lord knows she'd left enough messages, but none had been returned. Maybe she was away on a modelling job... or maybe she was just avoiding her. Things hadn't been so great between them when she had left and, knowing Babsy, she was probably sulking because Cherry hadn't called her from Miami.

The sound of the telephone interrupted her thoughts. Cherry deliberated over answering it. Maybe it was someone she didn't want to speak to — like Mr. E... But, of course, he didn't know that she was back. Yet. It was probably Nikki.

"Hello?"

"Hi baby."

It was Freddie Famous.

Latonya had finally found the piece of paper that she had written Cherry's London address on when she'd sent the limo round the night Freddie took her Subterania. From that it had been a synch to hire a private detective and get her home telephone number. She still couldn't believe Cherry's phone bill had actually been in the name of Cherry Drop — she'd always thought that that was her stage name. She'd handed the telephone number over to Freddie, who'd insisted on putting in a private call to Cherry. Latonya had wanted to be there, in case he scared her off again — after all, she had a lot riding on her too — but Freddie had been adamant that he wanted to call Cherry in private.

Cherry's heart began to thump a little faster. Even though she was thousands of miles away from him now; she still felt a tiny pinprick of fear at the sound of his voice.

She willed herself to remain calm and said, "Oh, hi Freddie."

Cherry had always known that Freddie was going to catch up with her sooner or later, but she had to give him marks of ten out of ten for getting there sooner. She knew there was no point in getting all nasty with him; that would probably just start a whole heap of trouble. And she didn't have time for his shit anymore. No, what she wanted was to have Freddie Famous out of her life forever. Permanently.

He was playing it all sweetness and light. "Baby, I've been so worried about you... We thought that you'd been in an accident or something 'cause you jus' disappeared. I mean, ya didn't leave a note or *anything*. How come you left so suddenly?"

For a split second, Cherry wondered if Freddie was actually brain dead. Trust him to ask the most obvious

181

question — he hadn't changed a bit. She answered in a serious voice, "I think you know why I left."

Freddie felt glad that she hadn't hung up already, maybe this was going to be easier than he'd thought. He hadn't even sent her any gifts yet. He began to feel confident that he was going to have Cherry back by his side in no time. "Oh baby, ya know that I was high. All that crazy bullshit was jus' the drugs takin' over, it wasn't me…"

She wanted to laugh out loud; he really must have thought her stupid if he expected her to believe that. Her voice was heavy with sarcasm as she said, "Oh really?"

"Yeah *really*. It wasn't like me at all! Cherry baby, you know that I would never hurt you. Ya know… I haven't been able to think of nothin' else but you since you went away. It's drivin' me *crazy* not havin' ya here by my side. I don't know if you know this but… it's all about you — I haven't touched another honey since ya left, baby. An' I've been cleaning up my act too. I mean, if ya want, I'll even go to rehab. I don't wanna fucked-up thang like powder to get between what we got, know what I'm saying? Look, I was too fucked-up to say it before, but I think… *I think I love ya, Cherry*. I mean, no other woman has ever touched me as deeply as you have, baby…" He paused. "An' my bed's so empty without you in it. I'm so lonely at night without you next to me."

Freddie had decided to lay it on thick. He knew that the honeys always found it hard to resist a nigga when he told 'em he loved them. If she got really difficult, he might even propose marriage. With a real long engagement period.

Cherry knew that Freddie was going to be all full of shit when he eventually tracked her down, and she was more than ready for him.

She pretended to stifle a sob. "Oh baby, did you really mean that, when you said you *loved* me?"

Freddie couldn't believe she was coming round so easily; he'd figured that it would take at least a week of grovelling to win her back. must have been all those sweet, honey-dipped lyrics he was droppin' on her. Well, they didn't call him 'Mr. Loverman' for nothing, sometimes he even amazed himself when he turned on the charm for a woman.

He let his voice fall into a low dramatic whisper and said, "I really do baby."

Cherry audibly stifled another little sob, "Oh Freddie that means so much to me... even though I'm so *scared*."

He reassured her. "Baby, you don' need to be scared of me. I told ya, the other night was jus' the drugs that had me actin' all crazy an' shit. I would *never* lay a finger on you! You know that. I mean, you're my lady, an' I love ya."

Cherry continued, "Oh, it's not that. I *know* that you didn't really mean to do what you did the other night... No, I'm scared because I think that your love is gonna turn to hate when you hear what I have to say."

Freddie wondered what she was talking about. Surely she hadn't found another man so soon? Maybe she had done something stupid, like sold their story to the papers. Or maybe it was just her build up to say that it was completely over. He urged her to explain.

"No way baby, I could never hate you. What's up?"

Cherry's voice cracked with emotion. "Well, it's funny that you should call me now because I just got the results today."

Freddie was confused, "Results? What results? What are ya talking about?"

She made a series of loud sobbing noises into the phone. "It's all over Freddie, I tested positive."

He was still in the dark, "Positive for what?"

"Well let's just say that it's a big disease with a little name."

Freddie was getting irritated. "Cherry will you just tell me what the fuck you are talkin' about!"

Cherry might have guessed that he wouldn't figure it out and that she would have to literally spell it out for him. "AIDS, Freddie... WE'VE GOT AIDS!" And with that she made a gut wrenching cry and wailed loudly into the phone.

Freddie let the full meaning of what Cherry had just said sink in. "Don't ya mean *you've* got AIDS, I mean ya can't catch it from oral sex and we never actually did full penetration."

Cherry prepared to drop her final bombshell. "It's no good Freddie, I hoped that that was true too. But I've checked with my doctor: I could have have given you AIDS from oral sex. In fact, the stage I'm at, he thinks I could give someone the disease by just breathing on them."

Freddie felt like he was going to collapse. "I gotta go."

Cherry pleaded, "But... but I thought you *loved* me."

"That was before you told me that you've more or less *murdered* me YOU FUCKING WHORE!"

Freddie slammed down the receiver, and Cherry fell back into her seat laughing. It had been perfect. He'd gone for it like a lamb to the slaughterhouse. Now if that didn't get rid of him, nothing would. Even if he had himself tested and got the all clear, he still wouldn't trouble her now that she'd told him she had AIDS. He'd be too scared to risk it. And even if somehow, with those tiny brain cells of his, he managed to work out her ruse, and realised she had been lying to get rid of him, he surely wouldn't be prepared to take the chance and find out. Now all she had to was work out how she was going to hard-ball him into letting her use those songs...

The Metamorphosis

FREDDIE FAMOUS CLOSED ALL THE CURTAINS in his suite. He put the 'Do Not Disturb' sign outside his door and pulled his phone out of its socket. Still fully clothed, he lay on the bed that he had once handcuffed Cherry to, and thought about what she had just said.

He had AIDS.

He was going to die.

It had to be some kind of nightmare and any second he was going to wake up. But, even though he was on his bed, Freddie was wide awake.

Having AIDS meant it was all over: his career, his money, the honey's — *everything*.

As the hours ticked by, Freddie thought about how much his life was going to change. It was funny how little the things that he'd considered to be important in his life, really mattered now. The limos, the clothes, the jewellery, the fancy hotels, all of the different honey's that he'd had... *it all seemed like bullshit now*. His records, his TV appearances, becoming a superstar, being No. 1 — none of it meant shit.

As he thought about his life, he searched for some sort of meaning, but found only emptiness. Hot wet tears began to slowly roll down his cheeks, as he came to the realisation that he had wasted his life. He had nothing of any real value to show for his years on earth. Sure, he'd sold a few records, but what had he done with all the money he had made? Had he built schools, given to charity, or helped the sick or the elderly? No, he'd spent it all on drink and drugs, he'd bought fast cars and fancy jewellery, and thrown it all at his various honeys and his crew.

And now he was going to die. His life was to be terminated in its prime. Freddie could hardly believe it. Surely he was too young? — barely a man really. And now he would never be able to experience the simple things in life, the things that any ordinary person could enjoy. He would never be able to

185

get old, or raise a family. What would his mother say if she knew that he was never going to give her any grandchildren? Freddie couldn't even bear to think of his mother, if she knew that her son had AIDS, it would kill her.

For two whole days and two whole nights Freddie stayed in his room alone. He didn't order anything from room service. He didn't even allow the maids in to clean up. All he could do was think about his imminent death, and how shamefully he had lived so far. What was going to await him on judgement day? What kind of life had he lived that would seal his fate?

Then at last he came to a decision, something that would help him find an answer to his prayers, and all the questions that he'd asked over the last forty-eight hours. On Sunday morning, Freddie rose to do something that he had not done for a long long time. Something that he hadn't done since he was living with his mother. He'd decided to go to church.

Still as shell-shocked as he was the first moment he'd heard Cherry's terrible news, Freddie washed and shaved off the two days worth of sweat, dirt and facial hair in a trance-like state. As if in automatic gear, he slipped into what he considered to be his smartest and most conservative outfit. When he was satisfied that his appearance was appropriate, he stepped out of the back entrance of the Taravala Hotel undetected, to discover that Miami was having a most unusual day — it was raining. Large, warm, heavy droplets of rain poured from the heavens. Scared that he might get drenched and ruin his carefully chosen outfit, Freddie hastily searched for the long, black stretch limo that was always waiting outside.

His Italian-American chauffeur was caught unawares. "Oh, it's you, boss. No-one told me you were going out."

Freddie remained impassive behind his black Armani sunglasses. "That's because I haven't told anybody. And if anybody asks if you know where I am, I want you to say 'no'. I don't want any of my people to know where I am, or what I'm doing. Have you got that Frank?"

"Sure thing boss, whatever you say. So, where are we going?"

"To the Pentecostal Church of Divine Intervention on Sunrise Boulevard."

Frank was incredulous, "What? You're gonna do a gig in a church?"

Freddie remained patient, "No, Frank, I'm gonna attend a sermon at church, and if you don't start burnin' some rubber, I'll miss it."

"No problem boss." Frank stepped on the gas, and headed off.

The Pentecostal Church Of Divine Intervention was small, but ostentatious. Elaborate stained glass religious murals filled every window, and the ceiling, which stretched high above the congregation's heads, was adorned with intricate carvings, the result of years of skilled craftsmanship. The floor was parqueted in a polished, red-brown mahogany, and a thick, ruby-red carpet flowed down the aisles between the pews. The preacher stood on a small, raised platform in front of the congregation. And a black gospel choir, resplendent in black robes with crisp white bibs, was clustered together on an upper level behind the preacher. The sermon had already started when Freddie arrived, so no-one paid him any mind when he found himself a pew at the rear of the church. Everyone else was already seated, mesmerised by the preacher's uplifting frenzied sermon.

"And I ask you, children of the Lord, with so much evil in the world today, what chance does the common everyday man and woman have to live their lives in peace? With so much *evil* in the world today, how can people like you..." He pointed to an adoring member of his congregation. "Or you..." He wagged a finger at someone else. "Or *all of you*..." He spread his hands out wide to include the entire congregation. "How can ordinary people like *us* learn to live our lives in the good, and honest, and pious, and humble way that the Lord intended us to?"

Freddie hung onto his every word, feeling as though all his prayers were about to be answered. These were the very questions that he himself had asked the Lord, as he'd lain awake for two days and two nights in his suite at the hotel.

The preacher held up his hands, rolled his eyes and looked up towards the heavens. "How can we learn to reach out a hand to our fellow man. *Who* will teach us how to *lu-u-rve* one another?"

He paused to let his rapt audience rack their brains for the answer to his soul-searching questions. "Let me tell you, my heavenly brothers and sisters. Let me tell you... the answer lies in Jesus." He slammed his hands onto the pulpit to emphasise his point. "Yes, Lord! *The answer lies in Jesus! If* you are in doubt about the right way to live your life, then I say look to JESUS. If you have problems that just refuse to be solved. Then I say JESUS will show you the answer!"

Several members of the congregation were now shouting hearty Hallelujahs and some Amens as they gave praise and approval to the preacher's good words. Freddie found himself in agreement, echoing their sentiments under his breath. He had known the answer all along. But it felt so good to hear the preacher confirm his thoughts. It felt so good to hear his answer straight from a man of God. Freddie felt his spirits begin to rise and his soul start to be uplifted.

Satisfied that his congregation had understood his point, the preacher continued, "Wasn't it JESUS who said that we should love our neighbour? Tell me, my brothers and sisters. If we all lived according to just these three little words that came from the sweet mouth of JESUS, would not the world be a better place? If we could all reach out with love and forgiveness toward our fellow man, *would not the world be a better place*? If, instead of fussin' an' fightin' and hating our neighbour and coveting his possessions, we could turn to him with *love*, WOULD NOT THE WORLD BE A BETTER PLACE?!!" He was working himself into a frenzy. "We would walk *freely* on the streets, our heads held high, our hearts *burstin' with love*, unafraid and certain that when we meet our fellow man along the way, he'd turn to us with love. Think of it! Our children would be able to play outside *without fear of harm*. Our doors could remain unlocked at night and war between nations would rage no more! *Forever* there would be peace and harmony on earth!"

Sweat was rolling down his brow now, and he paused to take out a carefully folded handkerchief and press it against his forehead and cheeks. After he had recomposed himself, he gave a crestfallen sigh. "But I hear the doubting Thomases amongst you. The ones who say it's impossible; that peace on earth can never be any more than a dream, that it's not possible for every man and woman to turn to each other with love. Well I say to you — that's the devil whisperin' in your ear. It *is* possible. I say that we *can* find heaven, right here on earth! And I say that EVERY man and EVERY woman *can* find *love* and *compassion* in their hearts!"

He stopped and let his voice fall to a dramatic whisper. "If they only look to Jesus… Look to Jesus… It's not too late to let *Jesus* save your soul."

Freddie felt close to tears. *This was his answer.* This was what he had been looking for! He prayed to the Lord that it wasn't too late for him to save his evil soul from eternal damnation.

The preacher continued, "Now, my beautiful brothers and sisters, I want you to turn to the person next to you, be they a stranger, or your very best friend, and give them a hug. Close your arms around them and let them *feel* your love and allow yourself to be comforted by theirs."

Everyone turned to one another and gladly did as the preacher asked. Freddie turned to the older woman sitting next to him, and gave her a mighty hug.

She responded to his warmth and said, "God bless you, my brother."

"And God bless you, my sister."

Satisfied that his flock was feeling the word of Jesus, the preacher went on. "Now, I want you all to join hands to form an unbreakable chain of love, and raise your voices to praise Jesus."

The congregation held hands and stood and echoed the preachers words: "I love you Jesus... We *love* you Jesus... We *adore* you Lord. We worship you Lord..." As they moaned and shouted their words of praise, they whipped themselves into a communal frenzy. Freddie began to feel an almost out-of-body experience as he gave up his spirit in praise to the Lord.

After about ten minutes religious fervour, the preacher asked them all to be seated. "Now, every Sunday new brothers and sisters come to join our flock. Lost souls, maybe even sinners, have come to us today in order to be saved from this hard and lonely hate-filled world. Heavenly creatures who have strayed from their rightful path in life. I ask you now, my children, to *welcome* them into the Lord's house, which is home to each and every single one of us."

The old lady next to Freddie turned to him and said, "Welcome to the Church of Divine Intervention my son."

Freddie bowed his head, humbled by her love. "Thank you mother-sister."

The preacher cast a beady eye over his congregation. "We have come to the time where we must ask if we have any sinners amongst us. Is there any poor unfortunate soul here who has fallen from righteousness and found themselves walking down the cruel, cruel path of evil?"

Freddie's eyes were locked onto the preacher, for he knew that these words were directed to him.

"Is there anybody amongst us who has sinned? Is there a *sinner* in the house of God? *Is there a sinner who wishes to repent and be forgiven in the house of God?*"

The congregation sat in silence, tense with expectation, barely containing their frenzied passion. The odd person still shouted out the occasional word of praise to the Lord.

The preacher continued, "Well I say to that sinner GET READY to repent your sins! Come and be *forgiven* in the house of the Lord. GIVE YOUR HEART AND SOUL TO

JESUS!"

Freddie rose from his pew as if in a trance, drawn by the preacher's words. He slowly walked down the aisle to the front of the church. He was now certain, beyond any shadow of a doubt, it was God's doing that had brought him to church that day. He felt eternally grateful and honoured that the Lord had answered his prayers and sent him to his and choked back his tears as he realised that the Lord had sent him to church so that he might be saved. So that he still might have a chance to enter the gates of heaven when he passed into the next world.

The preacher jumped off his pulpit when he saw Freddie walk towards him. He stretched out his arms and bade him to kneel down at his feet. "Welcome to the house of the Lord my child. How have you sinned?"

Freddie looked up at the preacher. His face was contorted with pain as he confessed, "Oh, father, I have strayed onto the path of temptation. I have led an evil life of *sin* and *debauchery*. I have used and abused women, drunk alcohol like it was water and freely taken a multitude of illegal substances."

The congregation 'oohhed' and 'aahhed', and several of the older members tutted at his confessions. Freddie continued, "I have been selfish and have wallowed in my own greed and sense of self-importance. Even though I am a rich and successful man, I've never once reached out a helping hand toward my neighbour."

The preacher's ears pricked at the words 'rich and successful' and he fervently pressed his palm of his hand against Freddie's heated brow. "I'll not lie my young brother — you have been *truly* sinful; and your path to the Lord will not be an easy one. You have made some grave and serious confessions, and your heart must indeed be heavy with the weight of your sin."

Freddie closed his eyes and kept his hot forehead pressed against the preacher's cool hand."Oh it is, Father! It is!"

"Tell me now. In fact tell *all* of us here today... Do you *repent* your sins?!!"

Freddie felt hot, salty tears begin to roll down his cheeks. "Oh I do Father, *I do*." He grasped the preacher's free hand. "Please Lord, I *beg* your forgiveness!"

The preacher rolled his eyes towards the heavens, "Lord, I ask you to take this *wayward* sinner into your loving bosom and *forgive* him, for he knew not what he did. He kneels here humble, and repentant before you, Lord, and I ask you to save his *evil* soul."

A young girl was sitting with her mother in the front pew right in front of the preacher and Freddie. As the scene had unfolded before her, she somehow felt certain that she'd seen him somewhere before. As the preacher asked the Lord to save Freddie's soul, she suddenly realised who he was, and she jumped out of her seat and shouted, "Oh my God! It's FREDDIE FAMOUS!"

The congregation rumbled with excitement, and the preacher, sensing a stampede, took control, "Stay still my children. *Would you be so bold as to interrupt the Lord's work*?"

His brow creased as he tried, along with the rest of them, to find the unshaven, snarling features that he knew as Freddie Famous, in the clean-shaven face of the smartly dressed young man that was kneeling before him. "Is it true, brother? Are you Freddie Famous?"

Freddie stood up and faced the crowd, his eyes were red and sore from crying, "Yes it's true. I was once a singer, who preached the evil word, and led young people astray and into temptation. But I'd like to tell you all here today, my good brothers and sisters, that *that is all behind me*. I hearby pledge to you today that I will spend the rest of my life serving the Lord, and spreading the good word!"

Everybody shouted cheers of praise and joy. The preacher turned to Freddie with a wide benevolent smile and said. "God bless you my son."

The Revelation

MR. E SAT IN THE OFFICE of Black Knight Productions. He hadn't seen Fingers or D in a few weeks, and Yam seemed to have disappeared off the face of the earth. The recording equipment in the studio hadn't been touched in all that time; there hadn't seemed much point without Cherry. They were all waiting for the deal to be signed. Without Denise to man the phone and take care of the paperwork, the office had been temporarily closed for 'refurbishments'. So the building that housed Black Knight Productions was like a ghost town.

But now Mr. E had to make preparations for Ashton — Big Red's son — to start recording. But before he did that, he just had one thing to do. The one thing that could maybe get him out of this whole mess with Big Red and get his business back on its feet again. He had to try and get hold of the two hundred and fifty thousand pounds advance he was going to get for signing the deal for Cherry.

He called B.U.L. Records and asked to be put through to Nikki Stixx.

"Mr. E, how can I help you?"

Mr. E was a little surprised to hear that Nikki was not being her usual exuberant self. If he didn't have a multi-million dollar deal almost ready to be signed with her, he'd think that she was giving him the cold shoulder. However, he refused to be discouraged by her unenthusiastic greeting and kept his tone jovial and friendly. "What's up Nikki! Everyt'ing cool?"

Not waiting for an answer, he quickly went on, "Listen, I've just spoken to Cherry in Miami, and you'll be pleased to know that she'll be heading back to England shortly. She's finally getting over her father's untimely death and is looking forward to recording some hit tunes for us all. I was just calling to check that all the contracts are still in order — and, of course, to see that you are still firing, and as gorgeous as ever."

Nikki could hardly believe what she was hearing. Could Mr. E really be this much in the dark? "I'm sorry... you said that you spoke to Cherry in Miami *today*?"

"That's right, she was telling me how she's about to buy her ticket to return to England — I t'ink she's had enough of the sunshine state now!"

Nikki almost felt sorry for him. "I don't see how that could be possible."

"What d'ya mean? All she has to do is call up Virgin or British Airways, or any one of those cats, and she'll be here within a matter of a few hours! If it's Freddie that you're wondering about, you can rest yuhself. Dat was only ever gonna be a fling anyways!"

"I meant it's not possible, because Cherry was with me yesterday here in London, and she's going through a B.U.L. recording contract with her lawyer right now as we speak."

Mr. E suddenly felt short of breath, "What? You mean she's in London, and you're planning to sign the deal with her direct?"

"Yes."

It simply couldn't be true, he felt like he was going to faint,. "But, but that's *impossible*, Cherry has got a contract with Black Knight Productions. Everything she does has to go through me."

Nikki was business-like and to the point, "I'm sorry Mr. E, but that's something that you'll have to take up with Cherry herself. As far as B.U.L. Records is concerned, we've signed no agreement with Black Knight Productions, and any commitment Cherry has made with you will have to be honoured from her share of the royalties. Look, I'm going to have to cut this conversation short, as I've a meeting to go to. Good luck with Cherry."

Nikki Stixx replaced the handset. What an idiot, to think that he was planning to hard-ball her into going to bed with him. *How wrong could you be.*

Mr. E was in a state of shock.

194

He was furious. Cherry Drop had messed with the wrong man this time, and she was going to discover what happened to you when you messed around with a Yardie. First, she'd gone off to the States without a by your leave, and *now* she had the nerve to be double-dealing behind his back, trying to take the deal from right under his nose! This time, the bitch had gone too far. There was no way she was going to get away with it. *Not when his life depended on getting that advance*. He had a water-tight contract with her scrawny lickle raas, and he would see to it, personally, that she'd never see a penny of whatever money that she earned for as long as she lived.

Still enraged, he called Carrington. He got the answering machine. Again. So that pathetic little piece of shit was trying to outsmart him as well, was he? Mr. E's blood began to boil. He needed to show certain people what happened when you fucked around with someone like him. Feeling mad as hell, Mr. E jumped into his black Mercedes. He was going pay someone a long over-due visit.

"No way! You're just being nice."

"I mean it darlin', the fashion editor thinks you're *gorgeous*. You make that other bird, Naomi Campbell, look like Hilda bloody Ogden!"

Babsy giggled in appreciation. Dave Armstrong was telling her how wonderful she looked in the photo session she'd done for the article in *The News* that was about to go to press.

"So, she really wants to use me for a fashion special?"

She's *begging* me to use you. It'll be for a lot of cash you know, we always pay our models *big* money. We can afford to, as we're the biggest selling Sunday paper in the country!"

"That's great Dave, I'll leave you to sort it all out. Listen… how did Yam's photos go? Do you think you'll use any of them?" Babsy secretly hoped Yam wouldn't be used

195

in the piece, and that the story would be from a 'me-and-my-best-friend' angle, like Dave had mentioned. She was very excited by the thought of being in a national newspaper, and was loath to share the glory with anyone else.

Dave cleared his throat. "Well, of course, he's not as nice to look at as yourself, but we'll probably use one small pic, so our readers can see what he looks like. Still, he's not gonna look too good on the same page as you. We might have to call the piece 'Beauty and the Beast'!"

He laughed loudly at his own joke and Babsy giggled back, "Ooo don't be mean!"

Dave wiped his eyes and calmed himself down. "Yeah, you're right love — that was a bit cheeky! Anyway, it was great speaking to you, and we all love the story. Have you cashed that cheque yet?"

Babsy felt the familiar rush of adrenaline that she got every time she thought about the eighty thousand pounds which now sat in her savings account. "Yeah, it's in the bank."

"Good girl, now, don't go spending it all at once yeah? I'll speak to you later, darlin'."

"See ya."

Babsy clicked off her mobile. She'd just deposited the cheque and was on her way back home, where Yam was waiting for her. As usual, when she thought of Yam, she felt herself getting irritated. He was such a kill-joy these days. The cheque had been made out in her name, and she had a good mind not to give him any of it, the way he was going on. I mean, how could any man have a woman like herself, who Dave had said was better looking than Naomi Campbell, and still be pining after a two-timing tramp like Cherry? As far as she was concerned, he should be over it by now. And there was no way she was prepared to waste any more time with someone who was in love with somebody else. She had a modelling and acting career to be getting on with. She didn't need to be dragged down by a no-hoper like Yam.

It was in this frame of mind, that Babsy entered the communal door to the house that contained the room she called home. The first thing she did was check her messages, on the notepad by the telephone in the hall. There was one from her agency, and two others from Cherry.

Babsy had instructed the other girls in the house to say she wasn't in, to tell Cherry, whenever she called, that they didn't know where she was or when she'd be back. Of course, she hadn't told any of this to Yam. At first, she just didn't think it was right that Cherry could run off to America, and then breeze back into their lives whenever she felt like it. Not now that she and Yam had got together. And then, since they'd done their interview in *The News*, she'd decided that there was no way she could let Cherry and Yam speak to one another, otherwise he might get all soft, and blow their whole story. *Not to mention the eighty grand*. She tore the sheet of paper from the notepad, and threw it in the bin.

Yam lay on Babsy's bed and aimlessly channel surfed the TV. He was feeling very depressed about the photographs he'd shot for their upcoming article. Somehow Babsy had persuaded him to go ahead but, as far as he was concerned, it had been a nightmare. He hadn't wanted photographs anyway. That was more Babsy's sort of thing; she was convinced that the photo session was going to be her 'big moment'. But Dave Armstrong had been adamant that the photographer should take some snaps of him. At least they hadn't insisted in caking him up with make-up and put him in stupid skimpy outfits like they had with Babsy. No, Dave had decided that he needed a 'natural' shot and they took some pictures of him in the alley outside the photographic studio. Hopefully they wouldn't even want to use them — they must have been awful. He hadn't smiled in one of them. The way Dave had kept talking about Cherry being with Freddie, while the photographer had been snapping away, had made him feel close to tears.

Now Babsy had gone to put their 'payment' in her bank account. Yam knew that the thought of forty thousand pounds should make him feel better, but the truth was it didn't. He felt like shit. He still had a horrible feeling about this article and was sure that slimeball, Dave Armstrong, was just using Babsy and him to dish the dirt on Cherry. And that was the last thing he wanted to do. Of course, Babsy didn't care at all about the rights and wrongs of it; the only thing she was bothered about was the money, and her stupid modelling career.

He hadn't known Babsy could be so naive. She seemed completely oblivious to the fact that this con-man, Armstrong was slimier than snot on a door handle, and he was just using them both until the next 'newsworthy' item came along. It made Yam sick the way Babsy had simpered and giggled at every one of Dave's pathetic jokes. *Cherry would have told someone like him where to go.*

As these thoughts ran through his mind, Babsy returned to her room, looking very annoyed at the sight of Yam, lying on her bed. She adopted a sarcastic tone of voice, "Busy as ever I see."

Yam ignored her, immune as he was by now to her put-me-downs. Why couldn't she ever say anything positive?

Babsy picked up a cushion that was lying on the floor and tossed it at Yam. "Hello? Anybody home? In case you hadn't noticed, I'm back from the bank."

Yam sat up and looked at her, "I've been thinking about this *News* story… I'm still convinced that we're doing the wrong thing. I've got a horrible feeling that this guy Dave is gonna stitch us up."

Babsy looked at Yam like he was a complete idiot. "Why would he want to do that?"

"Because he's a *journalist*. Look, Babsy…" Yam paused, more than ever, he was convinced the whole thing was going to the biggest mistake of his life. And that it would mean he'd never be able to see Cherry again. He *had* to find a way to make Babsy see his point. "Look, I've thought about this long and hard... I think we should give Dave his money back and call off the whole article."

Babsy gawped. "Are you mad? Why should we do a *crazy* thing like that?"

Yam was passionate and sincere. "Because what we're doing is *wrong*. It's *not right* to do the dirty on Cherry like this."

Babsy glared at him like he'd just murdered her mother. "You *what*? You want me to give up eighty grand to protect that lying bitch? You must be out of your mind! In fact you *are* out of your mind! Here you are with a beautiful girl like myself offering you all her love, and all you can think about is Cherry — someone who ran off with another man the minute your back was turned! When are you gonna get over it, Yam? You know what? *I don't need this*. I don't *deserve* to be with a man who's in love with someone else. Why don't *you* forget about the article and I'll go right ahead and keep all the money for myself. And then you won't have to feel so bad about selling out your precious Cherry!"

Yam stood up. He had to get out of there. If he didn't, he was going to do something they both might regret. Didn't she realise that this article was going to ruin his entire life? And if they went ahead with it he was probably going to lose the only person he had ever cared about? He could hardly believe that Babsy was capable of being such a bitch. She was acting like the devil in drag.

"You do that Babsy. I don't give a shit about the money — you can keep it. I'm outta here!"

He grabbed his things and stormed out of the house.

Babsy sat down on the edge of her bed. It couldn't have gone better if she'd planned it. Who would have thought that Yam could be so stupid? Now she could keep all of the money, *and* she didn't have to put up with his moping around the house all day! Fantastic!

She stretched out on her bed and fantasised about how brilliant her life was going to be when she was a supermodel and a famous actress. And then she went through a million ways in which she could spend eighty thousand pounds.

Cherry packed her clothes neatly away into one of the many cardboard boxes that were strewn all over the floor in her living room. It was Tuesday morning, and she had been awake for five hours. And she was still smiling.

She'd finally signed her recording contract the day before.

She played the events over again in her mind — there'd been photos, and everyone at B.U.L. had celebrated the deal with a glass of champagne. Her plan was coming together like clockwork. She felt certain she'd gotten rid of Freddie Famous for good, and her relationship with Nikki was going from strength to strength. And now, she was finally moving out of Byrant Court. Not that it had been so bad. On the contrary, Byrant Court had been very good to her — a half-way house between the Rosemead Hostel and her new good fortune. But she had no more use for it now, and it certainly had nothing on the newly refurbished three bedroomed, two-storey top-floor mansion flat that she was about to move into in London's fashionable Camden Town.

"Beep!"

The sound of the entryphone buzzer interrupted her thoughts. She went to see who it was.

"Yeah Cherry, I need to speak to you."

Cherry smiled to herself as she thought of Mr. E's timing. A few hours later, and she'd have been out of Byrant Court forever. She'd been wondering when he was going to catch up with her. "Come on up."

Cherry went to the phone and dialled Nikki. "Hi, it's me. Listen, I just want to let you know that Mr. E's arrived, so I'd like you to come over. Yeah, if you could arrive here in exactly thirty minutes from now, that should give me enough time to say what I've got to say. Remember *exactly* thirty minutes, okay? See you then."

Just as she replaced the handset, Mr. E knocked on the

door of her flat. She gave him a big, beaming smile.

"Mr. E! Long time no see!"

Mr. E was a little taken aback, he hadn't expected to get such a friendly welcome from Cherry. Maybe she had a short memory.

"Can I get you anything to drink?"

He decided to go along with the niceties — until he dropped his bombshell. "Yeah, I'll have a blackcurrant cordial if you've got one. Not too much ice."

"Cool, take a seat in the living room, whilst I go and make it."

When Cherry came back with a glass of cordial for Mr. E and a coffee for herself, he nodded at the room and said, "Movin' somewhere?"

"Yeah, I got a transfer."

"Oh yeah, where?"

Cherry didn't bat an eyelid as she lied: "Kent."

Mr. E didn't believe her for one second. But he really didn't give a shit where she was going, so he got straight down to business, "So, I hear dat you were down B.U.L. today Cherry."

"That's right."

"How's Nikki?"

"Fine."

"I hear you two are very close now."

"That's right."

They were both silent for a moment. Mr. E wasn't sure how he was going to broach the subject of Cherry's recording contract. Now that she was being so nice, it had taken the wind out of his sails a little bit. But it still didn't change the fact that the conniving little bitch was intending to cut him out of his own record deal. He bit his lip as he imagined what her neck would look like with his hands around it. Maybe that would knock the smile off her face.

Feeling cheery at the thought of what he had in store for Cherry, he smiled back at her. "How's the record deal coming along?"

She kept her cool. "Actually, I signed it this morning."

"You WHAT?" Mr. E nearly choked on his drink, "You've gone and signed the deal behind my back?"

Cherry stood up and put her coffee down on the mantelpiece. She looked down on Mr. E, who was sitting on her sofa. "That's right."

Mr. E was mad. Real mad. Who the hell did she think she was, calmly telling him that she had *fucked with him in the worst way imaginable* — and not even having the sense to look scared. Well, she was going to get a rude awakening when he reminded her of the contract she'd signed in the studio of Black Knight Productions. The same contract which stipulated that every single penny she earned for the rest of her life would go to him first. And he was going to make sure that she wouldn't even come *close* to receiving a brass farthing of those royalties. And the first thing he would do would be to get hold of that quarter of a million advance. Keeping his temper in check, Mr. E pulled a folder out of his ever-present black record bag.

He handed a thick document to Cherry, "I think you're forgetting about this."

She flicked through the pages and casually said, "Oh that."

Mr. E laughed inwardly. She really was stupid — she probably couldn't even read the contract, never mind understand what it meant. "I don't think you understand, young lady. *That* is a copy of the contract which, if you remember, you signed when we were in the studio of Black Knight Productions a couple of months ago."

Cherry handed the document back. "I know."

Mr. E marvelled at just how much of an idiot Cherry really was. There was nothing else for it, he would have to spell it out for her. "What it means is that you are in no position to be signing any record contracts behind my back. In fact you're not in a position to do *anything* unless I give it the okay first. And this contract states quite clearly that every penny you ever earn will go directly to me. *It ain't passing go and you won't collect two hundred pounds.* And, after all the nasty lickle double dealings you've done, you'll be lucky if you see a single penny of your royalties, not to mention that advance that I negotiated with B.U.L. Records!" He gave Cherry a victorious grin. "Put in plain English, so dat even a lickle rude gyal like you can understand. Your ass is mine!"

Mr. E cracked up at his own delivery. He hadn't lost his touch, when it came to adding a bit of humour to things.

Cherry listened patiently and, when he had finished, she asked calmly, "Mr. E, did I receive any legal advice, prior to signing this contract?"

He laughed again, "Of course not! You didn't need legal advice on this, you signed it on the basis of trust."

Cherry talked slowly and calmly, as if she was explaining Einstein's theory of relativity to a child. "According to British law, Mr. E, a contract is not legal unless all its signees have undertaken legal advice on its contents first? Usually, it's poor unsuspecting musicians who aren't clued up on music law. Or it's certain unsavoury characters who are too busy trying to rip people off, to do their homework properly. You were stupid enough to get me to sign a contract without seeking legal advise first. I took advantage of your ignorance in these matters and signed your stupid bit of paper; in case you tried to exploit me in the future. It's a bloody good job that I did. Those forms in your hand are worthless. And if any money is going to be paid to anyone, it shall be out of the kindness of *my* heart and not yours."

She leaned closer to Mr. E. She didn't want him to miss a single word of what she was about to say. "And I can assure you, my 'mysterious' friend, I do *not* have a kind heart. In fact I don't think I have even one kind bone in my body. Especially when it comes to evil fuckers like you."

Mr. E was stunned. *Had she gone mad?* Who the hell did she think she was talking to? And what was all that crap about the contract being 'worthless' — surely she was bluffing?

"Bullshit!" was all he could say.

Cherry smiled calmly and confidently, "I'm afraid not. When you *do* actually get some legal advice, you'll soon find out that it's one of the hard facts of life."

Mr. E felt anger rage through his entire being. Who did she think she was, trying to outmanoeuvre him? The Black Knight! He stood up, looked Cherry dead in the eye and hissed, "I think you're talking a load of fuckries. But let's say for one brief moment that you're right. Are you forgetting that without me you wouldn't even have a demo tape, never mind a record deal? I'm the one who's been financing your entire career up until now. Do you really think that I'm gonna stand by and let you fuck with me like this?"

Cherry stared back at him, and her eyes were ice-cold. "I guess that that's what happens when you fuck with people, 'Mr. Mystery' — you get fucked right back."

Mr. E was beside himself. She had to be the craziest bitch he had ever come across in his entire life! He leapt to his feet and stood nose-to-nose with her, growling through clenched teeth, "I should put my hands around your throat and throttle every last breath out of your nasty, lickle no-name self for even *thinking* that you can disrespect me like this!"

Cherry looked right back into Mr. E's fiery eyes. "Maybe you should, but I wouldn't try it if I was you. Nikki Stixx's on her way over. I called her when you rang the buzzer."

Mr. E stood his ground. He wasn't convinced Cherry was telling the truth. He had a lot of pent-up emotions raging inside of him, and he was in the mood for some kind of release. Maybe giving Cherry what she deserved was just what the doctor had ordered.

He opened and clenched his fists, his fingers itching to hurt her. "Maybe I don't give a shit if Nikki is on her way over. With the crap you two have been coming up with, she looks like she deserves to be shown what time it is as well!"

For the first time since Mr. E had walked into her flat, Cherry had to admit she was starting to lose her cool. She had timed it perfectly, saying what she had wanted to say and more. But, according to the clock on the wall, thirty-five minutes had passed. And Nikki still hadn't shown up. What if she'd somehow been waylaid? What if she didn't show up at all? What if Mr. E followed through on his threats? She didn't like the way he was looking at her. *The last time she had seen that look in someone's eye, somebody had been murdered.*

She tried not to let her growing fear show on her face. "What? And go down for *murder*? You might be a fool, but even you aren't so stupid you're gonna throw half your life away just 'cause you missed out on a recording contract."

Mr. E edged even closer. He felt like he was going to explode. "It might be just a 'recording contract' to you, but it's *everything* to me. If I don't get the advance from this deal, my whole business is goin' down. I'll be destroyed!"

This was just what she'd wanted to hear him say, *what she had been longing for him to say*, and Cherry found herself becoming lost in her moment of victory. She couldn't contain a triumphant ripple of laughter as she looked right back at him and said, "I know."

Mr. E felt a fury surge across his consciousness. Who the fuck did this bitch think she was? How *dare* she laugh in his face when he told her that he was going under? *Didn't she realise what was going on?*

Unable to contain himself any longer, his hands flew to her throat, and he began to squeeze. He wanted to squeeze every last laugh, every chuckle, every drop of joy out of her, along with every single last breath. He wanted to squeeze away her, the studio, Delroy Carrington and Big Red.

Cherry gasped for air as his fingers closed around her windpipe. As she felt her life slipping away, she tore at his chest with her fingernails. This wasn't how she had planned the meeting at all. She stared at the clock on the wall behind him — forty minutes had passed. Where was Nikki?

The Decision

LATONYA WAS BESIDE HERSELF. She'd been going crazy wondering whether or not Cherry had signed the deal with B.U.L. in London. And she hadn't seen Freddie since he'd locked himself in his suite two days ago. Whatever was going down, it obviously wasn't good. She had never, in all her time with Freddie, seen him act like this. The nigga was demented. Surely he wasn't turning into some sort of recluse over a woman? She didn't mean to diss a sista, but a nigga had to be plain stupid to act so fucked-up over a chick. He'd already missed an interview that she'd scheduled for him with *Vibe* magazine. You just don't diss a publication like *Vibe*. It was fine now while he was top of the billboard charts, but every nigga had his day. What about when his records didn't sell as well as they were selling now? Magazines have long memories, and they wouldn't be there to support him when he was on his way down.

And now, finally, he was 'summoning' her to his room. Well she was going to have a word or two with him when she got there, job or no job.

She knocked on the door, and then walked straight in. She stopped when she saw Freddie. She'd expected him to be looking a little off colour, after two days of sitting alone in his room. At the very least she'd expected to see his trade mark stubble and his bad-boy hair cut. Instead, she was shocked to find Freddie clean-shaven, and sitting up at the writing desk in his room, hair all neatly trimmed and wearing a smartly cut suit. He looked more like the Reverend Jesse Jackson than the rude boy of hip-hop. She was momentarily lost for words.

Freddie took charge of the situation, "Come in sister."

Latonya did as he said and stayed silent. Where was he coming from with all this new dialogue? Calling her 'sister'! That was a first. He usually called her 'bitch'.

Freddie's expression took the shape of benevolence. "I

have called you here today to inform you that I've come to a decision. It hasn't been easy, but then the things that really matter in life never are. I have been through a *life-changing* experience. A revelation. Which means that I will never be the same way again. This revelation has made me closely examine the evil way in which I previously existed."

He broke off his dialogue and paused to look at his boots and shake his head in shame as he thought of how he'd lived his life. "This revelation has made me realise that my life before today was *truly* sinful. I'd been tempted by the devil himself, and was caught up in spreading his evil word through my music, and by the bad example that I set for the young people of America. But I gotta tell ya, Latonya — that all that shit is all behind me now."

He looked her dead in the eye, his expression grave and serious."I have decided to give my life to God."

Latonya fought back the urge to burst out laughing. *Had Freddie gone nuts?* He must have been droppin' acid. She cocked her head at Freddie and asked, "Are you okay?"

Freddie smiled. "Oh yes, Latonya. I have never been so okay in my life! The Lord has blessed me with a visit and has given me a chance to save my soul before it's too late."

"Too late for what?" Latonya was starting to feel panicky. Freddie looked stone-cold sober and she was beginning to feel that he actually meant all this shit.

Freddie's face took on an even more sombre expression. "Too late for redemption, Latonya. The good Lord saved my soul before it was too late for *redemption* and I would have been forever damned…"

Latonya was in shock. For once in her life, she could truly think of nothing at all to say.

Freddie continued, "So I've called you in here to see if you want to join me, my sister. Are you willing to cast aside all your worldly goods, and dedicate your life to doing God's work? Latonya… do you want to save your soul?"

Latonya looked at her employer with horror. She couldn't believe that, in a space of a few days, someone could have changed so much. What could have Cherry told him on the phone to make him go off the wall like this? And now he was asking her to give up all her 'worldly goods', everything she had ever wanted, everything that she had worked her butt off to get. He *had* to be nuts!

She decided to keep calm, sit it a while and see whether he was going to keep this 'redemption' thing up. "Er, Freddie, I think that I'mo have to think about what you've said. Ya gotta understand that it's come as a bit of a shock to me. But I want you to know that I love ya, and that I'm here for you no matter what you decide to do with your life."

With that, she excused herself and left the room, hoping this was just a fleeting moment of madness, and within a few days, he'd be back to his normal bad-boy self. If not, she was going to have to find another job. There was no way she was going to do something crazy like devote her life to God. Staying with Freddie and giving up all her worldly goods just sounded to her like another way of saying that she would work for the nigga for free. And Latonya Johnson didn't do shit for free. Not in this life *or* the next.

A few days after their meeting, Freddie sat and stared at the envelope in his hand. He'd already fired all of his crew. No-one had been prepared to 'denounce their evil ways' and he wasn't going to finance their sinful wrong-doings for a moment longer. Of course, he'd felt sad that they could not find it in their hearts to embrace God in the way he had. But each person had to find the Lord in their own good time. He prayed for their souls, and hoped that it would not be long before they walked beside him on the path of redemption.

Freddie had been having some private counselling with Father Wright, the preacher from the Church of Divine Intervention. During these sessions, he'd confessed all of his sins to Father Wright and told him about his relationship with Cherry, including the fact that she'd told him that she'd given him AIDS. Quite sensibly, Father Wright had advised him to go for an test, because there was every possibility that he might not have caught anything from Cherry. Not to mention the possibility that she might not even have had the syndrome in the first place, and had used it as an excuse to get rid of him.

Freddie wasn't so sure, he somehow felt certain he'd caught the disease and was going to die. Why else would the good Lord decide to give him one last chance to save his soul? Besides, he'd always hated doctors and hospitals, and detested the idea of a blood test. He might have been the rude boy of hip-hop, but he usually fainted at the sight of a needle.

However, Father Wright had persuaded him, saying that by not going for the test, he was denying himself the truth. And that he would not be able to God's work properly without knowledge of the truth. He'd told Freddie to pray for forgiveness and to leave himself in God's hands. And to remember that, whatever the result of the test was, that it was God's will, and therefore for the best.

So Freddie sat and turned the envelope that contained the results of his AIDS test over and over in his hands. He hadn't been able to stop himself from praying to God and asking him to let him live. On more than a few occasions, he'd passionately begged God to let him live, vowing to dedicate himself to doing His work, if he would only spare him from the curse of AIDS. He still wanted to live more than anything else in the world. He was convinced that his future was here on earth, so that he could make a difference and use his wealth and his fame to help and guide the poor and the unfortunate.

His mouth felt dry as he uttered one last prayer before opening the envelope that would reveal his fate. "Oh Lord, I know that I have lived a life of evil, and have committed untold sins. But I truly, *truly* repent for what I've done. And if you could find it in your heart to forgive me and let me live, then I swear to you Lord, that I will dedicate the rest of my life to doing your good work. *I swear*, I'll be your nigga!"

Freddie choked back his tears. "Amen."

He tore open the envelope and saw the word: negative.

Tears of joy streamed down Freddie's face. He'd been saved! The good Lord had answered his prayers and given him another chance! He threw on his coat and made ready to go to the Church Of Divine Intervention, so he could share the good news with Father Wright. Even though he'd travelled the world, spent weeks riding on the top of the billboard charts, sold millions and millions of records, and won countless Grammys and other awards, Freddie felt like this was the best moment of his entire life. He'd never felt happiness in the way he felt now. And he was certain that it was all thanks to his Saviour, the good Lord in heaven.

"WHAT THE FUCK IS GOING ON!!?"

Nikki Stixx's mouth dropped at the spectacle before her. She couldn't believe what she was seeing. Cherry had always told her Mr. E was an evil man, but she hadn't quite believed her. She'd always presumed Cherry was just trying to paint a bad picture of him, in an effort to justify cutting him out of the record deal. Sure, she'd known that he was capable of bending a few rules from time to time, just like any other hustler out there on the street. But never in her wildest dreams would she have imagined he'd be the kind of monster who'd be doing what she could see right there and then with her very own eyes.

Mr. E had Cherry by the throat was holding her against the wall. Cherry's body was limp and all the colour had drained out of her face. *Could she already be dead?* Nikki cursed herself for not taking Cherry more seriously when she'd called. Now she knew why Cherry had been so adamant that she'd come around in exactly thirty minutes. She'd thought that Cherry and Mr. E would have just been having a row or something, and that Cherry had wanted her to come in so that it wouldn't have dragged on too long. How could she have known that Mr. E really was a violent lunatic, capable of anything? Capable of… of… *murder*. Nikki rushed forward. Surely she wasn't too late?

Mr. E turned round, startled at the sound of her voice. In his rage, he'd almost forgotten that she might be on her way up. He let go of Cherry's throat and she flopped back against the wall like a helpless rag doll. A million emotions ran around his consciousness. He squinted at Nikki as though she were an… an *apparition*… a dream that he couldn't quite focus on. How could Nikki, the woman of his dreams, his… *queen*… be in cahoots with a she-devil like Cherry? He'd been living for the moment when they would meet again, but he'd never imagined it would be in these circumstances. He would never have wanted her to see him like this — not after what they had nearly had together.

He felt an urge to put his hands back to Cherry's throat, finish off what he'd started. But common sense was already returning to his mind like a bad dream. Mr. E shook himself — he'd missed his chance and he knew it.

He turned and looked back at Cherry, the reason for his torment; and whispered in her ear as she flailed against the wall, still gasping for breath. "I'm gonna check out that contract tomorrow, and I hope for your sake that you're wrong. Either way, you haven't heard the last of me."

Cherry slowly lifted her eyelids with a look of pure hatred. "Whatever, asshole."

Nikki rushed up to Cherry all breathless and concerned, as Mr. E stormed out. "Darling, are you all right?"

Cherry was still coughing up all the phlegm that had risen to her throat, but her breathing was starting to return to normal. "Yeah… But if you'd arrived a second later, I doubt I would have been able to answer that question."

Nikki slumped against the wall next to her. "Oh thank God! I thought I was too late, that you were… you were…"

Cherry laughed bitterly. "Yeah, me too. He was really starting to lose it."

Nikki looked confused, "Just like you said he would. You know, Cherry, I had no idea, I'm… I'm so… *sorry*. Would you believe that I actually ran out of petrol? I had to fill up on the way!"

Cherry looked intently at Nikki. "No… But I'm glad you made it when you did."

Satisfied that Cherry wasn't dead, and that she was going to be all right, Nikki walked towards the telephone, "I'm calling the police, that lunatic should be locked up! Don't worry, he can't have got far, they'll track him down."

Cherry stood up straight and shook her arms and legs, in an effort to get the blood back into her head. It'd been a close call, but there was no mistaking the fact that she had met Mr. E head on and won! He'd even admitted it himself — *she had destroyed him*. Almost.

She turned to Nikki, who was dialling 999 and said, "Don't call the cops."

Nikki was confused, "No?"

"No…" Cherry felt suddenly exhilarated by her first taste of victory, "I have a much better idea. Let's have a drink to celebrate the demise of Mr. E instead!"

Nikki gaped at her, unable to believe that someone who'd been on the brink of being strangled to death could suggest celebrating. Surely she should call the police? But as she looked into Cherry's huge light-brown bambi eyes, she could see that she was deadly serious. *She really didn't want to call the cops*. Not for the first time, she wondered who Cherry really was, and what kind of person she must be to not want to call the police when someone had just tried to… to *murder* her. In a daze, she watched as Cherry came out of the kitchen with an ice-cold bottle of Bollinger, and poured the golden liquid into two long champagne flutes.

Hardly knowing what to say, she looked at the packed boxes that were all over Cherry's flat. "You're all ready?"

"Yep. Ready to start my new life."

For want of a better thing to do in, what seemed to her, a crazy situation, Nikki raised her glass. "To your new life."

The girls clinked glasses, and let the bitter-sweet, ice-cold liquid bubble down their throats.

The Conference

YAM SAT IN HIS MUM'S LIVING ROOM. It was late — about two a.m. — and his mum had gone to bed hours ago, leaving him with the house and the television control to himself, channel surfing to his heart's content and spooning as much of his favourite chocolate and strawberry ice cream down his throat as he wanted. He felt like a terrible weight had been lifted from his shoulders since he'd moved out of Babsy's. It was so refreshing to have a break from her sarcastic comments and all the digs she loved to make about him and Cherry. Now he was back on his own, he didn't even know why they'd got together in the first place. He guessed that it had just happened... But it had soon turned sour. They just weren't right for each other — you didn't have to be a rocket scientist to work that out.

Yam sighed contentedly. It certainly was nice to be back home, and his mum had been glad to see him. She hadn't said much, but he could tell how happy she was when she'd gone into the kitchen and returned with a huge plate, piled high with chicken, rice and peas and a thick steaming gravy.

Yam patted his stomach, his belly full. But underneath his joy to be finally free of Babsy, was a deep sadness that hung heavily in his heart and seemed like it was never going to go away. Without Babsy to occupy his mind, he thought about Cherry all the time. He missed her more than ever, and found himself asking the same questions over and over again. Why did she leave? When was she coming back? How was she going to feel about *The News* article?

Then something caught his eye causing him to abandon his thoughts. Freddie Famous' picture had flashed behind the newscaster that was on his mum's cable channel. Thinking he might find out something about Cherry, he hastily switched up the volume to hear the newscaster say, "Stay with us as we go live to Miami, where Freddie Famous has called an urgent and impromptu press conference!"

The camera cut to Freddie Famous, sitting at a long table which was covered with a white cloth. Father Wright and several key members from the Church of Divine Intervention were sitting on either side of him.

Freddie was holding court, addressing the reporters while the cameras flashed. "I've called this press conference in order to inform the public of some major changes I've made in my life."

A reporter butted in with a question."Freddie is it true that you and your wife Cherry Drop have separated?"

Freddie faced the cameras, "I would like to state clearly that Cherry Drop and I were never married. I repeat. We were never married. I know there was a rumour going round that we had a quickie wedding in Las Vegas, but that rumour was not true. I repeat, it was not true. Cherry and I have recently gone our separate ways, and we're no longer in a relationship... Now, I have called this conference in order to tell you—"

Another reporter broke in. "Is it true that Cherry is pregnant with your child, and is planning to raise the child in England as a single parent?"

Freddie shook his head. "No, that is not true. Cherry Drop is not, and never has been, pregnant with my child. What I'd like to tell you is I have—"

"Tell us about Cherry's affair with Michael Jackson. Is she recording an album at his ranch?"

Freddie stood up. If he wasn't a man of God now, he would have jumped over the table and kicked their butts. They were more interested in his broken relationship with Cherry, than his relationship with God!

"Look, I am *not* here today to talk about Cherry! She's no longer in my life! I am here to talk about GOD! As of now, I will be *dedicating my life to Him*. Because of this decision, *I want to urge the American public to stop buying my records*, as they are evil and will do no good! My former work is no longer relevant to the person you see before you today.

Friends, *I have seen the light*. I no longer want to lead my fans down the path of temptation and evil. With the help of my brothers and sisters from the Church of Divine Intervention, here in Miami, I'm going to record a gospel album. It will be a blessed platform from which I can spread the good word of God."

Freddie spread his arms high above his head and looked up to the heavens, making as if he were reaching up to the Lord Himself. A thousand flashes exploded as the cameramen rushed forward to get their shot. All over the world, thousands of press machines whirled into action and started to print the headline: 'FREDDIE FINDS GOD'. The American cable TV reporter turned to the cameras, her excitement at getting such a great scoop clearly visible, "Well, there you have it. This could well turn out to be the *revelation of the century*. The rude boy of hip-hop, Freddie Famous, has turned full circle and decided to give his life to God! You heard it first on CCN! This is Marilyn Bradley, live from Miami for CCN!"

Yam couldn't believe what he was hearing. Finally, his prayers had been answered. *Cherry had broken up with Freddie Famous and was back in London*. He felt a pinprick of hope, a possibility, that they were going to get back together. Surely this recent good news was a sign that he and Cherry were definitely meant to be... After all, as Cherry had said right from the start, it was fate.

His heart beat faster and faster as it filled with joy and he rushed to the telephone to call his baby. At last, she'd be able to explain everything to him and make all his pain go away. Yam's hand shook in his effort to dial her number as quickly as possible. He had no idea what he was going to say, but the way he was feeling, he would be just glad to hear her voice.

He heard a few muted clicks on the line, then the flat tone denoting an unobtainable number. His hopes momentarily shattered, Yam replaced the handset. Cherry's line was cut off. Maybe she didn't even live in Byrant Court anymore. As he contemplated what this might mean, Yam resolved to find Cherry. Even if he had to search the four corners of the earth to do so.

The following morning, Cherry woke up in her new flat in Camden Town. She stretched out like a cat in the middle of the huge four poster bed. Shafts of sunlight filtered through the skylight in the sloping ceiling of her bedroom. She looked through it to see a clear blue sky.

She jumped out of bed and walked barefoot across the reclaimed pine floorboards to her seventies-retro black and white-tiled ensuite bathroom. As she brushed her teeth, she realised she was still reeling from the newsflash that she'd seen on television last night. Could it really be true that Freddie had turned religious? Well it certainly made sense out of the letter he'd sent her...

A couple of days ago, she'd received a letter that had been redirected from her old address in Brixton. It was marked 'private' and had been mailed from the States using Fed-Ex. It was from Freddie, who'd painstakingly explained that he was making peace with all his 'demons' from the past and that he was writing to apologise for all the ordeals that he'd put her through. He hoped that one day she would find it in her heart to forgive him, and suggested that maybe it would help if she knew that he had managed to leave the 'path of evil and temptation' and that his soul had been 'saved'. He went on to write that he truly felt sorry for her having been cursed with such an evil disease, and to remember that if she put her trust in God, everything would be all right. He added that, if it was any consolation, he had no problems with her using the songs they'd recorded together, as he would have 'no use' for 'sounds of the devil' now. He'd concluded his letter with another apology for 'all the evil' that he'd inflicted her and had signed his name with a 'God Bless You sister'.

Cherry had thought that it all very strange, and had

wondered if it was a joke. But now she'd seen Freddie giving his press conference, it was all beginning to make sense.

She hastily threw on some crumpled jog bottoms and a T-shirt — she had to go out and buy the newspapers and get the full run down on what was happening with Freddie.

She pulled on her baseball cap, so as to remain incognito. Coming back to England had been weird. When she'd been with Freddie in Miami, she'd gotten used to all the attention they'd received. Freddie always seemed to attract a throng of adoring fans wherever he went. However, now she was alone and back in England, she'd found that she'd been attracting attention on her own. Of course, it had been nowhere near as ridiculous as that Freddie went through, but she did get the odd person coming up to her. Usually, they just asked for an autograph, or, more often than not, they asked if she could get Freddie's autograph for them. But occasionally, people had been abusive. It was always young girls, fans of Freddie's who hated to see anyone taking their idol away from them. One girl had even tried to hit her. Of course, Cherry was not too fond of this and had taken to wearing a 'disguise' in public. She soon discovered that if she dressed down, in a track suit or something, and covered her face with a baseball cap, nobody would recognise her.

Once she was in the newsagent's, she picked up a copy of each of the Sunday papers. The cockney newsagent took her change, gave her a wink and said, "Awight, love? Ya boyfriend's in there today!"

Cherry gave him a quick smile and hurried out of the shop. She didn't feel like being dragged into a conversation with her local newsagent about why Freddie had turned to God.

Once she was back in her fuschia-coloured living room, with a cup of coffee, she started to flick through the papers. As she ran through them, she realised that it was true. All the newspapers were confirming what she had seen on TV.

Freddie really was dedicating his life to God and he giving up his career in hip-hop to make a gospel album.

Suddenly her heart stopped. On the front cover of *The News*, there was one of the publicity photos that she'd taken for Black Knight Productions earlier in the year, and two small headshots of Babsy and Yam. The headline read : 'THE REAL REASON WHY FREDDIE HAS TURNED TO GOD!' and underneath it in smaller print it said, *'Turn to the centre pages to find out the real reason behind Freddie's amazing change of heart!'*

Her heart started to race as she turned the pages. Inside she saw a full-length colour photo of Babsy, scantily dressed in some sort of candyfloss-pink lacy lingerie. The caption above her read 'ME AND MY BEST FRIEND CHERRY'. The following article went on to say, 'Barbara Jacobs was the girl responsible for matchmaking the former love birds, Freddie Famous and Cherry Drop, before Freddie turned to God! Read all about how she and Cherry used to reek havoc in London's top West End clubs in their hell-raising wild-child days!

Before running off to Miami with Freddie to live it up in the lap of luxury, sexy stunner Cherry Drop, and her saucy galpal Barbara were going through young men like they were hot dinners, at Touchdown — a naughty nightspot in the heart of London...

Cherry could hardly believe what she was reading. What a load of bull! She might have guessed Babsy would sell her out just to make a fast buck.

She turned to the opposite page and her heart sank as she saw a photograph of Yam in some dingy London street, holding his baseball cap in his hands, and looking close to tears. The caption read: 'THE DAY THAT FREDDIE'S GIRL BROKE MY HEART'

With growing horror, she read the accompanying text: 'No-one could have been more heartbroken than Kenneth Brown, also known as DJ Yam, when his former fiancée, Cherry Drop, ran off and left him for a life of fame and fortune with Freddie Famous'.

Fiancée?!! Cherry read on, unable to tear herself away from *The News'* sordid pages. The article rambled on and on about how she and Yam were supposed to be getting married, but she'd dumped him when Freddie Famous had promised to help her career. It finished with a long quote from Yam: "It didn't surprise me to hear that Freddie Famous turned to religion when Cherry left him. She's an amazing girl, who was always very affectionate and loving. She had an incredibly high sex drive, and used to drive me crazy with all her night kinky and passionate demands for love making. After losing a lover like her, any man would be prepared to end his own life, never mind turn to God! I know I have found it virtually impossible to get over her. If it wasn't for the fact that I've found love with Babsy, I might have had a nervous break down. I have heard that Cherry is pregnant with Freddie's baby now, and can only wish her all the best." Then the reporter concluded, 'DJ Yam hung his head as he went on to say, "I still miss her though. My life has been missing a little bit of sunshine now that Cherry is no longer in it." So there you have it readers — the inside story on Cherry Drop, the real reason why Freddie Famous has turned to religion. Remember, you read it here first, in the nation's number one Sunday newspaper — *The News* — pages of fun for all the family!'

Cherry dropped the paper in shock. She felt like her whole world was caving in on her. Who would have thought that Babsy and Yam would go to *The News* and tell them a pack of lies? *And who would have thought they'd be in a relationship?*

As she pictured Babsy and Yam making love, she felt like being sick. Of course, she'd suspected that Yam might have found someone else, but her best friend…? How could he have stooped so low? How could *she* have stooped so low?

She wondered how soon it had all happened after she'd left for Miami. She'd only been away a few weeks, so they must have got together pretty fast. At least she now knew why Babsy hadn't returned any of her calls. Cherry literally cringed with embarrassment as she recalled all the intimate details that Yam had gone into in the article. How could he have dished the dirt on her like that, blabbing about their sex life to the entire nation? As she thought about it, Cherry began to consider the much wider implications of the article. Would B.U.L. want to terminate her recording contract after they read the sleazy story Babsy and Yam had sold to the press? They might say that the public would no longer be able to take her seriously as an artist, that they'd dismiss her as a talentless bimbo. They could argue that the whole thing would affect her future record sales.

Cherry didn't know what she would do if this fucked-up her deal. Everything she had worked for, all the sacrifices she had made, were tied up in her deal with B.U.L. If they pulled the plug on her now, her plan would be set back to square one. She'd find herself back where she'd started: penniless, alone and on the streets.

With growing desperation, she started to try and think of away to secure her future and avoid any devastation the weekend's events might reek on her career.

Nikki Stixx sat in her office and watched the video that everyone at B.U.L. was talking about. It was a tape of the press conference that Freddie Famous had given over the weekend in Miami. She stared at the screen with a mixture of horror and disbelief as Freddie urged his fans to stop buying his records on worldwide television. Nobody at the company had known anything about it — until, of course, it was broadcast on worldwide network and cable television.

The whole of B.U.L. was in pandemonium. Freddie Famous was making history within the recording industry. When she'd got to her office, the whole building had been in chaos, as everyone scrambled to meet the demands that were the consequences of Freddie's conference. The head of B.U.L. in New York, Dick Francis, had woken her up at six a.m. that morning to ask her about the situation. He'd wanted to know whether or not the break-up between Freddie and Cherry had had anything to do with Freddie's decision to dedicate his life to God. Since Nikki had been the one who'd signed Cherry, Dick made it quite clear that it was up to her to find out, and report any information back to him. Naturally, Nikki was very keen to uncover anything she could; if she fell in favour with Dick Francis, it would give her a lot of clout, *and make her a major player at B.U.L.*

With this in mind, she dialled Cherry's new telephone number. "Hi Cherry, how are you?"

"Okay." Cherry was apprehensive, Nikki was being all sweetness and light, but she knew she must have heard about Freddie.

"Have you heard the news?"

"Yeah."

"What do you think about it all?"

"I think it's… bizarre."

Nikki laughed. "You can say that again! He's got the whole company up in arms, everyone's going nuts over here this morning…! Have *you* any idea why Freddie has decided to turn to this religious crap?"

Cherry deliberated momentarily over whether to tell Nikki about the ruse she'd played on Freddie. But, she could see no real reason why B.U.L. should be aware of that particular piece of information, so she played her cards close to her chest. "No."

Nikki sensed she was hiding something. "Oh… it's just that I remember how *desperate* you were to get out of Miami that day you called me for a ticket, and I was wondering what made you want to leave so quickly. Is there something you're not telling me, Cherry? Did something happen between you and Freddie that I don't know about?"

Cherry stuck to her guns, "Oh come on Nikki, I think we're close enough now to not have any secrets with each other."

Nikki persisted, "Don't think I'm being nosy darling —

you know that normally I wouldn't pry into your private affairs like this. It's just that the head of B.U.L. called me first thing this morning from New York. They've got the article that was in *The News*, Cherry, and they want to know if there's any truth in it."

Cherry felt her throat go dry. She was genuinely worried now. Nikki was confirming her worst fears; maybe this whole Freddie thing really was going to affect her deal with B.U.L.

She kept her tone light. "Look Nikki, what I told you is the truth. Me and Freddie split up because I wanted to spend more time concentrating on my music. You know how difficult it is to combine a relationship and a career — people break up under that kind of pressure all the time. I haven't spoken to Freddie since I left Miami, so I don't know anything more about this whole thing than you do. If the suits in New York want to know why Freddie has turned to God, why don't they ask him themselves?"

Nikki gave up. She obviously wasn't going to gain any insights from Cherry. "Okay, you don't need to get defensive. I was only asking because nobody can understand Freddie's crazy behaviour. As it happens, this whole thing has turned out to be surprisingly profitable for us. People are going out in *droves* to buy what's being dubbed as 'Freddie's last ever album'. That is, before he does this gospel thing that he's talking about. We're selling more of Freddie's records than ever, in fact it's probably going to go down as the fastest selling record in history! Look, I know that this might be bad timing, but have you decided whether or not you want to use the songs that Freddie wrote for you?"

Waves of relief resonated throughout Cherry's entire being. *Maybe everything was all going to be all right after all.* She couldn't wait to tell Nikki the good news. "Actually, yes I have, you'll be glad to know that I'll be using every single song that I recorded with Freddie on my album!"

Nikki was elated, "That's great! If your album sells half

as much as Freddie's we're going to be very *very* successful! And his decision to turn to God can only help the sales of your album as much as it's helping his!"

However, Cherry still had doubts. "But... have you read *The News*? Don't you think that the suits are gonna worry that it might damage my credibility?"

Nikki laughed, "Are you joking? Darling, now's the time to realise that there is *no* such thing as bad publicity! With the kind of coverage we're gonna get off the back of this, you'll be in every magazine and on every television station in the world! It's gonna be HUGE Which reminds me — I didn't tell you about the rest of the conversation I had with Dick Francis. Apparently, he's already heard some of the stuff you've recorded with Freddie, and he thinks it's awesome. He wants your album to be top priority in every B.U.L. territory. So we've gotta start recording right away if we want an album finished and a single out before the end of the year!"

By the time Cherry had finished talking to Nikki, her whole body was covered in goose bumps. This was it. She finally felt certain that it was really going to happen.

phyllis blunt

The Reunion

IT HAD TAKEN HIM LESS THAN A WEEK to track her down. Earl's baby mother, Monica, worked at the telephone company, and it didn't take her long to get Cherry's phone number and address. And now he was standing outside her front door.

Yam looked up and saw that the lights were on. Which meant that she was in.

But what if she wouldn't speak to him after the article in *The News*? Yam felt the tears begin to prick once again at his eyeballs, as he remembered what Dave Armstrong had chronicled for the nation. How he'd covered every sordid detail, in sensationalist tabloid fashion. Paragraph upon paragraph of pure... *drivel*. Surely Cherry must hate him now! Even if, by some miracle, she did still love him — how could she ever forgive him for what he'd done?

He had to be crazy coming over here, thinking she was going welcome him back into her arms. But, maybe, if she knew that he had been against it all along, that he'd even refused to take any payment for it, that it had been Babsy who'd instigated the whole thing...

The thought of Babsy made him moan out loud. *How could he have been so stupid?* Not only did he go and sell Cherry's story, but he'd slept with her friend as well.

That settled it, if he really thought she would forgive him after everything he'd done, he *was* crazy! He should just go home and try to get over the whole thing.

He turned and started to walk away from the door. But he knew that it was no good. He felt that if he didn't at least try to make a go of it with Cherry, or at the very least explain what had happened, then life just wouldn't be worth living.

He walked back to the door and pressed the intercom.

"Hello?"

A flood of emotion came over Yam as he heard her sweet voice. His baby! It had been so long, that he'd almost forgotten how good she sounded.

"Cherry. It's me."

Cherry felt her heart stop. She'd recognise that voice anywhere. It was Yam. *Could Mr. E have sent him to track her down?* No, there was no way that Yam would be in cahoots with Mr. E. Still, you couldn't be too careful, she'd never have dreamed he could sell her story to the press either.

Whilst she was going over the possibilities, Yam was beginning to wonder if he'd just dreamed that he had heard her voice. The seconds ticked by, and still there was no reply from the intercom speaker.

He buzzed again, "Cherry it's me — Yam!"

"What do you want?"

Yam flinched, her voice was so cold. Still, he'd never expected a welcome party. "I just want to speak to you."

Silence.

"Please, just for five minutes."

Further silence.

Yam persisted, "I promise I won't take up too much of your time. I just want to explain what's happened."

"I'm not interested in your explanations Yam."

Yam felt himself growing desperate. He *had* to persuade her to hear him out. Otherwise he swore he would go mad. He couldn't hold back a small sob as he pleaded at the intercom, "Please Cherry, I beg you. *Please.* I'll only be a minute, I swear. I just want you to know the truth about what's happened that's all. And if you never want to see me again, I promise I'll leave you alone forever. *But please let me say my piece.* Just five minutes baby…"

As Cherry listened, she felt increasingly sure that his coming had nothing to do with Mr. E. Yam was never that good an actor.

"Okay, you can come up. But only for five minutes."

Yam didn't need to be told twice, and he pushed through the door before she could change her mind.

He must have rehearsed his piece a million times, but standing in front of her, face to face, words failed him.

Cherry, on the other hand, didn't waste time. "Well?"

Yam stared at his feet. He hadn't anticipated the whirl of confusion that had overtaken his brain the moment he looked once again into her huge amber-coloured eyes.

"Well I... er, I..."

Cherry felt herself growing impatient. "Look Yam, you begged me to let you come up so that you could say your piece. Don't tell me now you're here you haven't got anything to say. Or were you lying... just like you lied in that newspaper article?"

Yam was utterly speechless. How could he say his piece when all he wanted to do was throw himself at her feet and declare his undying love? *Didn't she realise how she made him feel?* He felt like was falling apart into a million tiny little pieces.

Cherry had just about had enough. She had too much to do without wasting time on an backstabber like Yam. "Look your five minutes are up, I think you'd better go."

"No!" The thought of having to leave shook Yam out of his reverie. "Cherry, I... I just want you to know that all that shit in the newspaper had nothing to do with me. I swear, I did *everything* within my power to stop it!"

Cherry wasn't buying it for a second. "Oh really? Was that before or *after* you did the photographs?"

"Before...! I mean after! I mean *both*!" Yam shook his head. It wasn't coming out the way he'd intended it to. He tried to make himself clear. "Look I had no idea that they were gonna write what they did. It was pure lies!"

"Oh, so you *didn't* start sleeping with my friend the minute my back was turned?"

Yam stared dejectedly at the floor. She had a point. And it was the one point that he couldn't justify.

Cherry's voice was impatient, "I think you'd better just leave, I really don't wanna hear any of this crap!"

"No! *Please* Cherry. I know I've made some terrible mistakes, ones that I'm sure you'll never forgive me for. But isn't there a way we can work this out? I... I still love you

Cherry… More than I've ever loved anyone in my whole life. And I swear that if you don't take me back, I'll never love anyone again."

Cherry looked at him in disgust. "Do you really think that after you've dragged my name through the mud in a national paper, not to mention telling the whole world about our sex lives *and* fucking my mate into the bargain — that you can really just show up here, say you're sorry, tell me you love me, and *I'm gonna turn round and forgive you?!* You must be stark raving mad! Get out Yam!"

"Oh no!" Yam felt himself fall to his knees. He clasped his hands in front of him as he looked up at Cherry and begged. "Please don't turn me away Cherry. I'll make it up to you. I promise!"

"Get the fuck out of here Yam!"

Yam felt all his sense of decorum fly out of the window. Tears were streaming unabashedly down his face. "But… *I love you* Cherry. Please let me back into your life!"

Now Cherry had definitely had enough. If she'd known that it would come to this, there was no way that she would have let him into her flat. "Get out, before I call the police."

Yam heard himself wail, "No! Please! Take me back Cherry! *I'll do anything.* I swear, I'll lay down my life if only you'd give me one more chance!"

Cherry's ears pricked, at the sound of the word 'anything'. "Stop talkin' shit! A bastard like you wouldn't even walk to the end of the street for me!"

Yam looked her and gasped, "I would! I'd do *anything.* Just name it Cherry!"

Cherry hesitated, and looked him in the eye, "Do you really mean that? You'd do *anything* I asked you to?"

Through his pain, Yam felt a faint glimmer of hope, a minute chance that Cherry might take him back after all. "Of *course*! Just tell me what I have to do."

Cherry's mind was working overtime, she'd just thought of a way to tie up all the loose ends, and complete her plan.

"Well, there might be just one thing that you could do…"

The Revenge

DELROY CARRINGTON SAT ON THE CLOSED lid of his toilet, fully dressed in his favourite Savile Row charcoal-grey suit, at his home in Kensington. Slowly, he fingered the cold hard steel of his trusty old Colt .45, as he turned it round and round in his hands. On the floor by his feet, an open suitcase holding half a million pounds in cash blinked back at him.

He was about to make the biggest decision he'd ever had to make in his entire life. This was it. He'd come to the final crossroad. And he had two choices. Either he was going to take the money that sat at his feet and run off somewhere... *anywhere*... in the hope that he could somehow start again. Or he was going to die. He was going to end his life forever.

And the way he was feeling at the moment, the balance was firmly weighted on the side of death.

Delroy thought about his constituency and, for the first time ever, he really didn't care. Even though he had worked his whole life and sweated blood and tears to achieve his level of political success... *he really really didn't care any more*. He was now convinced that, when you truly looked at things — not from a financial, or a social point of view, but on a deeper, *spiritual* level — things like having a seat at Westminster really didn't matter.

Delroy laughed out loud at the irony of it. After all he'd been through, who would have thought his final analysis would be that none of it really mattered anyway? So, in effect all those degrees and honours he'd obtained, ultimately signified nothing. One big, huge, enormous *nothing*. It was just mankind's way of trying to fill the... *emptiness* of existence with something they could consider purposeful and worthwhile.

He wondered how many men, in the face of death, would conclude that their lives had meant nothing.

His thoughts turned to Bernice and their two daughters.

Even his wife meant nothing to him now; he'd come to accept that. All these years, he'd brainwashed himself into thinking that he had loved Bernice more than any woman on earth. Now he realised that he'd just been fooling himself. How foolhardy he'd been to have cherished security, when life was really all about chaos and disorder. Lies and deceit. Even the children... He was sure his daughters would go on to live their meaningless lives without him, and that their inevitable end — like that every living thing on the planet — would be death.

Which was what he was facing now.

And he was *glad*. For death would put an end to the hardship, and the struggle, to the sorrow and the sadness, to the deep, everlasting, unbearable pain that he had come to call life.

Delroy Carrington looked into the barrel of his Colt .45 and felt joyous at the thought of the simple peace that it was about to bring him.

Mr. E drove his black Mercedes through the night, his eyes grimly focused on the road ahead. He had checked out Cherry's contract, and the bitch was right — it was not legal. Any case he might have had against Cherry would be thrown out of every court in the land.

Which meant that he was completely in the shit.

Big Red wasn't going to give him another chance to get the hundred grand. Next time, *that noose was going to tighten and squeeze every last breath out of his body*. Mr. E fingered the Walther PPK in the inside breast pocket of his pea-green Armani overcoat. He only had one chance left to save Black Knight Productions and all its affiliated companies, and that one chance was riding solely on the shoulders of Delroy Carrington.

He parked his car two streets away from Delroy's house, and pulled a Fedora hat low over his eyes as he skulked incognito across the affluent Kensington neighbourhood to the front gate. He stole around the side of the building until he came to a back entrance. Taking out a huge bunch of 'master keys', he set about picking the lock, a task he completed in a matter of minutes.

Once inside, Mr. E started to silently comb the house in search of Delroy and his family. The place was cloaked in darkness, and Mr. E had to quickly flick his torch into the corners of each room to keep his bearings. He carefully went through every floor, but came across no-one, nor any sign of recent activity.

After about half an hour of searching he stood in what looked like the master bedroom, ready to give up. There was no hope now. Delroy and his family had obviously gone away, probably to their house in the country.

If Mr. E didn't have so much riding on the guy, he would have laughed at the irony of it. The whole scenario — him finally breaking into Delroy's house, only to find that, for once, he really was 'out of town' — fitted in perfectly with the way his luck was going at the moment Maybe Black Knight Productions, just wasn't meant to be...

It was at that point that he noticed a tiny chink of golden light. Mr. E flashed his torch in its direction to discover that it glowed from around the edges of a door that was set discreetly into the back wall. Silently, he crept across the room and opened it.

Delroy jumped and looked up to see Mr. Knight's snarling features leering down at him. *So he had finally caught up with him.* How bitter-sweet — that Mr. Knight, of all people, should be there to witness his final hour! Any doubts he might have had about ending his life had suddenly vanished. It was a sign. Mr. Knight would be the perfect person to finish him off.

With a trembling hand, he lifted his pistol. "So, you've finally come for me have you? Well let's not waste any time. Take this."

Mr. E, alias Mr. Knight, looked in horror as he saw Delroy Carrington sitting on the toilet, fully clothed and waving a gun at him. *How could Delroy have known that he was coming for him tonight*? He spoke in the manner one might use to calm a wild animal. "Now, Delroy, let's not be too hasty…"

Delroy couldn't believe his ears, Mr. Knight, his worse enemy, was trying to convince him out of committing suicide! He held the gun out. "Come on, Knight, this is your chance. It's time to end all this crap!"

He couldn't deny it, Mr. E was scared shitless. He should have anticipated this… but how was he to know that Delroy would be waiting for him, sitting on a toilet with a gun? *Sitting on a toilet*, Mr. E grimaced inwardly. Delroy might be a politician, but he had no class. What kind of schmuck tried to murder someone whilst sitting on a shit-bowl?

Mr. E attempted a disarming smile. "Now look, there's no need for guns. I only came here to have a lickle chat wid you, and… and to tell you that I won't be troublin' you for any more change. So we can put all of our… our 'differences' behind us and consider the whole matter as being finished an' done with."

Delroy laughed high and loud, like a madman in an asylum. "You're a bit late Mr. Knight. I'm not in the mood for *'chats'*. I know that you came here to get the money! Although, I must say, Knight, you have impeccable timing. How on earth did you know I'd withdrawn it?"

For the first time since he'd entered the room, Mr. E noticed the suitcase at Delroy's feet. He peered over its open lid to see that it was filled to the brim with neat wads of crisp fifty-pound notes. They smelled so new, he could almost taste them. His mouth began to water as the answer to all his prayers stared him in the face. Mountains and mountains of green stuff, the one thing that he needed more than anything else in the world. It was a Godsend! He had no idea why Delroy was sitting on the john, waiting to kill him with a pile of money nestling at his feet, and he wasn't about to ask any questions either. With that kind of cash, he could pay off Big Red in an instant! On the other hand —

fuck Big Red — with that much cash he could leave the country forever! It was amazing how easily you could cover your tracks when they were paved with gold. He could start again, go to America... Jamaica... anywhere he fuckin' wanted to!

Delroy got tired of waiting for a response."Why the delay Knight? I know you want to shoot me, just like you shot poor Tootsie all those years ago."

Mr. E kept his back against the door, and wondered how he would be able to get away fast enough before Delroy caught him with a bullet. The suitcase full of money... *sizzled...* on the floor in front of him.

He decided to play for time. "Well, actually Delroy, there's something I haffe tell yuh 'bout dat." Nervously, he cleared his throat, and forced a smile. "Tootsie isn't really dead. She never was. It was just a lickle game that I played on you in order to collect some change over the years!"

"What?" Delroy tried to digest what Mr. E had just told him.

Jolly, like he was sharing a great joke with one of his closest friends, Mr. E delivered his good news. "Tootsie is alive Delroy!"

Delroy shook his head in disbelief, as he tried to digest what he'd just heard. "You're telling me that... all these years... *Tootsie has been alive?* But I saw her... all that blood! The hole in her head! The... the gun!"

Mr. E shook his head and attempted to keep up his jovial facade, all the while keeping one eye on the cash that was screaming up at him from the suitcase on the floor. "It was all just make-up and play acting, Del. Just like in the movies!"

Delroy paused for a moment, as he let the magnitude of what he'd just heard sink in, before letting out a high-pitched madman's laugh. "You mean to tell me that *all* these years you've been blackmailing me, it was all over *nothing?*" Delroy continued to roar with laughter, "Well isn't that just *perfect.* I was just thinking that life was one big meaningless nothing, and you've just come along and proved it!"

Thinking that Delroy must have gone stark raving mad, Mr. E nodded and kept his now fireproof grin in place, in a continued effort to show that it had all just been in fun.

Delroy tossed his gun at Mr. E's feet. His expression was deadly serious as he said, "Well that doesn't change a thing. If anything it just makes me even more determined to go through with it. Kill me anyway Knight."

Mr. E stared wide-eyed at the gun at his feet, Delroy really had gone... *crazy*. What was he thinking of — throwing away his only hope of survival? Nobody could be that stupid, surely? It had to be part of some kind of trap. *Had Delroy somehow set some kind of trap for him*?

But it was the break that he'd been praying for. Mr. E wasted no time in picking up the gun and pointing it at Delroy. Genuinely confused, he loosened his collar and said, "Now, what the fuck is going on?"

Delroy looked at Mr. E like he was a retard, "What do you mean, what's going on? I'm waiting for you to kill me, *that's what's going on*."

"What? You *want* me to kill you?"

Delroy couldn't believe it. This chap made a monkey look like Albert Einstein. His voice dripped with sarcasm. "Are you always this on-the-ball Knight?"

Mr. E kept the gun pointed at Carrington. "But why would you want me to kill you?"

Delroy looked at Mr. E like he was a very dim child. "Because I want to die, obviously!"

"But *why* would you want to die?"

Delroy looked incredulously at Mr. E. "Haven't you heard?"

Mr. E was getting frustrated, "Heard what?"

"It's all over. My constituency, my bid for the leadership of the Liberal Democrats. Everything."

"Whaddya mean it's all over?"

Delroy started to lose his patience. "Good God, man. Where have you been? Haven't you read the papers? I lost the election — my career, everything I've ever worked for! My wife has left me. She's taken the children and ran off with another man, gone to live in Nigeria with him. She's been having an... an affair with this man for years. She's taken everything... all my money — she completely remortgaged the house, and cleaned every penny out of our joint savings account. She even took the cars! I'm ruined Knight... I have nothing left, apart from the remains of my constituency fund sitting here in this suitcase. And now I'm even going to lose thanks to your unscheduled arrival!" He let his head drop into his hands and started weeping.

"It's all so damned hopeless. I can't bear it anymore! How am I supposed to go on? You've *got* to kill me Knight. Put me out of my misery!"

He went over to where Knight was standing and took hold of the hand in which Mr. E was the gun. Then he sank to his knees and pointed the barrel to his head. With tears streaming down his face, he begged, "You *have* to help me! *Please* pull the trigger. I can't take it any more!"

Unbelievable. If it had all been in a movie, Mr. E would have laughed. Not only was Delroy *begging* him to shoot him, he was practically handing him a suitcase full of cash at the same time. There must be a God up there somewhere. Even though he'd had his share of problems, he had to admit that he was the luckiest nigga alive.

His finger itched at the trigger, as he prepared to squeeze it and blast away Delroy Carrington forever. He was about to become a very rich man.

It was at that point that he felt the sharp edge of cold, hard steel at the back of his neck, and a voice say, "What the fuck is going on?"

Mr. E went ice-cold. *So it was a trap after all*. He knew that the whole thing was just too good to be true. He stayed silent and kept his gun pointed at Delroy's forehead until the voice said, "I think you'd better drop that gun, Mr. E."

Mr. E dropped the pistol. Suddenly, Delroy grabbed his trouser legs and started screaming, "For God's sake, just kill me! Why are you torturing me like this? Wasn't it enough that you… that you *hounded* me all my life? Do you have to go on torturing me, even in my death? Can't you just end it?"

He fell sobbing at Mr. E's feet, which caused Mr. E to stumble back. As he did so, he felt the gun at the back of his head slide to the right. It was his chance: his attacker had slipped his guard! Without missing a beat, Mr. E reached behind his head and tried to grab the weapon. He cursed the six inches of steel as it slid fleetingly into his hands and slipped icily through his grasp. But his attacker lost his footing and stumbled to the right. Mr. E swirled round to see a man, all dressed in black with a balaclava an his head. The only visible part of him was a pair of dark-brown eyes glinting through the slit.

The panic in the man's voice was clearly audible as he steadied himself and said,

"That's enough, Mr. E. If you don't stop… If you don't stop fucking around, I'll kill you right now."

Delroy Carrington lifted himself up and kneeled on his hunches. Tears were still streaming from his eyes, and he rubbed his aching head in frustration. The irony of it! Here he was in a room with two men, and at least two guns, and he was finding it impossible to get killed. He was even failing at death!

He turned to faced the masked attacker. "Look, I don't know who the hell you are, but would you mind just blasting one of those bullets through my skull, before I go stark raving… *mad*! The suitcase by the toilet holds half a million pounds in cash, and it can be all yours if you would just kindly pull the trigger…"

Behind the Balaclava, the attacker's eyes widened. "Oh my God — you're Delroy Carrington!"

Mr. E looked on in amazement. What kind of fool-fool trap was this? First Delroy was begging the other guy to kill him, and then the attacker was greeting him like a fan. It was crazy. There was no way that this guy could be in cahoots with Delroy Carrington. *Or could the whole performance just be another part of their trap*?

The masked attacker kept talking, "I don't understand. What have you got to do with Mr. E?"

Now Mr. E was certain. Something definitely wasn't right. This guy didn't seem to have a clue what was going on. If the attacker had been an accomplice of Delroy's, he would have been referring to him as Mr. Knight, not Mr. E. So whoever had sent this... *buffoon*... had to know him as Mr. E. Big Red wouldn't have sent such an idiot along to get rid of him, he would have sent Mr. Ice, or Little Stevie-Jack-Shit.

The attacker was still babbling on. "Why would Mr. E want to kill you? Who does that money belong to?"

Delroy was completely ignoring him. Seemingly having given up on any hope of ending his life, he had contented himself to bury his head in his hands, his body shuddering up and down to his loud and piercing sobs. Mr. E, however was hanging onto his every word. There was something... familiar about this guy... He was certain that he'd heard his voice... *somewhere*... before.

He moved forward an inch and said, "Listen, maybe we can come to some sort of an arrangement, I—"

"Don't move, or I'll shoot!"

As the attacker yelled, the penny dropped in Mr. E's skull like a dead-weight. It was Yam! *The stupid muthafucka in the balaclava was Yam!* But how could it be? What possible reason would Yam have to be pointing a gun at him?

He inched forward again, "Yam?"

Nothing.

"Yam, is that *you* under that hat?"

Still nothing, but the way the attacker's eyes darted about behind the slit made him feel he was on the right track.

"Why are you pointing a gun at me, Yam?"

The voice was clearly fearful now. "Stay back!"

That was it! It was *definitely* Yam! He would recognise

that voice anywhere! "Yam! Have you gone mad?!! What has possessed you to make yuh so fool-fool that you would try and kill your old spar Mr. E?"

"You can cut the 'old spar' routine Mr. E — you're no friend of mine. Cherry's told me all about you, and all the evil shit that you've done to her!"

Cherry! So it was Cherry who'd sent him! He might have guessed that rude gyal would be behind this! But why would she want him dead? *Was the deal really so important to her that she would want to kill him for it*? Mind you, he'd always known the bitch was crazy…

"So it's *Cherry* that's gone an' put this fool-fool idea inna yuh head!"

"Maybe. We're back together and, once I've taken care of you, we're gonna get married. And we'll never be apart again!"

Mr. E was really confused now. The whole thing wasn't making any sense. "What are you talking about Yam? What's you and Cherry getting married got to do with *killing me*?"

Yam gulped. When Cherry had told him what she wanted him to do, his first thought had been that she was absolutely crazy. But then she'd come clean with him… She'd given him the missing pieces of the puzzle that made her such a mystery. Tears pricked at his eyes when he thought of how he'd cradled her in his arms, when she'd been crying her heart out. He still couldn't believe what she'd gone through. Or who'd put her through it.

All of his baby's pain and misery was down to one man, and one man only: Mr. E.

He felt pure rage surge back into his consciousness. How could Mr. E have done such things to his girl? How could anyone be so… *sick*… And now he was acting all innocent, like he didn't know *exactly* what was goin' on! Well those days of lies and deceit were over. Yam was going to give him what he deserved. He was going to become his retribution.

He looked back at Mr. E with eyes of one hundred

percent hate and said, "Because while you're still alive, she can never commit to a normal relationship. She'll *never* be able to experience love. The only way she can get over all the shit that you put her through — the only way *I* can get over all the shit you put her through — is if you are no longer on this planet!"

"And so she's sent you to do her dirty work!"

"No. *I* want to do this. I love Cherry like I've never loved anyone before, and anybody that harms her has harmed me. You *deserve* to die for what you did to my baby!"

Mr. E was dumfounded. Yam was off his head! He was talking like a madman! "Whaddaya mean — what *I've* done to your baby!!? I haven't done shit to her! She's been fillin' you lovesick head with pure rubbish! Yam, you know me — have you ever seen or heard of me harming a living soul in my life? Cherry's lying!"

"Bullshit!"

"Oh yeah? Well, did she tell you about the deal that she's signed with B.U.L. Records?"

"What?"

"Oh, so she forgot to mention that little detail did she? How convenient! She's already signed the deal, Yam. She did it with Nikki Stixx last week! How can you two run off and get married if she's supposed to be recording an album for B.U.L. Records?"

Yam faltered. This was news to him. If what Mr. E was saying was true, then it was a pretty big thing for Cherry not to tell him. Could she really have signed the deal? Why hadn't she told him about it? But... the way she'd cried in his arms and and... *everything*.There was no way that what Mr. E was saying could be true.

He stood his ground."I don't believe you."

Mr. E was adamant, "I swear to God it's true! Why d'ya think she's moved all of a sudden? I bet her new place is a lot phatter than that run-down council flat she used to live in!"

Yam thought about Cherry's new flat — the designer

furniture, the prime location — and Mr. E's words began to slowly make sense. She *did* seem to be living large all of a sudden. He'd bet she couldn't afford that kind of lifestyle on her giro. He grasped for a reason — anything that would make it possible that Mr. E was lying. Anything that would show that Cherry wasn't using him all over again…

But it didn't change what Mr. E had done to his baby…"You still did what you did! Why would she want me to kill you for any other reason than you abused her?"

Mr. E took another step forward, another inch closer to the gun that Yam was pointing at him. It was all beginning to make sense to him now. His voice was low and quiet. "Remember that contract I got her to sign back at the studio? The same contract I got all you guys to sign? Well that piece of paper means that every penny she ever earns has to go to me first — because, as you know, I'm the one who looks after the money. But she doesn't want the money to go to me first. You wanna know why? *She wants to keep it all for herself.*" Seeing that Yam was drinking in his every word, he took a chance and inched a little closer, saying, "Y'see, She's just signed a deal, the same deal that I negotiated on behalf of all of us, for at least quarter of a million pounds. *And she wants to make sure that none of us sees a penny of it.* Every single member of Black Knight Productions has been cut out of the deal — including you. Of course, when I found out about this, I paid her a visit, made it quite clear that she wouldn't be seeing a red cent of it, because of the way she tried to cut the deal behind our backs. Can't you see she's just using you Yam? The same way she's used all of us!"

Yam gasped for breath. He felt like he was going to faint. Could it really be true? Could Cherry still be taking him for a mug? But she had cried… she'd told him all those… *things*… told him that she loved him.

Mr. E was face to face with him now. And he could see that Yam wasn't going to go through with it. There were too many doubts.

Yam slid off his balaclava and stared forlornly at Mr. E.

He felt like he was dying. He felt like Mr. E had struck him down dead with his revelations.

Mr. E took hold of the gun.

Carrington was still crouched down, whimpering into his hands.

"Delroy."

At the sound of his name, Delroy Carrington looked up, and Mr. E shot him twice in the head.

Yam froze to the spot in terror. Did he really see what he just saw? *Did he really see Mr. E take his gun from his hands and shoot someone dead?* And that someone was not just any old body, it was Delroy Carrington, the distinguished and highly renowned politician. There was blood everywhere.

"Oh my God! What have you done?!"

Mr. E moved quickly, "Shut the fuck up, Yam, and help me move the body."

"What?"

"Help me move the body! We've gotta get rid of Carrington, before we get the money."

Yam could hardly believe what he was hearing. He had just witnessed Mr. E perform cold-blooded murder, and now he was asking him to help, to be an accomplice. "Are you mad?"

Mr. E looked at Yam like he was about to ask him the very same question. "Have you seen that suitcase? There must be a least half a million there in cash!"

Yam still couldn't believe it. "So, not only are you asking me to be an accomplice to murder, you're also asking me to help you steal the dead man's money!"

"Yeah... *And*? Of course, you can't have the main bulk of the cash, but I'll give you some dollars for what you've, er... what you've been through today. Call it a 'helpers fee', or you could call it hush money — hell, you can call it what the fuck you like. Just fix up yuhself quick, I don't want Delroy's neighbour's to start wondering whether they heard gun shot just now, and finding us here at the scene of the crime."

Yam looked at Mr. E and realised Cherry was right: the guy was truly evil. He was the devil incarnate.

"I'm calling the police."

"Are you crazy!?"

"Look, I'm not about to be involved in *any* of this. You're a complete mad man!" Yam turned to get out of the bathroom and find a telephone.

Mr. E could hardly believe what he was hearing. Yam was quite probably the most stupidest man on earth if he thought that he, Mr. E, was just going to stand there whilst he turned him in to the police! Grabbing Delroy's gun from the floor, he rushed up to Yam and slammed it as hard as he could against the back of his skull.

As the pain reverberated through his brain, Yam felt himself go limp, and the whole world went black.

After he'd dropped, Mr. E gave him another blow, just to make sure that he was unconscious. He turned back towards Delroy, and prepared to get his hands on the suitcase full of readies. He'd deal with Yam later.

Then a strange sound kept popping through his thoughts, he wasn't sure, but he could swear that he could hear the sound of clapping.

Clap clap clap clap clap. "That was a great performance, Mr. E. Or should I call I call you Mr. Knight? Or maybe I should just call you 'The Muthafucka That Ruined My Life!'"

Mr. E turned round. He knew this voice only too well.

Cherry was holding a Magnum and she was pointing it right at him. His eyes darted around the room as he tried to locate his piece.

"Don't even think about moving, you stupid piece of shit. I'm not Yam. I won't think twice about blowing your fucking brains out. In fact that's exactly what I came here for."

She glanced at Yam's unconscious body. "Nice to see that if you want to do a job properly, you've gotta do it yourself."

Mr. E looked her in the eye. He had to get out of there,

quick, with the suitcase of cash. "What's your problem? You don't have to kill me to keep the money for the deal. You were right — my contract with you is worthless. I can't get a single penny out of the deal you've just signed with B.U.L.! You've got what you want. So just let me take my money and get the fuck out of here. I swear, you'll never hear from me again."

Cherry seemed to think that this was hilarious. She let out a deep throaty chuckle.

Mr. E felt bile rise to his throat. What more did she want? *Why would she want to kill him?* All he wanted was to take his money and leave... *The money!* The bitch must want the money! And now she was going to kill him for it! He tried to keep the desperation out of his voice. "Look, you don't have to *kill* me over some dollars. I'll be willing to share it with you. Hell, I was even gonna share it with Yam, but he got all stupid on me and wanted to run to the police!"

Cherry still said nothing, but she burst out laughing again like Mr. E had just cracked another really funny joke. "You stupid little shit. Are you fucking deaf? Didn't you hear me? I said that I came here to blow your worthless brains out!"

Mr. E stared at her. He'd known it from the very first moment he met her. She'd had it in for him from the start. "But why?"

Cherry imitated his voice in a high-pitched whine. "But why? *Are you blind?* When are you ever gonna truly look at me?"

What the hell she was talking about?

He squinted at Cherry. There *was* something different about her today, she had all her hair tied up in a black scarf, which matched her all-black outfit, which made her look like a fuckin' burglar or something. Still, she did look different without all that horse-hair flapping about her face. She looked like...

Mr. E felt a hint of recognition... there *was* something vaguely... *familiar.* There was something... well... *different...*

She wasn't going to wait for him to come up with the answer, "I guess that it must be hard to recognise little Marcia Jones after six years. Funny how much a girl can change between the ages of seventeen and twenty-two."

At the sound of that name, Mr. E felt a knife go into his heart. He hadn't heard that name since... since...

"You fucking bastard! Did you *really* think I was gonna let you let me take the rap for that wanker's murder? Didn't you realise that the first thing I was gonna do the minute they let me out of the slammer was come and find your miserable arse?"

Mr. E stared like he was seeing a ghost. Now she'd said it he could see some resemblance in her features. But she looked so... so... *different*. Marcia Jones had been a skinny little teenager with a tiny afro-puff. It had been hard to get her any work at all really. She had looked like such a child that he could only really put her with the perverts. The really sick fuckers who got off on abusing teenagers... She wasn't even that good at his scam. That was why... why she had been so... expendable. But Cherry was so womanly. Still, that's what happens between the ages of seventeen and twenty-three: a girl becomes a woman.

"But... but... Marcie? I... I can't believe it's really you. I mean..."

Cherry wasn't even listening, "Ya know, the first time I met you in the studio, I was so scared you were gonna recognise me. That my plan would be fucked. But you hardly even looked at me; it was like you just looked right through me. I bet you don't even notice your whores. The only thing that you probably saw were dollar signs! 'Cause that's all women are to you isn't it, Knight? They're just a means to an end! That's when I knew that my plan was gonna work. That when I knew I was gonna be able to destroy you. Destroy you the way that you destroyed me."

Now that it was actually happening, Cherry felt strangely

calm. She'd dreamed of having this opportunity so many times it hardly seemed real. She felt like she was acting in a play she'd rehearsed a million times. And she'd cried so many tears over this moment that now she felt no emotion. It was like she'd dried up inside, like she had no tears left.

Mr. E's head was reeling. "Now Marcia let me explain… That was all years ago I—"

"Shut the fuck up! The last thing I wanna hear is your explanations. I've heard them all before remember?" She tossed him a pair of handcuffs, "Put these on, we're going for a drive. Make sure they click twice — we don't want you to break free or anything, do we now?"

Mr. E silently put on the handcuffs. He could see she was deadly serious. Who would have guessed that Marcia Jones would have come back to haunt him like this?

Once he'd clicked the cuffs in place, Cherry came over to check them, grazing the side of his skull with her Magnum whilst she did so. Then she reached into his breast pocket until she found the place where he always kept his mobile phone.

She looked at Mr. E and said, "When I give you the nod, you're to say, 'There's been a murder at number ten, Wilton Place in Kensington'." She pushed the steel tip of the Magnum against the pressure point at his temple. "And If you fuck it up, I'll kill you."

She dialled 999, and Mr. E slowly repeated her words.

She clicked off call, wiped the phone free of her prints, and threw it on the floor next to Carrington's dead body.

Mr. E was incensed, "What the fuck are you doing? That's my phone that you're leaving at the scene of the crime!"

Cherry smiled, "I know. Now shut the fuck up, and get the fuck out. Unless you want the cops to find you here red-handed."

Yam watched the news with a morbid fascination. An artists

impression of Mr. E flashed on the screen. It was amazing, if he hadn't had seen him with his own eyes, he would have sworn that Mr. E hadn't even existed. The police hadn't been able to find a single photograph of him. Not one.

The newscaster read her autocue: "The Police are still looking for this man in connection with the murder of leading politician Delroy Carrington. They also want to question him with regards to half a million pounds in cash that Delroy Carrington drew out of his party's campaign fund, the day he was found dead in his London home in Kensington. The former boyfriend of pop singer Cherry Drop was held for questioning…" Yam gulped as he saw one of his snarling DJ promotion pictures flash on the screen. He looked like a fucking axe murderer… "But Kenneth Brown was released earlier this year, due to lack of evidence. The police are convinced of his innocence in connection with Mr. Carrington's murder, and he has since been assisting them in their search to find the man they believe to be the killer, a Mr. Knight', sometimes known as Mr. E."

A gorgeous air brushed publicity still from one of Cherry's videos flashed onto the screen. "Pop star Cherry Drop was called in for questioning. However, despite her connection with Mr. Brown and Mr. Knight, she is not connected with the murder, as she was with her A & R representative from B.U.L. Records at the time of the crime."

Yam sank back into his mum's sofa. He couldn't help replaying the events leading up to, and after the murder over and over in his head. Cherry had refused to have anything to do with him after what happened. Why, she hadn't said — but he'd guessed it was because he'd let her down with regards to Mr. E. It looked like she had been right all along. Mr. E was a… sick… fuck. When he thought about the way Mr. E had calmly popped Carrington twice in the skull… *all that blood*… it made him want to retch. And now it was all over.

The police had actually thought he'd done it at first. But

when they found the phone and matched up the call that had been made, they realised that someone else had been at the scene of the crime. And you didn't have to be a genius to realise that there was no way that Yam could have popped Carrington, and then knocked himself unconscious. Twice. It turned out that one of Carrington's secretaries had recognised Mr. E from the police's artist's impression, and had informed them that Mr. E had been blackmailing Carrington, and had caused a ruckus at his offices just a couple of weeks before the murder! Now all they had to do was find him...

Yam wondered if they ever would.

Or if Mr. E would remain a mystery to the very end.

Huge imposing skeletons of dinosaurs towered over the proceedings. A large, bony Brontosaurus bowed its bleached-white knuckle head over the long, long trestle table that was draped with a crisp white linen cloth. The table's thin legs almost bowed under from the weight of the feast that graced its top. Canapes, finger dips, smoked salmon and cream cheese sandwiches, blue cheese and red onion rings, tiny vegetable spring rolls with sweet-and-sour sauce, spicy chicken wings, crispy breadcoated lobster and plenty of red and white wine and champagne. The assembled photographers and journalists hovered around its bounty like vultures over their dying prey, cramming as much of the feast into their cavernous bowels as was humanly possible and swilling as much alcohol as they could stand down their stringy necks.

They were all congregated in the Natural History museum on London's Brompton Road, for a party that had been thrown by B.U.L. Records. As Nikki Stixx surveyed the scene, her chest swelled with pride. It was an impressive crowd. All the best people were there, and the press had turned up in droves to see their new idol. Stepping onto the slightly raised platform that was at the head of the room, she tapped the microphone that was standing there and cleared her throat in a bid to get their attention.

"Okay everyone. If you'd like to gather round, I think we're ready for you now!"

She gave them all what she considered to be her most gracious smile and started a round of applause as Cherry took the stage. As Cherry glided through them, the photographers and journalists parted like the red sea. She was wearing huge bright-red platform shoes. and was dressed from head to toe in a technicolour, almost see-thru floor-length dress that clung to her every curve. It was a one-off design that had been made especially for her by Azzedine Alia, one of her many new friends. Her hair had been blow-dried and curled to perfection, and her face had been painted until it resembled a work of art, by Razz, her personal make-up and hairdresser.

She stepped behind the microphone and gave them all a dazzling smile. "First of all, I'd like to thank you all for coming…" She paused as they all gave her a raucous round of applause, and a few of the guys called out a few wolf whistles and cheers.

Still smiling she continued, in low, husky tones: "And I would like to thank you all for the tremendous support that you've given me over the past few months."

She had to make another pause, as the crowd broke into another round of cheers.

"What 'ave you got to say about the Delroy Carrington murder?"

Cherry gave them a serious look, and addressed the reporter who'd shouted out the question. "Honey, the only thing I ever planned to murder was the record charts!"

They all roared with laughter.

"And lastly, I would like to say…" Cherry paused to flutter her eyelashes at the press. "I would like to say, that I'm not the kind of girl who has one-night stands, so I expect some kind of commitment from you guys — so we can have a long and happy relationship!"

She gave them a pantomime wink, "And don't go cheatin' on me with any other girls!"

Everyone cracked up at Cherry's gag, and she shouted above the laughter, "Enjoy the party!"

As she stepped down from the platform, a thousand bulbs flashed in her eyes as the photographs rushed over to get what they'd come for: a colour picture for the front page of tomorrow's newspaper. Cherry stopped and posed happily for them, smiling a big, beaming lipglossed smile the whole time. Gradually she made her way through the throng to get to her dressing room out the back.

Nikki Stixx surveyed the scene with a sense of satisfaction. Everything had gone brilliantly. She had masterminded Cherry's career, and the whole thing had been an unprecedented success.

Her new personal assistant, Sandra G came up to her. Sandra G was a pretty young black girl with short hair, that was cropped close to her skull and bleached a bright blonde. She had a lean, muscular body and was wearing black hipster denim jeans and a skimpy vest top. She sidled up close to Nikki, and handed a glass of champagne to her new boss, saying, "She's wicked isn't she?"

Nikki nodded, "She's a natural. I always knew she would be. From the very first moment I laid eyes on her."

Sandra inched closer to Nikki, continuing, "What do *you* think about the whole Delroy Carrington scandal?"

"Who knows? Cherry's caused a stir with the press since she landed on B.U.L.'s doorstep. The controversy has been good for sales. Which is the only thing I'm bothered about."

Sandra was lost in thought for a second, then she whispered, "Nikki… who is Cherry — really. Where does she come from? Do you know her real name?"

Nikki turned round to face her new P.A. She rested her hands her shoulders and looked serious as she said, "To tell you the God's honest truth Sandra, I don't know anything about her. And I don't care either. The only thing I know about Cherry Drop is that she's going to be a major MAJOR star, even bigger than she is now, and she's going to be with us for a long, LONG time. And we're all gonna make a hell of a lot of money!"

She gently pushed Sandra in the direction of the food table and gave her a playful slap on her shapely butt. "Now be a darling, and get me a selection of those delicious canapes before these hounds devour the lot!"

Cherry sat in her dressing room surrounded by a selection of the lavish bouquets of flowers that had been sent by her fans and well-wishers. She carefully wiped off her make-up and brushed her hair into a simple ponytail. Slipping out of her Azzedine Alia dress and Vivien Westwood shoes, she pulled on her old cut-off jeans and a tiny black T-shirt, together with her trusty old lace up boots. She picked up a tiny black leather rucksack... and the suitcase.

She couldn't resist a last look before she sneaked out of the party. She flipped open the suitcase to see Delroy's campaign fund winking back at her. Half a million pounds. Cash. Enough to keep her going, until she was settled.

Undetected by the revellers, who were too busy enjoying the party to notice a young, clean-faced ponytailed girl slipping through their midst. She stepped out of the Natural History Museum and let the bright sunlight hit her face. A cool, gentle breeze ran through her hair, as she walked away from the city, down the long length of Cromwell Road going, God knows where. A huge, imposing billboard stretched out behind her. On it was plastered a full-sized poster with a stunning blue-tinted close-up of Cherry's face. It read:

BURSTIN' THE CHERRY
THE INCREDIBLE NEW SINGLE
FROM THE NO.1 ALBUM
BY RISING STAR
CHERRY DROP

BESTSELLING FICTION

I wish to order the following X Press title(s)

❑ Single Black Female	Yvette Richards	£5.99
❑ When A Man Loves A Woman	Patrick Augustus	£5.99
❑ Wicked In Bed	Sheri Campbell	£5.99
❑ Rude Gal	Sheri Campbell	£5.99
❑ Yardie	Victor Headley	£4.99
❑ Excess	Victor Headley	£4.99
❑ Yush!	Victor Headley	£5.99
❑ Fetish	Victor Headley	£5.99
❑ Here Comes the Bride	Victor Headley	£5.99
❑ In Search of Satisfaction	J. California Cooper	£7.99
❑ Sistas On a Vibe	Ijeoma Inyama	£6.99
❑ Flex	Marcia Williams	£6.99
❑ Baby Mother	Andrea Taylor	£6.99
❑ Uptown Heads	R.K. Byers	£5.99
❑ Jamaica Inc.	Tony Sewell	£5.99
❑ Lick Shot	Peter Kalu	£5.99
❑ Professor X	Peter Kalu	£5.99
❑ Obeah	Colin Moone	£5.99
❑ Cop Killer	Donald Gorgon	£4.99
❑ The Harder They Come	Michael Thelwell	£7.99
❑ Baby Father	Patrick Augustus	£6.99
❑ Baby Father 2	Patrick Augustus	£6.99
❑ OPP	Naomi King	£6.99

I enclose a cheque/postal order (Made payable to '*The X Press*') for

£ _____

(add 50p P&P per book for orders under £10. All other orders P&P free.)

NAME _____

ADDRESS _____

_____

Cut out or photocopy and send to:
X PRESS, 6 Hoxton Square, London N1 6NU
Alternatively, call the X PRESS hotline: 0171 729 1199 and place your order.

X Press Black Classics

The masterpieces of black fiction writing await your discovery

❏ The Blacker the Berry   Wallace Thurman   £6.99
'Born **too** black, Emma Lou suffers her own community's intra-racial venom.'

❏ The Autobiography of an Ex-Colored Man   James Weldon Johnson   £5.99
'One of the most thought-provoking novels ever published.'

❏ The Conjure Man Dies   Rudolph Fisher   £5.99
'The world's FIRST black detective thriller!'

❏ The Walls of Jericho   Rudolph Fisher   £5.99
'When a buppie moves into a white neighbourhood, all hell breaks loose. **Hilarious!**'

❏ Joy and Pain   Rudolph Fisher   £6.99
'Jazz age Harlem stories by a master of black humour writing.'

❏ Iola   Frances E.W. Harper   £6.99
'A woman's long search for her mother from whom she was separated on the slave block.'

❏ The House Behind the Cedars   Charles W. Chesnutt   £5.99
'Can true love transcend racial barriers?'

❏ A Love Supreme   Pauline E. Hopkins   £5.99
'One of the greatest love stories ever told.'

❏ One Blood   Pauline E. Hopkins   £6.99
'Raiders of lost African treasures discover their roots and culture.'

❏ The President's Daughter   William Wells Brown   £5.99
'The true story of the daughter of the United States president, sold into slavery.'

I enclose a cheque/postal order (Made payable to 'The X Press') for

£ _____

(add 50p P&P per book for orders under £10. All other orders P&P free.)

NAME _____

ADDRESS _____

Cut out or photocopy and send to: X PRESS, 6 Hoxton Square, London N1 6NU
Alternatively, call the X PRESS hotline: 0171 729 1199 and place your order.